Contents

Prologue

When the polite knock first rumbled on the minority leader's door in his office at the Virginia Assembly, he already knew it was one of his colleagues from across the aisle. One doesn't just stroll into Jim Harkson's office.

"Tom, nice to see you on this side of the building," Harkson greeted him with all the polish and sincerity of a 13-term professional politician.

"Jim, I'm glad I was able to catch you. I wanted to talk to you about HB2312," Thomas Plankton III said with wild-eyed enthusiasm.

"HB2312?" Harkson said as if completely in the dark, releasing Tom's hand from the collegial shake as he looked up at him quizzically.

"The Fitzgerald bill," Plankton stated firmly and with a mild hint of irritation at Harkson playing coy.

"Oh yes ... this is your project, I understand?" Harkson asked skeptically.

"It is, but we have a growing number of sponsors and patrons. I was hoping you would join."

"Really? This bill strikes me as both unnecessary and, well — to be honest, just election-year political chicanery," Harkson said, cutting to the chase.

"It's a great bill, and it'll give law enforcement the flexibility it needs to keep our best officers in the fold past mandatory retirement. It's truly bipartisan," Plankton pitched, in full stump speech mode.

"It is? Well, you don't have any bipartisan support yet. Why's that?" Harkson said wryly as the political chess game began.

"That's because you have not yet blessed the bill and *released* your caucus to support it," the younger but just as able Plankton quickly offered with a smile.

"Tom, all I know about this bill is it was offered by a legislator seeking re-election in a hotly contested, purple district. *And* that legislator wants to tie his name to this Fitzgerald character, who is apparently quite popular up there. That's how I see it," Harkson said, staking out a seemingly firm position.

"Jim, I could see where you might think that way, looking at the bill from only one political perspective. But *you* made the key point here. Fitzgerald is one hot commodity, and the people of that district and this commonwealth love him," Tom said, his eyes narrowing on Harkson.

"I hear he's some kind of local legend in your end of the commonwealth, but I don't know much about him, frankly. The political calculus doesn't change much for me." Harkson said as he paced the floor of his office, giving little wiggle room from his original view.

"It should change the equation, Jim," Plankton stated matter-of-factly and confidently as he stepped in closer to the minority leader. "Let me help with the math. What's going to happen here is that HB2312 will advance with the majority and no bipartisan support. That's going to put *your* team and *your* candidate in that hot election on the wrong side of the issue. Frankly, if we were playing politics, we wouldn't *ask* for your help. We'd move the bill, take our chances and claim all the credit when it passes."

"So … you are just here doing me a favor?" Harkson chuckled, leaning back on his windowsill to send the unmistakable message that he was not rattled, but now paying closer attention.

"I want to pass it, Jim. I want to make sure it is done *this* session. *And* I don't want it stuck in committee or falling short in some last-minute deal. If you sign on, that doesn't happen. It's no longer a political issue. It's a win-win," Plankton declared.

Harkson actually saw the logic in that reply. He paused a minute, looked at Plankton and offered an opening: "I have a meeting on offshore drilling in 15 minutes. That, my friend, is *never* going to pass, by the way. *But* ... tell me a couple of your best Fitzgerald stories while I wait for the others to arrive."

"You're gonna love this one," Plankton began.

Chapter 1: She Bop, He Bop, and We Bop

"I told you, everybody *loves* to bang. They bang their neighbors. They bang their co-workers. They'll bang anyone … other than their own spouse. That's what the 'poo-tang philosopher' told me," Detective Parker explained to the young sheriff's deputy guarding the crime scene. Deputy Hogan might have chuckled if he weren't still green from looking at the carnage of a brutal murder on display right on the floor in front of him.

"Hogan, you look like you're gonna puke, kid. Don't toss your cookies in front of Fitz!" Parker warned the rookie.

"Hey, Fitz, listen to this crazy statement by the vic's lawyer. This blowhard reminds me of my third wife's lawyer."

"What was her name?" Fitz shot back.

"You mean the wife or the lawyer?" smiled Parker.

"Pick one," Fitz laughed.

Detective Ronald Roland Fitzgerald was old school. He'd seen more bodies than a Navy combat corpsman. He'd been around a long, long time — long enough for people to call him only "sir," "detective" or "Fitz." That's it. You did not call him Ron, Ronnie or Ronald. In fact, the only thing the legendary chief detective despised more than his first name was his middle name. *And* the only thing Fitz hated more than his middle name was unscrupulous lawyers.

In precise order, Fitz hated divorce lawyers more than any other type of lawyer. Criminal defense lawyers were a very close second. Fitz really hated those guys. He once told a Loudoun County Circuit Court judge that criminal defense lawyers were just "uncaptured criminals." Fitz hated lawyers so much that he didn't even like the prosecutors he worked with, except a "couple of the old 'Nam vets." Of course, the lawyers he really liked were his daughters,

5

including his number-one daughter, one of Loudoun County's three deputy commonwealth's attorneys. But she didn't fit his general view of lawyers, as she was first and foremost a Fitzgerald.

Fitz was "in his 70th year," as his father would have said about anyone who recently turned 69. He was built like a man half his age, not like a man with 44 years on the job. In all those years Fitz had worked hard not to become bitter or jaded, but the suburban invasion of the county that locals called LoCo had really gotten under his grille. None of those 44 years of service did he find more trying than the last 15. Loudoun County had changed dramatically, and to Fitz, it was not necessarily for the better.

"It's not the work, the crime or the dead bodies," Fitz told his various sergeants and lieutenants. "It's the A-holes. They're Loudoun's new cash crop." As Fitz saw it, most people invading the new Loudoun County were either "dickheads" or "dot-heads."

Fitz had missed the sensitivity and inclusion training last month — and the last three decades. It's not that he was a racist. In fact, Fitz would tell you, "I have held dying soldiers of every race, color and creed … they all bleed out red." Still, Fitz was raised in a different time, and by an older generation who often grouped people by race, ethnicity or religion, and he wasn't about to soften his word choices for the "PC police."

"Seriously, Fitz, do you want to talk to this lawyer about the dead girl, or do you just want to read my statement about it?" Parker egged him on. Parker knew the answer, and he knew the question alone would stick in Fitz's craw. It was just the type of tweak only Fitz's longtime partner could get away with, the type of petty little fight only he would pick with the man most men revered.

Fitz was right out of central casting for a 1970s alpha-male misogynist, but by every calculation Sheriff Detective Fitzgerald was

6

a certified badass. You don't survive in today's politically correct culture with attitudes and opinions like those Fitz dispatched freely and loudly unless you were a living legend. That's Fitz … decorated Silver Star Marine, UVA law degree, Tom Selleck build, Archie Bunker disposition.

Detective Parker loved Fitz — most days. All the sheriff's officers feared and revered him. He solved cases, kicked ass and made no apologies. He was a cop's cop and a victim's cop. You know who loved Fitz more than anyone? The families of violent-crime victims. Fitz worked every case as if one of his seven daughters were the victim. Yes, Fitz had seven daughters.

"Parker, you no-account, New Jersey, carpetbagging guinea, of course I am going to talk to the A-hole. I want to solve the case, kid. Otherwise, I'd read your Dick-and-Jane scribble from the interview. You know what would happen then? The f'ing killer would be drinking mai tais on your deck while banging your latest girlfriend," Fitz bellowed out, chuckling at his own ruthlessly predictable, ethnic bitch-slapping of his partner.

"Tell me this A-hole lawyer's name?" Fitz asked just loudly enough for the lawyer to hear.

The 6-foot-4-inch lawyer answered for Parker. He leaned in, looked down at Fitz and said, "My name is Alan Bodine. B-O-D-I-N-E. It's pronounced *Bo-DINE,* like fine *wine.* You getting this, or do I need to slow down?" Bodine says, his tone marinated in sarcasm and contempt.

Alan Bodine was the life of every party. His whisper was like a rock concert. The managing partner of a Leesburg, Virginia, divorce firm, Bodine was famous for making witnesses cry on the stand, even his own. By all accounts he was a hell of a trial lawyer and nearly as great as he claimed to be. Bodine loved to mix it up — in court, on his deck, just ordering dinner or on the baseball fields where he coached youth sports. In any good squabble, if someone yelled "fire," Bodine reach first for the gas can, then for the fire extinguisher.

"Oh, yes sir, I got it down here all correct-like, Mr. *Bo-dean*," Fitz spit back at him, looking him dead in the eye. If this were a blinking contest, these two boys might be here a few decades.

"I'm Detective Fitzgerald, *Bo-dean*. My friends, both of them, call me Fitz, pronounced like I don't give two … *shits*."

"How do you know the vic … Bo-*dean*?" Fitz smiled as he tweaked the lanky, crane-necked lawyer who was still looking down, sizing up Fitz from the detective's last deliberate mispronunciation of his name.

"Well, Mr. Fitzgerald, why don't you call my office, make an appointment, and I will make some time to speak with you when you have had the opportunity to collect and compose yourself."

"Bo-*dean*, you're not leaving my crime scene until I know everything that you know about this woman. Would you like to tell me here and now, or would you like my partner Joey Buttafuoco over there" (he pointed at Parker) "to arrange for a ride to the station for you? We can turn on the pretty lights just for you. You can pretend it's a parade, something we commonly do for Ashburn VIPs like yourself." Fitz said, sarcasm dripping from his lips like the juice of a summer peach.

"Tread lightly, Columbo, or this might be the last case you work. You want to take me in? Man up and make the call. You want to get my cooperation? Stop waving your pecker around and ask some intelligent questions," Bodine growled. He never flinched, not a wink, not a blink, not even a pause in his piercing stare.

Detective Parker moved in deftly as Fitz stepped toward Bodine. The last time Parker saw that blank look on Fitz's face,

Parker spent five hours explaining to internal affairs why Fitz was justified in beating a perp within an inch of the kid's life. In the world of adult male wanker-measuring contests between men who should know better, this one was going to need a yardstick.

"Fitz, Mr. Bo-*dine* is counsel for the victim and came to the scene at the family's request. He's been *nothing but helpful* so far, and no one could calm down the victim's 10-year-old son, Jason, other than Mr. Bo-*dine*. Maybe we can take five, look through our notes and let Mr. Bo-*dine* get a drink and collect his thoughts if he is still willing to help," Parker said, trying to deescalate the situation with both some sugar and the careful, correct pronunciation of Bodine's name.

"Ten minutes, Mr. Bo-*dine,* does that work for you?" asked Fitz as his and Bodine's eyes stayed locked on each other.

"Yes, Detective Fitzgerald, thank you," Bodine said coolly, but with just a hint of a smile.

"Jesus Christ, Parker, are you fucking handling me now?" Fitz asked as they walked away. "Maybe you can come by later and wipe my ass for me too? Or, maybe you can just cradle the balls and drink the gravy, you pansy." He was more than just a little miffed at Parker stepping into the interaction.

"Hey, that tall jackass is smarter than shit, connected as hell and the only guy we know of right now with any useful information about this victim. I wanted to make sure he didn't bust our balls and slow this investigation's launch." Parker said with surprising resolve.

Fitz pulled Parker in closer to be sure his words carried no farther than Parker's ears. "For fuck's sake Parker, I just wanted to see his reaction and study his face. You stepped on my read. That big pompous dick might have been screwing this girl ... lord knows she was apparently servicing everyone else. Your 'po-tang philosopher' there might have been taking his payments by bumping uglies with this gal," Fitz looked at Parker, clearly no longer kidding around he continued.

"*Never* rule out the loudmouth who's always talking about getting ass or having gotten ass. Your victim here, despite her current *unfortunate* appearance, was one mighty fine looking woman, and fancy pants over there fancies himself as the guy in the room every woman wants."

"So, you were just busting him for a reaction?" Parker asks as if a rhetorical question.

"Of course."

"Well, OK. What's your take on Bo-*dean*?" Parker asked with a laugh as the two moved in unison away from Bodine and toward the door.

"You mean *Bo-DINE* like *pig swine*?" Fitz muttered, proud of his own little quip.

"I think that guy might be the biggest A-hole in an ocean full of them here in Loudoun County, but he doesn't have the balls or meanness to do *that* to this woman. My guess is, he has info that will help us get this investigation going. Heck, it might even lead us to the killer, whether he knows it or not. Still, I refuse to rule him out until we know much, much more. The guy's divorce lawyer scum ... to the extent that isn't redundant."

"Jesus, Fitz, we have worked a few sad-sack cases, but *that's* some crazy shit someone did to that lady," Parker said surprisingly sombered by the surreal scene on the floor before them.

"Yeah, I know, and we've got to find the sick bastard, even if it means playing patty-cake with Bo-*dine*. Put Mr. Big Stuff on ice, delay the interview and start without me if you must. I have to get some real American fucking coffee before I sit and listen to Bo-*dean*," Fitz declared as he began moving more swiftly toward the front door.

Parker loved this guy, and sometimes he forgot that no matter how much experience he had, Fitz was painting with oils while the rest of the detectives were still using crayons.

Fitz bolted across the manicured lawn, around the yellow tape, and hopped in his '71 Chevelle. He was the Chevy version of Starsky and Hutch and threw in his favorite mix tape. Yes, mixed tape.

CDs? No.

iPod? Are you kidding me?

Streaming music service? Not a chance.

Detective Fitz had a prize collection of "mixed" cassette tapes from classic rock to what he called "real country." But when he was feeling frisky, he couldn't resist a good '80s mix. His girls got him hooked on the genre.

Fitz burned rubber as he headed off for "real American" coffee, which to him meant Dunkin' Donuts. As he headed out from the crime scene, Fitz treated the entire Section Two area of what was once sold as the Sky Meadows neighborhood of Brambleton, Virginia, to Cyndi Lauper's cult classic, "She Bop."

"*She bop, he bop and we bop, I bop, you bop and they bop …*"

Fitz was tapping the wheel as he thought, "Maybe if she bopped instead of banged, she wouldn't be hog-tied, face down in her own blood and vomit with a Swiffer sticking out of her ass. Sorry it ended that way for you, sweetheart. I'll find this piece of shit."

He considered briefly his Dunkin options, and he was not pleased at all about where he knew he had to go.

Chapter 2: Take the "L" Out of Lover and It's Over

"Is there anyone in this neighborhood who you haven't screwed?" Jack Jensen asked his wife of 13 years, with a calm, almost expressionless face. The question stunned Jennifer "Jenny" Jensen. She had just walked into the couple's bedroom, a bit tipsy, giggling and seemingly in a great mood for the first time in weeks.

"What the hell are you talking about?" she yelled, almost sobering up before the words finished shaking the Jensen's so-typical Ashburn bedroom.

"You fucking whore. Do wash your mouth out from the neighbor's cum before you kiss our kids goodnight?"

Jack had been pacing the floor for two hours, and every mean thing he wished he'd said for the last eight years was queued up and ready to fire. In his mind, Jenny had treated him like shit, almost making him into a submissive cuck, robbing him of his manhood, confidence and pride. To him, she had become a cold, manipulative, money-grubbing, selfish witch who rationed sex to him and didn't even pretend anymore to enjoy it.

The two hadn't made real love in years, and the sex was awful, sporadic, robotic and pedestrian … on its best nights. In Jack's world of conspiracies, she had to be having an affair. And now he knew she was. All she cared about was her appearance, her fitness, her clothes and going out, just not with him.

Jack remembered when they first met. She made love to him the way men wished their women would do. She couldn't be contained in bed, and it was hard to keep up with her. Jenny was down for it all, and while most men are stuck trying to get their wives to keep the lights on, Jenny was always introducing things Jack never heard or thought of.

All that stopped years ago, and Jack never really knew why. She bore two kids, and then basically became their mother and his irritating, conceited roommate who merely tried to keep up appearances for their friends.

Jenny Jensen had sex with her husband like she did the laundry — sparingly and without joy. It was, to her, a chore.

Laundry ... check.

Shopping ... check.

Clean the house ... check.

Let my pathetic husband ball me for 60 seconds ... check.

Jack Jensen was ready for this fight. He'd wanted it, and he'd practiced for it. When she walked through that bedroom door, he was primed to call her out because he knew, without a doubt, she was cheating on him.

Now, staring at the 41-year-old, 5-foot-7 beauty he'd promised to love and cherish, he couldn't help but wonder whose semen was dripping down and soiling her panties under those "fuck-me blue jeans" she was wearing. "What a cold, mean, vicious, heartless little tramp," Jack thought.

Jenny Jensen was hot by any standard. In fact, she was ridiculously beautiful and irresistible. If you gazed upon her once, just once, you would remember the image.

Her frame was adorned with thick, vibrant, natural long brown hair. If she dyed it, she must have gone to the pro of all pros. It was that young, spry, shining, chestnut color that just doesn't come out of a bottle, not even from a pricey salon. God made that hair, and like most of Jenny, he was paying close attention to detail that day.

Jenny Jensen was like Jessica Alba's hotter, older sister. Born to a Syrian mother and an Italian father, Jennifer Antoinette Maria

13

Mariucci Jensen didn't have a single physical flaw. Her Mediterranean skin was supple, like that of a 22-year-old. Her eyelashes were freakishly long and childlike. They crowded around her huge brown eyes, creating a perfectly manicured landscape. God made eyes like her once, and he stuck them in Sally Fields. Then one day he woke up and said, hold my holy water, I can top that. He set out and then made Jenny Jensen's eyes.

Jenny's dad used to tell her that her beautiful set of eyes could win a man's heart for life — or haunt him for eternity. It looks like he was right on both accounts.

Jenny may not have always been the model of propriety, but she was the model of proportion. She had broad, athletic shoulders, with just visible traps from years of CrossFit training. Her biceps were fashionably tight and fit. Somehow God gave her perfectly sized and shaped breasts, both of which seemed to know the proper way to stand or lie for any occasion or outfit. Jenny had an ass like a 16-year track star and the long legs of an equestrian. In fact, she wore her riding boots daily even though she had never been on a horse. Some boots are custom made for riders, Jenny's legs were custom made for boots.

Jenny walked with a confidence and swagger that sent the unmistakable message that she knew she was a rare beauty, and onlookers' fawning was expected *and* welcomed. Yet, somehow, she wore that look with a gracious smile. She was — remarkably the girl next door who never really lived next door to anyone.

For Jenny Jensen, a man could swallow a lot of pride. For Jenny Jensen, a man could eat a large pile of crow. For Jenny Jensen, a man might go insane.

Jack Jensen long ago had lost his mind for Jenny.

Tonight, in a jealous rage, he was ready to snap.

Jack Jensen was a pillar of the Brambleton community. "Coach Jensen," as most kids knew him, was smart, funny, caring and the type of coach most parents wished they could find for their kids. Jack Jensen coached every sport there was, seemingly. He had time or made time for every kid, from bench warmer to star. Every dad was tired of hearing about Jack Jensen, and every mother wanted to take her kids to and from practice in the hope that they might get some Coach Jack time.

Jack Jensen was a catch. No man could be that athletic, that good-looking and that alpha male while seemingly being the world's greatest dad. Moreover, by day, he was a modern superhero.

Jack Jensen was a federal agent. He was a G-man. Jensen was FBI, working as part of its terror interrogation team attached to the interagency High-Value Interrogation Detainee Group "HIG" unit created by President Obama. Jensen's schedule put him in odd places around the world at odd times. He never talked about his work — ever. But somehow it was hard to imagine Coach Jack breaking an international terrorist. The man purportedly headed the unit, and whatever people thought about his personality and good cheer, Jack Jensen got answers from terrible people about the worst of deeds.

Tonight, Jack was determined to get answers about the worst of betrayals.

"Jack, why would I ever cheat on such a kind, sweet, compassionate, loving man like you … such an accomplished lover … with that little Irish dick you can't keep hard for five minutes?" Jenny responded. "Maybe if you could fuck like a real man, I wouldn't be out there looking for a someone who knew how to make love to woman," Jenny Jensen fired back as she launched an unexpected counter-attack. In that big moment, her weeks of fear and panic turned to rage.

Jack Jensen was ready for war. He was ready to make Jenny cry. He was ready for the sobbing, the apology, the confession, the remorse and even the begging for forgiveness. Jack never expected Jenny Jensen to test the one thing everyone agreed Jack had … his manhood.

Whatever was happening at the Jensen house for the last seven or eight years, no one, absolutely no one in their little slice of Pleasantville had an inkling that the Jensens were less than perfect. Jack and Jenny. You didn't have a party in Brambleton without Jack and Jenny. "Hey, honey, Jack and Jenny are coming over, right?" That was the mantra in the huge subdivision that the neighbors sometimes called Bram.

Brambleton, Virginia — it's a made-up town. Heck, it's not even really a town. Ironically, neither is it merely a subdivision of the larger area known as Ashburn, which also isn't its own political subdivision.

In the early 1990s Brambleton was nothing but cow pasture. Now, if you asked Detective Fitz, he would say, "It has even more bullshit." Brambleton is what developers and planners call a planned community. It sits on the eastern rim of Loudoun County. Seemingly, it is at the end of one of Dulles International's four runways.

The now made-up town with its "town center" is part of a larger area of made-up towns all consolidated under the umbrella name of "Ashburn," which some in the area jokingly refer to as "Cashburn." None have local governments. They are instead policed by the County sheriff and ruled by Home-Owners' Associations, which make sure you cut your grass, paint your fence, and park the right way in front of your house.

The homes are big, and they really are built like crap. All are expensive, and most are soulless, vinyl barns crammed together like

16

the fake town on a set in a bad Jim Carrey movie. The neighborhood is like a beige Rorschach test, where earth tones are poured out in vinyl and brick structures, shoehorned onto postage-stamp lots, all dotted with pedestrian landscaping that lacks color and imagination. It looks magnificent on a brochure or webpage.

Brambleton is a metaphor for modern America and certainly for the Jensens. Most of its homes are oversized and overpriced. Most are filled with cheap toys, crappy furniture and the gaudy taste of two-income families wealthy enough to be house poor and with poor enough taste and judgment to have bought those houses. Most of the homes have brick fronts, and from the street, at the right angle, they are very impressive. If, however, one were to look behind that façade, one would see a house wrapped in plastic, built with illegal labor and low-quality materials. Those dreadful, cookie-cutter homes with the pleasant, street-facing exterior are a mirage, just like those beautiful Jensens.

From cow pasture to make-believe town in 20 years, Brambleton built thousands of those houses, a town center, and all the idyllic amenities to attract dual-income professionals from inside Washington DC's beltway to outside its confines. In Brambleton, you are either a lawyer, a doctor, an engineer, or an IT professional or you work for some law enforcement agency of the federal government. Brambleton is armed to the teeth with federal agents of every kind, and Jack Jensen was just one of them. Many houses were filled with school-age kids and stay-at-home moms or work-from-home couples.

Jenny Jensen sold real estate. Well, take that back. Jenny Jensen put her picture on signs to sell real estate, and by God, those properties sold. If Jenny held an open house, every male Realtor in Northern Virginia would show. Jenny was quite good at her job, and she understood the local market. She also knew how to use every gift God gave her.

The Jensens were Team Brambleton. Their kids swam with the Betas, where Jack coached, and Jenny ran the fundraisers. The swim team was miserable for most parents. One local Brambleton dad, the town crier, said that swimming was "the worst sport ever created. It was four hours at the pool and four minutes in the water for your kid." That might be true, but it was four hours at the pool with Jenny and Jack Jensen.

When her kids were little, 5 and 3, Jenny once wore her bikini to the swim meet. Attendance improved nearly 140 percent the following week, including singles, dads and young teenage boys having no relationship at all to the swim team. Seven years later, the boys no longer swim, but the local dads still ask, "Is that Jensen mom coming to the meet?"

Local legends abounded about the Jensens, but none had them as anything but Brambleton's sweethearts. With two boys, Jack Jr., 12, and Jason, 10, the Jensens were part of the Brambleton baseball mafia. Their kids played Little League and travel baseball. They got professional instruction, and the Jensens were fixtures at every field in Loudoun County, from Tillett to Byrnes Ridge. Jack was always on the sidelines coaching, and Jenny was surrounded by a gaggle of baseball moms all rooting like mad for their future major leaguers.

Baseball might be dying across parts of this country, but in America's fastest-growing county and its wealthiest, baseball is exploding. If you have a son in Loudoun County, he has likely played baseball or lacrosse, and he has likely taken private lessons from some "guru" or former major leaguer who, for $100 bucks an hour, will help your son make it to the show too. The Jensens' boys were studs, like their parents, and Jack and Jenny were deep in the travel baseball culture.

Jenny loved her wine, and Jack loved his Jenny — so it seemed. Jack didn't drink often, but when he did, the parents gathered around to hear him tell stories of playing baseball in the minor leagues. Jack always had a positive word for the players and parents. Jenny, seemingly, hung on his every word. If you found yourself on the back deck of a Brambleton baseball happy hour, you would find Jack and Jenny. You would have loved them. The neighbors wanted to be them.

Just last year, the McDougals were joking at one party, where the Wegmans wine was flowing, that they were going to go home and make love like the Jensens. Jimmy Mac said of his wife, "If she can play Jenny, I'll play Jack." The whole group laughed, though everyone else seemed drowned out by Mary's famous cackle. Jenny said, "Keep the lights off so you don't break character." No one thought she meant to be mean, but let's face it, Jimmy and Mary McDougal were *not* Jack and Jenny, and everyone got that joke.

Whatever charade the Jensens were living in their little slice of made-up America, it was over tonight. Jack was going to have his interrogation. He just didn't realize that Jenny actually might be the toughest suspect he ever had to break.

"Real man?" Jack shouted, not quite as a question. "This real man is the father of your children, you two-dollar slut." The unflappable Jack Jensen had just lost it completely. He was red-faced, the vein in his forehead bulging, his voice shaking right before it exploded.

She broke the professional interrogator just that quickly.

"How does your favorite faggoty song from your gay frat house go … 'Take the L out of lover, and it's over,' " Jenny quipped, without even batting an eyelash.

Jack Jensen lurched at her.

Chapter 3: Five Creams, Four Equals, Extra Hot

Fitz knew that the closest Dunkin' Donuts was up in the Broadlands. "Christ," he thought, "if there is one make-believe place I hate more than Brambleton, it's the white-trash version of Brambleton known as the Broadlands." Sheriff Tankersley once invited Fitz to an election event in the Broadlands, thinking that being seen with his famous star detective might be a good campaign photo op.

Fitz responded to the invite by simply telling Tankersley, "I hate farms."

The sheriff said, "Broadlands isn't a farm, Fitz."

"No? Why do they grow so many fucking turds there? It's a fucking turd farm," Fitz said matter-of-factly. Fitz didn't go to the event.

Turd farm or not, Fitz needed the coffee and wanted it from a drive through. This was a brutal murder, with an "A-hole" lawyer as a witness, and it was going to be a long night. So, Fitz was headed to the turd farm if only to get a decent cup of "fucking American" coffee. The truth be told, he had been to the establishment many times.

Fitz banged a left off Truro Parish into the complex and nearly fishtailed his old girl with the instant right at the Dunkin' Donuts. He soared around the back of the building, and the speaker at the drive-up scratched out what sounded like a Long Island Rail Road subway announcement, with a heavy Indian accent. Fitz had no idea what was said, but he barked his order back at the device.

"Gimme a large coffee, real goddamn coffee. I want *five* creams, *four* Equals, and make it *extra hot*."

The device crackled again, and all Fitz thought he heard was something about "Sweet' n Low."

"Hey, Juggdish ... fucking Equal. The blue shit. Four packets of the *blue* stuff go in the coffee."

"Ahh — Detective Fitz! Long time. Drive around."

When Fitz reached the window, he saw a familiar face. "Hari, thank Buddha it's you — this is extra hot with the Equals, right?"

"Fucking-A Detective Fitz," Rohit Hari smiled. "I have put an old-fashioned doughnut in for you, too, on me."

"For fuck's sake, Rohit, why do you hate me?"

"Mr. Fitz, you love old-fashioned, right?"

"Doc says no more doughnuts, Rohit, but if you keep the secret, I won't tell him. Besides, he's an Indian, too, and I have no idea what he is saying *either.*" Fitz smiled. "Wouldn't you know it, the only decent guy left in eastern Loudoun had to fly 8,000 miles to fucking get here," he thought.

"*And*, the only person in this county who knows how to make American coffee is a damned Indian. Jesus, we're fucked."

"No charge, Mr. Fitz."

"Thanks, Rohit. Say hello to the Mrs.," Fitz yelled as he peeled off. He didn't have time to argue again with Rohit. The man never let him pay, ever. Fitz hated it. He didn't want to owe anything to anyone, and he damn sure hated the idea of getting free doughnuts and coffee on the job. He'd had this fight with Rohit before, and the man wouldn't listen. So Fitz snuck in once a week and put twice as much in the tip jar on the counter just to be square. OK, maybe not everyone in the Broadlands was a turd.

When that store first opened, Fitz was in there getting coffee when a kid, as he would say, "all hopped up on something" held-up the store at gunpoint. Fitz talked the kid down even after the suspect grabbed a hostage, Rohit's wife, Irma. It was probably the command in Fitz's voice, a Marine thing, or maybe the way Fitz held his gun without shaking that convinced the druggie to stand down.

Just as Fitz thought he had defused the entire situation, the robber panicked and lurched for his gun. Fitz put three holes in his chest, about an inch apart. For Rohit, Detective Fitz never pays for coffee, and the same old-fashioned doughnut he ordered that night, seven years earlier, was always part of the deal.

Fitz never talks much about the incident, but as with many of his exploits, the other sheriff's officers always do. They say Fitz wasn't going to shoot the kid, but when he realized that the whole 20-minute ordeal made his coffee cold, he figured that was justification for a "clean shoot."

****

"Yes … fuck. Tell him to wait. Tell him pretty-please. Tell him he is tall, handsome and smart. Tell him old Fitz will come back and caress his ego for him."

Parker was on the other end of the phone pushing Fitz to return quickly as Bodine was getting ready to leave. "What the hell are you doing? Did you go inside and shoot somebody again?" Parker asked.

"Hey, it's not my fault they built 12 million houses between here and Brambleton, and they still have the same two-lane road that Gomer-fucking-Pyle used in this backward county in 1950. I will be there in three minutes. Sit on that Bodine A-hole."

Fitz used the F-word as if he collected a freshly printed Benjamin for each discharge. For some reason, however, he never said "asshole." He shortened it to "A-hole," which he thought gave it more kick.

****

Jeff Handly was white as the proverbial ghost.

"Dead? What do you mean, dead?"

"No ... no ... I know *what* dead means ... I mean .... dead how? Dead when?"

Handly never picked up his phone during K-state games, ever. But this was the third call in two minutes to his cell *and* his house phone. After screaming for his wife, Jane to pick up the phone, his cell rang again. It was Caylee Bodine. Caylee was sobbing as she tried to give the news of Jenny Jensen's death to Jeff Handly. She didn't have any details. She said her husband had called her quickly to explain why he left dinner abruptly and why he hadn't returned home and likely would not do so before daybreak.

Handly's voice sputtered as his words stumbled out of his mouth.

"Oh my God. Oh my God ... no ... no ... my God."

Handly dropped his phone as Jane dashed down the steps and then in from the kitchen. She saw the game on pause and looked quizzically at Jeff, half-irritated at being summoned by her husband who famously sat comfortably with his butt in the chair-and-a-half as he barked out commands. She hadn't been home too long, and she suspected Jeff didn't even know she'd been gone. She was trying to change fast and clean up when she heard the clamor.

Jane instantly knew something was wrong, the way any wife of 20 years can read the smallest tell in a husband's face, posture or mannerisms. Without any verbal communication, Jane Handly knew

Jeff hadn't called her to grab him a beer, fix him a snack or throw him an extra blanket.

Jane Handly knew, just looking at her husband, that something terrible had happened.

Handly blurted out, "It's not Jackson or Jeremy."

Even in shock, Jeff Handly knew his wife's mind was racing, processing and panicking about their boys. Jackson was off at college, and Jeremy was safe and sound in the basement on hour 17 of playing Fortnite.

"Jenny's dead. Someone murdered her."

Like an NPR public service message, the announcement came out clearly, matter-of-factly, without the expression one might have expected. Handly was hoping his serious, monotone delivery might blunt the devastating effect of the words on his wife.

Jennifer and Jane, or Jenny and Janie, were a complete set. You would just as soon travel around Loudoun with one jumper cable, or serve only salt without the pepper, than see Jenny without Janie or Janie without Jenny. They were the queens of the baseball moms. They went to church together, walked their dogs together, grocery shopped together. At any Brambleton party or soiree, Jenny and Janie were no less than 10 feet apart. Indeed, if one had the wine bottle, the other was holding the opener.

Janie Handly defined the word attractive. In her mid-40s, the athletic blonde was not in any way the natural beauty that was Jenny Jensen. She was simply attractive, fit, strong, confident and joyful. Janie was happy, and she wore her happiness like skin. She carried it daily, gave no effort to it; it was a constant reflection of her. The smile drew you in, the easy laugh made you comfortable and the southern charm was as real as fresh cane sugar.

Janie Handly would have been a great poker player, because even with the worst hand, she would be flush with a smile.

Right now, maybe for the first time in her life, Janie Handly was expressionless, joyless, nearly lifeless. Her eyes went cold, her skin turned gray and every ounce of what made Janie magically attractive disappeared in an instant. She seemed to first sway, then stutter, and then she sprinted from the room to the small half bath in the foyer off their kitchen.

Jeff Handly will never forget the sounds he heard next.

Janie threw up. Then she threw up again — and again. When she stopped, the wailing began. This wasn't regular sobbing; this was a soul pouring out every pain it ever felt, praying it could find a bottom.

"Sweetheart … let me in. Honey, are you OK?"

The wailing continued, and Jeff Handly slumped against the hallway wall, hand over his mouth, as he began, for the first time in his adult life, to sob openly for the pain of his wife. He couldn't even process what was happening.

****

As Fitz rolled back up Conquest Circle, the whole street could hear the unmistakable, rhythmic thumping of bass coming from his car. Van Halen's "Mean Street" thundered from the custom, eight-speaker sound system. It was the perfect tune for the night, even if the vanilla neighborhood of Brambleton's Section Two housing was often anything but mean.

In reality, Fitz thought, "a murder like this happens in a place exactly like this. But, this isn't stranger/danger crime. This isn't a home invasion, and it damn sure isn't gang- or drug-related. Christ, this isn't Sterling, Loudoun County's MS-13 headquarters," he thought. "This is *Brambleton*."

In fact, as Fitz pondered it, Loudoun County was not just a very rich county, it was a county with very few murders, making him one of the loneliest homicide detectives around. "Most murders here are domestic violence," he reminded himself.

His mind processed it all. "Senseless murders, drive-by shootings, rapes, muggings and criminal violence, those happen on the streets of broken cities with sick, dying and broken cultures. This was Brambleton, and that murder was a crime of passion. Someone hated Jenny Jensen so much, they went psycho-sicko on her. Or, maybe, someone loved her so much he went psycho-sicko on her." Fitz knew one thing about the killer: "Jenny Jensen and the killer were once definitely romantically involved. Or the killer wanted to be."

"This is home ... this is Mean Street," the radio blared as Fitz screeched to a stop, two doors down from the Jensen home. "What a shit show," Fitz thought to himself. "You have a murder in suburbia, and every deputy and EMT in the county is here like we are doing an active shooter exercise."

Fitz dismounted from his seat like an eager teenager, but on his face he wore the disgust of his years as he surveyed the situation on the street. "Christ, what is going on? Does Tankersley think he's fucking invading Brambleton? Charlie sent fewer slopes into the battle of Huê," he muttered.

"Sir?" asked the deputy who didn't realize Fitz was not talking to him. Tentatively the junior officer asked, "What was the battle of Huê?"

"Son, if you ever want to get out of newbie status, you may want to read a damned book. You know, the kind without naked chicks. Huê. The Tet Offensive? Have you ever heard of Tet, boy?"

"Ah, Tet? Like, Vietnam," the young deputy answered with little confidence.

"No shit, Sherlock. Viet-fucking-nam. Look up the battle of Huê. Report back to me and let me know if you find anything about me shooting about 6 million barefoot, straw-hat-wearing jungle rats who scurried into the city. Never saw anything like it, kid. You shoot one, and two more pop up."

"Yes, sir, I will look it up," Deputy Johnson promised.

Just as Fitz saw the medical examiner, his last thought from his back and forth with Johnson was, "I survived 25 days in the battle of Huê just to wet-nurse a publicity-hound sheriff in some make-believe town of A-holes. I wonder why I bothered ducking."

Parker met Fitz at the front door just as Fitz was picking up his gait and shifting into fourth gear hoping to catch up with the ME.

"We got a problem, boss," Parker said, exasperated.

"You mean, other than the dead lady with the Swiffer up her ass?" Fitz replied, completely dead-panned.

"Fucking Bodine apparently told Mrs. Fucking Bodine about the murder."

"Well, that's great timing, really. I was just lamenting not dying in some jungle hellhole at the hand of some slope whose land we had no fucking business being on. Thanks for the pick-me-up."

"Sorry, boss, Bodine insisted on making a call or he had to leave. I had no idea the schmuck would leak the murder to his wife."

Well, my day might be shitty. *And* that poor Jensen lady's day is definitely shittier. *But,* imagine being *Mrs. Fucking Bodine* … that's an entire shitty existence. Where is Bo-*dean,* that A-hole?"

28

****

"What's the fish special tonight? Wait, before you tell me, let me ask, is it any good? Without letting the server answer, Bodine continued, "I only ask because the last time I was here, the fish special tasted like ass." Bodine's voice carried over the din of the bustling crowd at Blue Ridge Grand Cafe.

"Well, tonight it's tilapia served over …," the young waitress began, before a nearly manic Bodine cut her off.

"Let's make this simple. Does it taste like ass? Or, does it taste like fish? Or maybe, at least a fish's ass? Or, is it more accurate to say, fishes' ass? You do know that in some situations, the correct plural of *fish* is indeed *fishes*," Bodine continued as if part of his own vaudeville act.

"In this situation, the correct description of my husband is 'horse's ass,' " Caylee Bodine jumped in, trying to save the poor server and order in a time and manner shorter than the famous scene from *When Harry Met Sally*. The two younger Bodine boys were giggling as the couple's only teenager cringed at the whole event, wishing he could find an eject button for his corner seat.

"Look, seriously, last week's fish was ass. I just want to know would you eat this fish, and if so, do you have any taste in food?" Bodine inquired, quite pleased with the scene he has acted out.

"People tonight have been raving about the tilapia, sir," The 23-year-old, blonde-in-a-bottle waitress stated, as if talking to someone who had made an honest, thoughtful inquiry. She'd done this dance with him before. "He was a good tipper, and honestly a decent guy, for an old man," she thought. So she smiled and used her

29

wares like any smart young server dealing with a self-absorbed, male blow-hard two decades past his prime.

"Fair enough. Are they raving because it tastes like ass or because it is overpriced?" Bodine retorted.

"None of the other customers tonight, or even this year, have mentioned an asslike taste," she said with a sheepish smile.

"Look at you being funny. That's my job, missy. Now give me the tilapia, and don't let Hector or José back there cook it to death. It's already dead. I'll have the house salad, with the dressing on the side. It's a honeymoon salad," Bodine emphasized.

"A *honeymoon* salad?" she foolishly inquired.

"Yes, a *honeymoon salad* — lett-uce alone, no dressing. Get it?"

"That's funny, sir," she said, without any real indication she thought so.

"Alan, the kids need to eat, it's already late." Caylee was decidedly unamused by tonight's "look at me, I am Alan Bodine" performance.

"OK, honey, please keep the wine glass full and upgrade me from your garbage white wine number one to your garbage white wine number two. The house wine tastes like a Boone Farms reject," Bodine stated as if fact.

"Calyee, don't eat that damn bread. You eat one bite of that and you will have to run 10 miles on …."

Alan Bodine fought his strong desire to ignore the ringtone from his phone that stopped him cold, but he knew he couldn't. Jenny had told him to set a special tone on his phone for both of her boys' numbers. Alan heard that ring … froze … looked at his phone and nearly jumped out of his seat, saying with authority, "Baby, I got to take this."

Bodine bolted up the aisle and headed off to the back corner of the restaurant by the restrooms, where it was most quiet and private.

"OK, son. Calm down. Are you safe right now? Good. I will be right there," Bodine assured Jason Jensen, a sobbing, nearly hysterical 10-year-old on the other end of the call.

Bodine was moving with purpose in that moment. He stopped at the table, looked his wife in the eye and with every measure of authority, he announced in a deliberately low tone the following clear, unmistakable message.

"I have a work emergency. Listen carefully. I can't talk now, I've got to go and I have no idea when I will be back. It's *serious*. I will call you when I can."

The tone, the look and the low voice told Caylee Bodine all she needed to know: Don't ask questions now. This must really be *serious*.

"We'll walk home or find a ride." Caylee assured him. She added, "Be safe."

Caylee Bodine was pure elegance. She was a super mom, marketing wizard, and loyal, loving wife. She was in every way the perfect match for Bodine. She was smart, sassy, irresistible and completely impervious to the Bodine personality and its need to dominate in any public forum. His antics rolled off her back because she knew something that only Bodine's best friends knew — he was a great dad, a loving husband and one hell of a coach. The Bodine persona was for show and a necessary outlet for him.

To those who didn't know Bodine, that persona made him one of the most irritating men on earth. But Bodine was fiercely loyal, and his friends would march behind him through hell in a gasoline suit to back him up. Undoubtedly, that was why Jenny Jensen trusted him in her most dire moment.

Chapter 4: Detective Trump and the Empty Tank

"Hogan, what the heck is going on out there? Did we make an arrest? I need an update. I must get with Brad and prepare a statement. We don't want a panic. Murder and Brambleton don't go together. This place is fast becoming the population epicenter of eastern Loudoun. I want to assure those residents that they are safe, and that the Tank has their back." Sheriff Tankersley nervously demanded information from the only deputy who would take his call.

"Sir, I have nothing on the investigation status."

"Where the hell is Fitz or Parker?" he demanded. "I called Fitz twice and Parker three times. Are they in hot pursuit of a lead? Why the hell isn't anyone answering my calls? I am the goddamn sheriff in this county."

Hogan thought long and hard before answering. He might have been green, but Hogan knew two things to be true. First, the guy on the other end of the line was his boss and everyone's boss. Second, the last thing Parker and Fitz said to him was "don't tell Tank a fucking thing or he'll dispatch an urban assault vehicle to our crime scene."

In that long pregnant pause, Hogan was calculating whom to piss off: the actual sheriff or Detective Fitzgerald — the man the actual sheriff wished he could be. "Easy choice," he thought. "I'm with Fitz."

In that microsecond, Hogan processed the same piece of advice he'd heard from about 15 sheriff's officers in his first year on the job: "Never, and I mean *never*, screw over Fitz. If you have his back, he'll have yours. In any fight, pick Fitz."

"Detective Fitzgerald high-tailed it out to pursue a *hot* lead, sir. Parker is in with a witness. To my knowledge, sir, they don't have the perpetrator, but they both think there is no immediate threat to the public … sir."

"That's all you have, Hogan?" Tankersley asked incredulously.

'Sorry, sir, that's it. Detective Fitzgerald was in a hurry, and … well … he doesn't answer to me, sir," Hogan said feigning a sheepish voice.

"No kidding, Hogan. Fucking Detective Trump there doesn't answer to me either, and I am the *real* sheriff. When you see either one of those two, you tell them the boss insists they check in — immediately. *You got that?'*

"Yes, sir," Hogan barked for effect.

"Repeat it back to me, Hogan, just as the Tank said it to you."

Hogan complied, and the phone line went dead.

"What a dick," thought Hogan. "Who voted for that schmuck? Who calls themselves 'the Tank'?"

Sherriff Linden Bradford "Tank" Tankersley grew up in an old Virginia household where he was known as a frail, sometimes shy boy called "Lindy" by his mother. His father rarely acknowledged him at all. From an early age, it was clear that while "Lindy" *might* be the product of his father's loins, he *surely* was the disappointment of his life.

His dad shipped "Lindy" Tankersley off to Hargrave Military Academy over the meek protestations of his mother. At Hargrave, "little Lindy" attempted to play any sport that would bolster his credentials as a man. He found that his skills never matched the needs of his insecurities. "Hargrave will make a man out of him; his father was heard telling his mother."

Tankersley might be the only kid since the 1950s to actually be stuffed in a locker by classmates who were sure old "Tank," as he began calling himself sophomore year, was more interested in peeping at them than the girls down the road at Chatham Hall.

At James Madison University, one of the premium frat houses accepted "Tank" as a pledge even after a unanimous vote to reject him. A few calls engineered by his father to the chapter's national headquarters granted him a rare reconsideration. He was the less-than-lovable Kent Dorfman of the house.

Tankersley majored in weightlifting, performance-enhancing drugs and a long series of failed and awkward dates. Some claim Tankersley met his first and only love at JMU … staring right back at him in the mirror. Tankersley loved weightlifting. He didn't need a friend for that activity. He also didn't have to be athletic to participate, and with some synthetic help, he found hours in the gym turned him, appearance-wise, into the man neither he nor his father ever thought he would be.

The squat, barrel-chested, 5-foot-9 Tankersley listed himself in his profile as 6 feet tall, which wasn't even true with his high-heeled shoes and lifts. By his late 30s, Tankersley had been a Loudoun sheriff's officer for 16 years. During that time, he became known among his fellow officers as "Drunk Tank." He had an uncanny knack and seemingly singular focus for arresting motorists for drunk driving. His sergeant once said, "Tankersley never met a drunk driver he couldn't take, in an unfair fight, using his weapon."

Tank Tankersley was unlikable, unimpressive and untrustworthy to nearly every group he encountered since prep school, except Loudoun voters. Go figure. The people who knew him least liked him most.

While Tank was busting drivers, he was also using family money to rack up advanced degrees in criminology and business management. The people of Loudoun might never have gotten the Tank if he had been accepted to law school. It turns out his undergrad 2.6 GPA and his 149 LSAT couldn't get him into George Mason law school, even with a call from his dad or his dad's best friend, a former U.S. senator. Some numbers are just too low even for the whitest of privilege.

Still, Tankersley looked great in his uniform. He also had two master's degrees, one an online MBA. His years of weight training and biannual commitment to teeth whitening made him a poster-child politician. When no other Republican was willing to take on the Democratic sheriff, there was Tank Tankersley, family money in hand, ready for the surprise election result of the decade. Tank rode 12 credits of public speaking and a backlash against the sitting president, combined with low voter turnout and his opponent's poorly timed scandal of adultery, all the way to a 273-vote win.

On the morning after the election, as fellow sheriff's officers moaned about Tankersley somehow winning, Fitz declared the winner to be "Sheriff 'Empty Tank.'"

When Tank was putting his management team together, he asked Fitz to be his deputy. He figured Fitz would give him credibility, and he surmised that Fitz was too old and too uninterested to run for his job. He also knew Fitz didn't respect him, but he thought he might like the title and raise before retirement. Tankersley was, if nothing else, a professional schemer.

Fitz famously declined the "generous offer," telling his closest friends, "I would rather have my manhood laminated." Of course, he told Tankersley that he was not cut out for a desk or politics but preferred to finish his time on the job solving cases. All of that was true.

****

"Brad, draft me a statement right now! I want to get out in front of this murder, and I have Channel 9, Channel 2, Channel 7, and the effing pit-bull from WJLA 24/7 News bird-dogging me."

"Tank, I am not sure you want to get out in front of the cameras until we get anything concrete from Fitzgerald. You might …."

"Screw that old bastard, Detective Trump," Tankersley barked at his public affairs chief, Bradley "Brad" Smith.

The Tank just loved to call Fitz "Detective Trump." Of course, he kept that mostly to his own inner circle. In fact, Tankersley was a bit concerned he let the crack slip earlier to a junior officer. He assumed Hogan had the good sense not to talk behind his sheriff's back.

Tankersley was no choirboy, and he was as salty and faux macho as the next insecure pretender with a life history of hiding from confrontation. Tankersley hated how Fitzgerald could seemingly say the most outrageous insults, about everyone and any ethnic group, and still be respected and fawned over by every law enforcement professional carrying a badge from New York to Florida.

After the rise of the irreverent candidate and now president Donald Trump, Tankersley started calling Fitz "Detective Trump." Obviously, Fitz hadn't yet heard about it.

"If you go out there, sir, we have to keep it very generic. No danger to the community, no reason for panic. Appears the victim knew the killer, stuff like that," Brad advised Tankersley.

Brad Smith was an old media pro and one of the better management team hires by Tankersley. Smith had contacts with every media outlet in the District, Maryland and Virginia — or as folks in the area call the three distinct groups that make up the DC area, the DMV. Smith knew how to horse-trade for time, offering media contacts great morsels to slow-roll stories or to get favorable coverage for Tank or the department. He knew which reporters had an ax to grind and which were the true professionals.

In modern local reporting, there weren't many old pros left. Many of the local reporters were nothing more than script readers and pretty boys and girls. They were easy to please and easier to shake for a real public relations expert. Mostly, they didn't ask hard questions on live camera, which no PR pro wanted of his subject.

The magic of Brad was that he staged Tank well, wrote him great copy and kept him on message. Tankersley had many flaws, but he knew what they were, and he trusted the team that guided him to his improbable win. Tank stayed in his lane. Still, as suggested by his time flexing in front of the mirror, the Tank had a not-so-subtle addiction to press coverage.

With a murder in Brambleton, where he had strong electoral support and many community connections, the Tank wanted to get out in the media and *be* in charge. He wanted to show the community his reassuring side.

Brad Smith knew he was holding a tiger by the tail, but he had bigger concerns than Tank. Peggy Felts from TV's WUSA9 was hot on this case, and she had details about a gruesome, almost macabre murder that neither Smith nor Tankersley could even confirm.

****

"Brad, pick up ur phone. Stop ducking me or I'll run the details on Bram w/o ur input." That was the text Brad Smith received from his old friend and sometime nemesis, Peggy Felts at Channel 9 in DC.

Brad just heard about the murder three minutes before getting that text *and* four calls on his personal cellphone all from the dynamic, persistent, resourceful pain-in-the-ass, Peggy Felts.

"Crap," thought Smith, "I haven't even talked to the boss, and fucking Felts has more info on this case than our lead detective. Shit."

Peggy Felts should have been more successful, really. She was like Diane Sawyer and Geraldo Rivera. She was smart, did her research, asked tough questions and wasn't afraid to mix it up. She was a reporter at heart with the bubbleheaded, bleach-blonde appearance of a news reader. Peggy had some wear on the tread, but you would have to be up close with fluorescent lighting to find it. Peggy had to be in her mid to late 50s, but her 28-year-old physique and always sharp-dressed appearance, layered with confidence and just the right application of base, made her look decades younger. She once said to a friend of her career, "I am an old pro in a young-looking woman's body still competing in a man's game."

Peggy spent plenty of time at various affiliates as an anchor, but she loved the reporting. And she could travel with or without a crew. She had no problem shooting her own B-roll and setting up the camera and staging her interviews on the fly. The lighting, the sound, the background, it was always right, even if she was a one-person crew.

She saved the local CBS affiliate money, and she brought it the ultimate professional able to cover any need. So Peggy got a lot of leeway on the stories she wanted to cover. More than that, Peggy wasn't going to be led around by the nose by some junior news producer. Peggy basically reported to Peggy and the station owner — who didn't mess with Peggy.

"U know what, FU Brad, I'll stake out every DD in LoCo & find Fitz," she texted next.

"Mother of pearl," thought Brad Smith. The last time Felts and Fitz mixed it up, the interview was picked up by the national network. Felts pushed Fitz on camera about an officer-involved shooting where Fitz shot and killed a serial rapist, apparently hitting him with six shots to the head.

In the on-camera interview, Fitz explained, "The assailant fired on me while I was in pursuit. I ducked behind a dumpster and took fire again. I used a diversion to distract the shooter and approximated my line of fire from the last known direction from which he shot."

Felts pounced on the recollection, thinking it incredible. "Detective Fitzgerald, are you telling me you got lucky and hit that man with six shots to the head from 60 feet in the dark?"

"No, ma'am, luck had nothing to do with it. The rapist's last victim was the mother of a six-year-old girl. The rapist forced the girl to watch the attack. I suspect the shooting was divine intervention."

"Are you saying God helped you shoot that man six times?" she asked, stunned.

"No ma'am, I get on my knees every day and thank God for my life. This was the first time he ever thanked me in return."

CBS ran that clip thinking Fitz came across as a deranged, cowboy cop. America thought he came across as a superhero. The final medical examiner's report and an independent investigation confirmed that Detective Fitz did, indeed, hit his armed target in the head six times, in the dark, from 74 feet.

****

"Bodine is in the family office, down the hall, first door on the right." Parker said. "I told him *not* to call anyone else about the murder unless he is calling his own counsel."

"Let me check with the doc first and find out what Sully knows," Fitz said as he processed the night's events. He'd rather know more than less when he speaks to Bodine, and getting some details from the medical examiner would help him on timeline issues, he thought.

Dr. Marcus Sullivan was the chief medical examiner, and he rarely met the dead bodies outside of his lab unless they were homicides. Sullivan had been in this job for nearly 20 years, and while Loudoun County didn't give him many murders, he was an experienced medical examiner who made his bones in Baltimore City long before he came to the exurbs of Virginia. In Baltimore, as a junior medical examiner, Sullivan saw more murder victims than he could ever recall, and there too he had seen nearly every manner of death.

In 34 years in the business, he never saw a Swiffer, or its predecessor, the mop, sticking out the backside of victim. He'd seen a mop handle shoved down the throat of drug mule once. He saw a guy shot in both eyes with a rivet gun, and he more than once had to reassemble dead bodies from puzzle pieces of sawed-off and severed limbs. In short, he'd seen worse, but he'd never seen *this*.

"Sully, what do we have?"

"We have a homicide, Fitz. And if I had to guess, this was a crime of passion where the killer freaked out and tried to make it look like something else after the death."

"Do you have a time of death, doc?"

"The victim died sometime between 9:50 and 10:30 p.m., based on the body temperature, morbidity, lividity, rigor and discoloration changes in the bruising."

"Defensive wounds?" Fitz asks.

"That's just it. There are none. Based on the wound on the back of her head, it appears she was struck from behind and likely knocked unconscious or was so dazed as to be defenseless."

"Was that the cause of death?" Fitz inquired.

"I can't tell for sure. The wound is significant, and based upon my initial examination, she was hit more than once. It's hard to be sure given the location, the bruising and the amount of blood and tangled hair. I can tell you this, detective, the killer apparently rolled her over here and then choked her. That's my hypothesis because of the lack of defensive wounds."

"You think if she was choked first, she would have fought back, and you would have found evidence of that fight, is that it, doc?"

"Correct. She had virtually nothing under her fingernails, and she had no bruising on her extremities. For example, if she were attacked from the front, she would have reflexively raised her hands to protect herself from the blow. I see no evidence of that, nor do I see any other external injuries to show she was engaged in a struggle with her attacker."

"All this other crap — it is postmortem?" Fitz said more as a declaration than as a question. By "other crap" Fitz clearly was referring to Swiffer situation.

"Of that I am certain. The only caveat is she does have one split nail and just a very small shaving of what I think is epidermis under two fingernails on her right hand. It is unlikely they come from this attack based on all the other physical evidence in the room, but Fitz, we need to know from whom it came."

Doctor Sullivan never broke from his formal, rhythmic, scientific approach to describing the facts as he saw them. That included his best effort to speak proper, formal English.

"Is it possible, Sully, that she had an initial altercation with her killer, say her husband or a lover, and he came back later and finished the job?"

"That type of speculation, detective, is entirely possible, but the proof of such a supposition falls more squarely in your field rather than my own."

"Is everything bagged and tagged?" Fitz asked.

"No, detective, we thought this time, sir, we would just, how do you say it — wing it." Dr. Sullivan said with his best effort at a wry smile.

"I just wanted to know how close ..."

"I understood, detective; I was just trying to get your dander up for my own jollies," the doctor said smiling broadly from a mouth full of crooked teeth.

"OK, doc, when the team starts getting results, can you make Parker the point?"

"Yes, detective."

"Doc, one more question. Are you sure she was tied like that after death, and the moppy-Swiffer-thingy inserted last?" He wasn't so much questioning Sully's findings as much as he wanted to hear the precise explanation. He thought asking it this way would prompt a pinpoint, detailed explanation, the type he might find more useful.

"The ligatures are well tied, using a common knot. That is to say, no particularly special skills were necessary or employed. The lack of marks on the skin where the ligatures are pulled more tightly show she was already dead when applied," Sully explained before continuing. "I suspect she was killed, her pants removed, then she was tied up. Afterward, the killer, for effect, inserted the … what did you call it … thingy?" Sully surmised as Fitz watched him carefully.

"Doc, how do we know she ever had on pants? Maybe she was in a love romp, got in a dispute with her lover, got up, and he struck her from behind in a rage?" Fitz described, even re-enacting out the possibility in a form of charades.

"Detective Fitzgerald, I can't prove or disprove your theory. However, I note with interest the following additional facts. A pair of boots was recovered in close proximity to the body. The boots are some distance from the door, which means it is highly unlikely they were removed upon coming home. They are nowhere near the sofa, nor are they in some sensible distance from the fireplace hearth. Thus, I have hypothesized they were removed by the killer postmortem and left in the disorderly fashion in which they were found and photographed."

"So, you don't think she peeled them off to get down with her lover, is that your point?" Fitz pushed him.

"It is highly unlikely. In addition, there is the matter of the pants and undergarment, if any."

"Do tell, doctor, have they been bagged and tagged too?"

"They, sir, are not to be found anywhere on the ground floor of this home. Thus, she would have had to be walking around with just this top and her riding boots, which, with her son in the home, seems highly unlikely."

"Wait …you are saying the killer took the pants and panties?" Fitz asked, raising his right eyebrow.

"I am saying, Fitz, that the pants, skirt or undergarment, if any, are not here."

"Well, Sully, we do know that it's not a skirt," Fitz declared.

"How, sir, do we rule that out?" asked the man Fitz loved to call Sully.

"Doctor, I have seven daughters, aged 48 to 18. Trust me, one doesn't wear a skirt with that top," Fitz deadpanned.

"Again, detective, that is an area of *your* expertise, not mine. As for undergarments, I don't know what kind, if any, she might have been wearing."

"I have an idea about that, Sully, but I won't bore you with it now. Let's get on the results of any fiber, blood, hair or prints, and we can start ruling people in or out," Fitz commanded, signaling the end of his immediate inquiry.

Fitz turned and walked toward the foyer, bellowing out a sincere "thanks, Sully" as he departed.

"Fitz!" Dr. Sullivan yelled surprisingly. "I believe you are correct. I can't imagine what skirt would work with, let alone complement, that top."

In a macabre and gruesome murder scene, sometimes trite humor was the only available release for decent people looking to decompress.

****

"It's Parker. Have we located the husband?"

45

"Not yet, sir, no sign of him. Car's in the driveway. No service or cab company has sent a car here, best we can tell," said Detective Galloway.

"We issued a BOLO for him. We've contacted his agency, and it's been remarkably unhelpful."

"What is the agency?" Parker snapped.

"FBI, sir."

"Please tell me, please, Galloway, just fucking lie if you have to, that the husband is just some paper-pushing flunky among the FBI's 35K employees and not a fucking G-man, agent-type," Parker groaned audibly.

"FBI identified him as a special agent attached to the HIG. It wouldn't even tell me what he did for the group. Heck, it wouldn't tell me what the HIG even was. The guy literally told me to Google the group for more information. The stiff then said to me, quote, 'Agent Jensen's movements are not subject to disclosure without authorization from the Office of the General Counsel of the Bureau.' "

"Well, Galloway, looks like you got the canoe captain."

"Canoe captain?" Galloway asked, missing the refence.

"Yeah Galloway, the douche canoe captain." Galloway chuckled over the line.

The rivalry between FBI agents and local law enforcement, often called "LEOs" by federal agents, was real. In fact, it was painful sometimes with big-city or large, sophisticated jurisdictions. The reason was simple: FBI agents are the gold standard in federal law enforcement and always have been. The problem is, they keep telling everyone that.

In sophisticated cities and large, wealthy jurisdictions, the LEOs often have outstanding career pros who don't like having their jurisdiction or expertise challenged. Most LEOs respect the expertise that the FBI can bring to an investigation, in particular its world-famous profiling division and its strong, sophisticated cybercrime division.

When it comes to old-fashioned cop work, most jurisdictions see FBI agents as less experienced, less sophisticated and less street smart than their own best and brightest. The truth probably lies somewhere in between those two starkly different perceptions.

One thing FBI agents and LEOs agree on is this: Neither likes to deal with FBI brass, a group best described as "arrogance on steroids. Perhaps the name Comey rings a bell?" Parker thought. "Many jurisdictions have great special agents in charge, but there is just something about the bunker mentality and God complex that emanates from the seventh-floor executive management team at FBI. Nobody likes those guys very much." With the recent EMT scandals involving President Trump and Secretary Clinton, the reputation of the group has been further sullied, and the politics has increasingly split field agents from brass.

Most FBI units reporting out of or taking direction from the DC headquarters are under fire, under duress and seemingly unable to play nice with anyone.

Parker knew about the HIG. He knew the interrogation unit has some of the FBI's best agents, and the work it is doing worldwide is little known, but its contributions are immeasurable in the fight against terror threats abroad and at home. Jack Jensen, as it would turn out, was a critical part of that unit, and if the FBI brass were going to make local LEOs jump through hoops on a regular request, you can bet the hoops would be damn small and mighty high on this request.

"The guy tucked his kid into bed tonight, according to the kid. So he can't have gone far in this short period of time. I hope the FBI isn't hiding him out on some federal facility." Parker said to Galloway, more ending his thoughts aloud.

"Should we get the sheriff to make this request?" Galloway asked.

"When I tell this to Tankersley, he's going to spend three days trying to figure out how many FBI hand jobs he can give before he pushes them for real information. Fuck and double fuck," the colorful Parker said to himself. Parker knew that the FBI had to cooperate quickly on Jensen, even if only to verify his whereabouts. How would he get them to do that?

Chapter 5: You Can't Handle the Truth

"Mr. Bo-*dine,* thank you for your patience," Fitz started with his best effort at playing good cop.

Bodine leapt in, cutting him off with his commanding style. "Have you located Jack Jensen?"

Fitz studied Bodine carefully, not wanting to escalate the initial moment into a discourse that Fitz did not completely control. Interrogation was a bit like trial work. Fitz may never have practiced law, but he understood both the science and art of trial work. He knew too how keenly those skills folded into interrogation. In trial, a lawyer who best keeps control of the room, is best positioned to win.

Fitz spent more time in courtrooms than 99 percent of lawyers. He was the perfect witness in any criminal case. Some of that came from four decades of honing his craft, fencing with trial lawyers and understanding all the traps. Mostly, Fitz understood that the power of trial work wasn't merely in what was said or how it was said. It was in staying calm while systematically evaluating all that was taking place in the room.

A good trial lawyer knew, heard and saw everything in the courtroom. He saw every skeptic, he found ever true believer and he or she could read an audience. This powerful skill guided with precision the selection and omission of every word said or unsaid. Likewise, that experience and talent told a great trial lawyer when to look at the jury, the judge, the defendant, or even up to the heavens. Mostly, that intuition guided a trial lawyer to whichever juror needed a personal appeal. All of this was about control.

The power of interrogation is also the power of observation. In a perfect world, Fitz would have more time to observe Bodine.

But he'd already learned so much from their first, short, machismo contest.

Of course, the success of a great lawyer, great witness and great interrogator depended on one intangible trait that could not be learned. The power of persuasion comes from the credibility of the witness, the lawyer or the interrogator.

With greater clarity … the power of persuasion in the great lawyer, witness or interrogator comes from the *perception* of credibility. Fitz may have been many decades removed from law school, but he always remembered the sage advice of his trial advocacy Professor, a former judge.

Fitz remembered fondly Judge Kelley, an old Virginia trial legend who later was elevated to the bench. Judge Kelley told his law students, "Remember, it doesn't matter if you are telling the truth or stone-cold lying. What matters is whether you appear unshakably credible." He noted, "Most great witnesses and lawyers with that natural credibility were truth-tellers." Fitz took comfort in that. The judge said that "credibility oozes from some witnesses, and it often comes from strong, confident witnesses who don't worry about what to say, how to say it or how they appear."

Fitz found Kelley to be right nearly 100 percent of the time, though he noted the rule broke down sometimes when dealing with true sociopaths. But Kelley was right about one other important witness reality: "A nervous witness may or may not be telling the truth, while a strong, confident witness is usually truthful."

Bodine was confident. He was strong. He was, Fitz thought begrudgingly, impressive. Bodine looked you in the eye. He never shrunk from the moment. He sat with the posture of a man ready to get down to business. He had not one single sign of concern. If Bodine were hiding key facts or involved in this murder, Fitz would have been shocked, just based on his total of these eight minutes of observations. Still, this process was just in the opening minutes, and time would tell if that credibility was a skillfully polished veneer or the timber of a rock-solid witness. Fitz also knew that Bodine the trial lawyer would be fighting to control this interrogation.

"Do you know Jack Jensen?"

"Of course I know Jack Jensen. His boy Jason played on my Little League team and is now on my travel baseball team," Bodine barked as if annoyed by an obvious waste of his time.

"You didn't answer my question," Bodine then interjected again.

"My apologies, Mr. Bodine. We have not yet located Mr. Jensen. Is it OK if we return to my questions so that we can draw closer to meaningful leads in this case?"

"Proceed," Bodine said calmly as he retreated from the front of his chair, seemingly unfazed and unimpressed.

"Am I to understand you represent the victim, Mrs. Jensen, in her pending divorce? Isn't that an awkward, if not an ethical dilemma for you?" Fitz asked.

Bodine returned back to the front of his chair. "Wait, what? I am a divorce lawyer and commercial litigator, but I don't represent Jenny Jensen as her divorce lawyer. From where did you get that idea?"

Fitz was pleased to keep Bodine from being too relaxed. "I heard you were her lawyer, from Mr. Parker, and I assumed that it was for the purpose of divorce. You are saying that is not true?"

"I *am saying* that is not true."

"For what purpose do you represent her?"

"Normally, I obviously would not be able to discuss …."

"Yes, Mr. Bodine, I seem to recall from studying for the bar exam that your professional relationship and whether or for what purpose you met is all part of a privileged relationship. But, according to my medical examiner, your privilege concerns died between 9:45 p.m. and 10:30 p.m. tonight. I think you have seen the evidence — that is your client's dead body?" Fitz worked to rattle Bodine.

"Correct, the privilege has expired under these circumstances. Did you say you took the bar exam?" Bodine asked, genuinely surprised.

"Yes Mr. Bodine, I graduated from UVA law, and I took the bar exam, though I never practiced. Law school was enough of lawyers for me," Fitz said without any hint he was kidding.

"Damn, detective, you're only part Neanderthal? Fascinating."

Fitz was momentarily pleased with himself, having both made Bodine uncomfortable and made a connection with him in a matter of minutes, two excellent interrogation techniques.

"Mrs. Fitzgerald can testify with greater specificity as to the size and scope of my caveman persona."

"I bet," laughed Bodine, who suddenly felt a strange new respect for the detective.

"You were at this murder scene nearly the same time our units arrived, correct?" Fitz used his open-ended cross-examination technique, wondering if the seasoned lawyer would simply answer the question or feel compelled to fill in with an explanation.

"That's correct."

"And ...."

"Is there a question to follow, or should I deduce one from the tone?" Bodine asked.

Fitz shifted in his chair. He understood now that Bodine was *not* going to do his work for him. It wasn't that Bodine was being deceptive Fitz thought. He really was so good at what he did, and so well trained, that he was not going to volunteer and fill in testimony without a question. That could make this process long, tedious and irritating to most investigators. "Frankly," Fitz thought to himself, "most lawyers can't shut up. They are not great witnesses. Bodine clearly has taken a few thousand depositions, and he likely remembers and follows the advice he gives his own clients."

Fitz decided to test his theory. "Alan, do you know what time it is?"

"Yes, detective," Bodine answered with a coy smile and perhaps even the smallest of winks.

Fitz now understood, Bodine was prepared to answer only the question that was asked, not one that was implied. If he was going to fill in the blanks, of course, Bodine would have told him what time it was.

"Alan, do you have any spare time to do much outside reading for pleasure?" Fitz asked.

"No."

"One simple, guilty pleasure of mine is reading murder mysteries," Fitz continued.

He left a pregnant pause after the sentence, inviting Bodine again, to perhaps fill in the blanks and jump in with active cooperation. The pregnant pause, lawyers call it, a great weapon in interrogation and depositions.

Most people get nervous and given the chance to fill in the silence in an uncomfortable situation, they start talking. Sometimes, a lawyer can use this technique in a deposition and find a witness still spilling his or her story 20 minutes later, with no new question pending. If you ever filmed what happens under a table during depositions, you would see a defense lawyer with a client who has diarrhea of the mouth actually kick his or her client to shut them up.

Fitz's second test of the pregnant pause technique proved again he wasn't going to elicit active cooperation from Bodine, but he decided to push forward with a few more tries.

Fitz took a long fake sip of his now cold coffee, settled back into his chair and continued.

"Have you ever heard of Kinsey Milhone?"

"No."

"That's a shame; she's a brilliantly written fictional character. She's the protagonist in a truly fabulous series of books known as the alphabet murder mystery series written by the incomparable Sue Grafton."

Again, Bodine was unmoved. Still he was clearly engaged, watching Fitz closely and wondering, "Where the hell is this headed?"

"Sue Grafton wrote a book for every letter of the alphabet except Z. Each was a murder mystery. Her main character was a female, private investigator who she brilliantly created with the opening book in the series. I am up to about K."

Again, Bodine wasn't biting, and to be honest, he was starting to wonder, "Who the fuck names their kid Kinsey, even in fiction?" But Bodine refused to show Fitz any interest in this obvious frolic and detour. He decided to enjoy the ride and see where it went.

"I love the writing because it is short, crisp, funny and thoughtful. Grafton captures these seedy people well, and the plots are unpredictable. The reads are easy, and they are a guilty pleasure. Truth be told, there are very few holes in the legal or criminal justice side of her stories." Fitz continued on trying to bait Bodine.

"Interesting as your cultural habits are, detective, is it possible we can proceed so that I may get home before my youngest graduates from high school? He's 10." Bodine couldn't help himself. He was now downright irritated by this delay.

"I thought we were bonding," Fitz laughed, recognizing that he was drawing Bodine's interest and ire. "Well, Alan, poor Ms. Grafton recently passed away," he continued in a fatherly tone. "And her first book reminds me of you and this current situation between us, that's all."

God, Bodine wanted to ask, how so? But there was no way he was going to give Fitz that moment.

"In her first book, the murder victim was a smart, cold, calculating, insufferable divorce lawyer. The guy was a real A-hole."

Parker chuckled, "Any chance his name was Bodine, boss?"

"I would have led with that, Parker," Fitz smiled as he played off his partner. "However, since our divorce lawyer guy here has a sudden interest in moving along, I will get at the point.

"That would be nice," a now visibly irritated Bodine jumped in.

"The first book was titled *A is for Alibi*." Fitz emphasized for effect.

Bodine broke down and asked, "Your point, detective?"

"My point is to ask you, sir, do you have an alibi? More precisely, Alan, did you murder Jenny Jensen?"

Bodine paused, quite perceptively. "It's a compound question," he replied trying to gain back some control of the process.

"So, it is. Please split it and answer both."

"Yes, I have an alibi. No, I didn't kill her," Bodine said tersely.

"Alan, do you know any facts about who murdered her or why?"

"No."

"Alan, I want to believe you. Now that we have that out of the way, can I ask you to embrace more substantive answers so that we are not here all night with you trying to get me to ask the precise, correct, follow-up question?" Fitz smiled at him again. "That way, I can get home to see my daughter graduate high school … this coming June."

Detective Parker's New Jersey persona had simply had enough of this dance.

"Bodine, for crying out loud, pal, we have a gruesome murder, a missing husband, your strange, perfectly timed appearance here and the remarkable statement of a 10-year-old boy who said, and I fucking quote, 'My mom told me if anything bad happens to her, call 911 and then immediately call Mr. Bodine.' "

****

Jenny Jensen didn't really believe in God. She went to church because, well, she wanted to believe. She wanted there to be something more than what she knew, which was that when you die that's it. In fact, the whole idea of the "invisible man in the sky" was an absurdity to her. She went to church for her kids. She went to church for her family's community reputation. She went to church because her dad would have wanted her to do so. She went to church with her best friend, hoping her faith would wash off on her. In some secret part of her tortured soul, however, she went there hoping someone or something would prove her wrong.

Lying there in that strange bed — with her heart still pounding in her chest, a bead of sweat rolling down her forehead as her perfect skin glistened from the sheen created by that experience — she thought, "Wow, if there is a god, I think I just saw him."

Jenny Jensen had never made love like that before. She'd made love more than anyone she knew, and she had been with many men, too many, really — but this was crazy. This was like a cheap dime-store, lusty-busty novel, wrapped in modern porn.

Her legs were trembling, her fingers nearly stiff from clenching the bedpost. All in one, she was euphoric, yet completely drained. In bed, with sex, she had always been in charge. She was the teacher, the giver, the lover. She provided the experience, and the partner brought it home as a remembrance to keep close or to drive him insane. Here, she was reduced to a starry-eyed teenager. Sick with love, soaked like a marathoner, and not one damn bit guilty about it. Love … like this … couldn't possibly be wrong.

"How have I never experienced this before," she thought.

Jenny had had sex with nearly two dozen men in the past eight years. Sometimes she wondered, "Am I just a dirty whore?" With each lover she often asked herself, "What am I looking for?" Yes, the thrill was amazing. Mostly, she loved the adoration, the fawning, the begging. She loved the power. Sometimes she actually reached orgasm, but mostly her pleasure came from luring in the prey, making them get off and leaving them wanting more.

Those insane sex romps were simply one-off events. Strangers, friends' husbands, clients, a rival Realtor and even her neighbor's husband in the bathroom of the fish-taco joint — while the two families were eating dinner together. It all meant little to her other than the adrenaline rush. She might as well have been jumping out of planes.

This experience — a long time in the making — it was new in every way.

****

Janie Handly had been in that bathroom for three hours. About an hour after the wailing turned to sobbing and sniffling, the room went quiet. It was too quiet. Jeff Handly had been drinking now for the last two hours, and for the last hour of that he had been downstairs trying to keep his son busy so that the boy would not stumble upon his mother. Handly's son was "perfectly oblivious," he thought. "We are talking about a 14-year-old boy, in his boy cave, with snacks, mainlining his Xbox."

Jeff Handly's mind was racing. His heart was pounding. He had gone from shocked to angry to panicked to a disgusting sense of relief. He couldn't believe Jenny was dead. He never really wanted her dead. In fact, all he really wanted was her — just one more time.

Handly was certain Jenny got so close to Janie just to torture him. Her head games were unreal. She lured him like the weak middle-aged, male prey that he was, used him and then left him. Of course, she left him with a memory of the most amazing sex he'd ever had, the price of which was his soul. That memory haunted him, but mostly, it was the weight of the guilt and shame he carried every day that wore on him.

"Janie was a saint and beautiful," he thought. "Like a fool, I risked all I had … all that we had … just to be with Jenny. It clearly meant nothing to her."

Handly lived with that guilt for two years. It took him a few months after that reckless, insane night to realize that to Jenny, he was a one-trick pony. He went from following her like a puppy looking for another treat to outright resenting her presence. The worst part was, he had to eat that resentment every day and pretend she was the best ever — all for Janie.

The woman was dead now, and Handly was just hoping that with her was the only other proof of his infidelity and weakness. "Jesus," he thought, "I have lived in pure fear that one day, that sick, twisted woman would tell Janie … and that would become the new last time Jenny Jensen ever fucked me."

For now, he had to gain his composure. He was drunk, he was pathetic and he was riddled with too many thoughts and emotions. His wife, however, needed him. Maybe this event, crazy as it was, would give them a clean slate. He'd never stopped loving Janie, even in his act of idiocy and infidelity.

Like a fat man gorging on cheap carbs and belching regret, the drunk Handly promised himself, "no more." He resolved to be Janie's rock. First, however, he had to find a bit more than resolve to get off the couch. Half a bottle of Jack Daniels, two Coca-Colas and a 55-gallon drum of guilt and shame were a potent mix and a sizable anchor for a middle-aged man.

"Stay clueless, kid," he said in a loud voice toward his teenage son.

Jeremy Handly was yelling into his headset with the volume cranked. He was in the final four of yet another game of Fortnite. He had no idea why his dad let him play into the wee hours, nor did he care. This time, he was finally going to take down his best friend CK, the Fortnite legend of Bram Middle School. There was no shot on earth that Jeremy Handly ever heard his father's pathetic, out loud lament.

Handly staggered up the steps and poured himself out of the basement, staring right at that bathroom door. The door between the woman he loved and the man who had foolishly betrayed her. He drew a deep breath for courage and resolve and thought one more time of his affair with Jenny: "Thank God, Janie didn't know."

"Janie. Jan-ie … come on, honey. Let's talk about this. Jeremy will be up soon," he said in his best, I'm-a-loving-and-caring-husband voice.

The door, shockingly, popped open. Janie was still a shade of gray. Her eyes were puffy, red and both underlined by and accented with dark bags — bags that never before sat on that face. Janie's hair was bedraggled. It was something between bedhead and hat-head after a week of rain and high humidity. The woman before him wasn't sad and upset; she was broken. The Janie Handly who existed before the news of Jenny didn't exist in the human shell now before her husband.

"We need to pull ourselves together for the boys and Jack. My god, Jack must be losing his mind," Jeff Handly heard his own words slide from his mouth.

"Jack can't help Jenny now," Janie said robotically.

****

Jenny Jensen sidled up to Coach Bodine right before he was about to give his famous pregame speech to his 10U travel baseball team. Jenny's son had been on Coach Bodine's team long enough for her to know when she could squeeze in and get a word with the coach during his frenetic pregame routine.

"Alan" she said firmly as she approached him on the fence line at Lions Field.

Bodine turned and made a familiar hand gesture in the form of a stop sign, like he was directing traffic.

"Alan — now!" she said louder than she wanted, but not so loud that anyone else could hear.

Bodine didn't miss the cue. Whatever the "emergency" was, it was real. Jenny Jensen was the perfect travel mom, which meant she wasn't about to give coaching advice or some suggestion to have the team wear pink laces for some cause or another. He suspected it might be that her son Jason was under the weather.

He approached the fence line and leaned toward Jenny.

"Hey, Jenny, not a great time, what's up? Jason OK?"

Jenny Jensen put on her famous smile. For all who would witness this interaction, she wanted to ensure that it would look innocuous.

"Don't do anything but smile or chuckle," she said authoritatively. "Pretend what I say is funny, stupid, meaningless pregame chatter. But treat what you hear as gospel — the absolute truth," she continued.

"Someone is stalking me. I think they want me dead. My marriage is over, and I don't know if the stalker is Jack or someone Jack has paid. But it could be several people. I know this for sure — someone is trying to kill me." She paused, looking at Bodine with that same have-a-great-game, you-are-the-best-ever smile on her face.

Bodine let out a laugh, a made-for-TV roar produced for the busybody, Ashburn parent types who might be watching their interaction.

"I hear you. How can I help?" he asked with the most genuine, transparently phony smile he could muster, all for those eyeing them from the stands.

"When can we meet alone, where no one will suspect anything? It has to be today or tomorrow."

"Caylee is down in Fredericksburg with the 14Us. Stop by the house tonight at 6 p.m." Bodine said with another forced and contrived chuckle.

He walked toward the dugout and yelled out to the coaches, "Put Jason at short and bat him cleanup, by order of Coach Jenny Jensen."

Jenny yelled across the field, "Hey, that's not true!"

"You can't handle the truth," Bodine barked in his best Jack Nicholson impression.

"Hawks! Noses on the fence, mouths closed, ears open," Bodine bellowed to his team, loud enough to be heard in Prince William County.

"Who wants to have fun today?"

Twelve voices exploded in unison, "Meeeee!"

"Is it fun when we are not baseball ready?"

"No, coach."

"Is it fun when we don't throw strikes?"

"No, coach."

"Is it fun when we take strikes down the middle?"

"No, coach."

"Is it fun when we swing at balls out of the zone?"

"No, coach."

"Is it fun when your pitcher is working his butt off and you are guessing the airline company of the plane flying overhead?"

"No, coach."

"Is it fun to take strike three — ever?"

"No, coach."

Is it fun to lose games to teams we should beat?

"No, coach."

"Good! Let's go have some fun."

Chapter 6: *Semper Fidelis*

"Reagan Catherine Fitzgerald, do you have a minute for your father?" Abby Fitzgerald yelled up the center-hall steps to her youngest daughter.

Reagan Fitzgerald was the classic product of Irish Catholic parents who, fertile and fit, sometimes think the biological clock driving reproduction has run out when it has not. The youngest of Detective Fitz's seven girls, Reagan was a senior at Loudoun Valley High School. She was 18, and her mom, Abby, was thrilled beyond belief when she realized, at age 48, she was going to have another baby.

Upon the news that his wife was pregnant yet again, Detective Fitzgerald jokingly called for an investigation before puffing out his chest and spending a week bragging about his virility.

Fitz didn't engage in much meaningless conversation. If he was going to talk to people, it was going to be about classic rock or preferably his girls. Fitz had been raising daughters since his first was born in 1970. In February 2000, his amazing wife give birth to his last child. He jokingly called her his Y-too-many-K's baby. By every calculable measure, she was spoiled, at least by Fitzgerald standards. Of course, Mrs. Fitzgerald would tell you, "Fitz spoils all the girls."

Fitz loved those girls. For the manliest man in America, no one knew more about braiding hair, picking out dresses, giving makeup advice, mending broken hearts and holding tea parties. Fitz knew the name of the 107 Barbies amassed by all his girls. In the most miserable of times, under the worst circumstances, real or hormonal, Detective Fitzgerald was the perfect counselor.

Misogynist and profanity expert by day, Fitz was the Dr. Phil of his house by night. His wife, Abby, was always amazed at his quiet patience with the girls and so thankful that from 48 to 18, these women — well, except for maybe Quinn — would talk to and listen to their father on any issue, fearlessly. Today, she knew Fitz would be tested as almost never before.

Fitz started this day, the very same day of the Jensen murder, the same way he started every day. He was up at 5:30 a.m. He would run his one-, three- or five-mile neighborhood loop. He would finish with 500 pushups in the basement, where his workout space included a rack of mixed cassette tapes that made the south wall of his basement look like an old Sam Goody store. He showered in the basement too, because every other bathroom in the house was in use. Then he would arrive upstairs, where Abby would greet him with some Dunkin' Donuts coffee she ground and brewed freshly for him.

Abigail Elizabeth Kelley fell in love with Fitz in the third grade. She figured out what it was by the eighth grade. Then, in her sophomore year of high school, she told him. When she did, he confessed his love to her on the spot, with a sweetness and tenderness she had never forgotten and they had never lost.

In a world of bile, where marriage had become disposable, the Fitzgeralds were the model for true love. Their marriage was passionate, hysterical, loving and adventurous. It was comfortable but only for those reasons. If they worked at it, no one had ever seen the labor.

Abby was every bit as strong if not stronger than Fitz, a point she proved giving birth to their first child while her teenage husband was fighting in Vietnam. Their marriage, like any great pairing, however, wasn't a competition. It wasn't about keeping score or managing each other. It was a love story among equals, passionate for each other and devoted to their family. It was a timeless love affair.

64

Abby met the man she called "Fitz" or "Fitzy" at the landing of the basement steps that morning. She had his Yeti in her hand, and she used the magic words that caught his attention.

"Fitzy, I need your help today."

This meant there was a "daughter issue." More specifically, the use of the term "Fitzy" rather than "Fitz" meant it was serious, he wasn't going to like it and she was warming him up with the charming pet name that she used in advance of either being amorous or needing a favor.

Fitz was sure Abby wasn't about to ask for a morning of lovemaking. The detective in him did now wonder if last night's better bottle of wine and the evening's passion that followed might not be connected to this morning's favor. Fitz didn't care either way. Heck, after last night, he would shoot someone if that was the price of the evening's events.

"Your daughter informed me yesterday that she was joining the Marine Corps upon graduation," Abbey stated with the unmistakable emphasis on the words *your daughter*.

Fitz busted out laughing. "Christ, she really hates you."

"Fitz, this is not funny. I don't think she is joking. She has a stubborn streak longer than her father had at 18. You might recall that crazy bastard turned down an athletic scholarship to be an infantry Marine in a hot war," Abby charged, using a line she often dusted off for just such occasions to describe Fitz and undesirable characteristics he obviously gave to her otherwise perfect children.

"Well, she's not joining the Marines this year, or in the next four years, so don't sweat it. Where is my little princess?"

"She's in hour two of the shower and makeup process. She should be down in a few minutes. Can you talk to her?"

****

Bodine's LS Hawks crushed their 10U opponent. The Hawks had lost only 12 games in three years, having won 12 tournaments and amassing an overall record of 73-12. Bodine prepared his team practice plans like he was going to trial, and not one minute was wasted. This was not a 1970s Little League practice with 12 kids picking daisies while a coach threw blooper balls for batting practice.

Bodine had five coaches, and everyone had a specific assignment. The practice moved like a Marine Corps boot camp, and Coach Bodine even built in water breaks, which were taken in fast, 45-second intervals between drills. Bodine was hard on the kids, but he believed he wasn't merely building baseball players, he was building young men learning to work hard, work as a team and fight to get better. Bodine left nothing to chance, and the results showed on the field. They likewise showed in the courtroom.

At home, Team Bodine was also the model of a well-raised group of boys who respected their parents, said "yes sir" and "no ma'am" to their neighbors and always kept an orderly and spotless home. Just as on the baseball field, however, Bodine punctuated that hard work and order with fun, and his boys worshiped him. If you spent five minutes in the presence of Bodine and his sons, you would see the affection he unabashedly poured on them when they were being good boys. Likewise, you would see the order he kept when the boys stepped out of line.

Bodine liked order, and that forced him to work harder than his opponents. He worked harder in his law practice, on the baseball field, and on his family relationships. Tonight, he thought, "I have some hard work ahead."

At 6 p.m. on the button, Jenny Jensen's car pulled up in front of Bodine's Brambleton home. Even though it was a beautiful spring evening, Jenny hustled from her sporty, white Range Rover to Bodine's front door as if it were a cold, windy winter day. She knocked more than causally. Bodine had seen her the whole way from his office window, yet he was not fast enough to open the door before the second, impatient, stronger rat-a-tat-tat sounded. He was both surprised and a bit miffed at her impatience.

"Come on in," he said as she rushed past him before the official, formal invite was completed.

"Thank God you're home," she said, surprising Bodine with a tone that indicated there was some question about whether he remembered the pointed exchange from four hours earlier on the baseball field. "Are you alone? Is it safe?"

"Hey, Jenny, relax. We're all set for this meeting. You're safe. It's just us. I sent Max down to CK's house. Jill's making the boys dinner. It's just us. Caylee won't be back from the other games until about 8:30. Let's talk in the office."

Jenny took two steps into Alan's office at the front of his house and froze, like kids hearing the bell at recess at a Catholic grammar school.

"Can we do this somewhere else?" she nervously asked.

"You mean leave the house?" Alan looked, somewhat puzzled.

"No. God, no. I don't want to be in front of any windows, that's all. I have no idea if I was followed."

"Jenny, your very conspicuous vehicle is parked prominently out front. This isn't exactly a secret meeting of the allied leadership," Alan said looking at her a bit taken aback by her squirreliness.

Jenny Jensen may have been the coolest, calmest, most confident woman Bodine ever met. He was certain that she was playing everyone, and she never, ever seemed to sweat an interaction. She lived her life as if she knew exactly what was going to happen next, she expected it and it always turned out as she wanted.

Now, she was as nervous as a long-tailed cat in a room full of rocking chairs. She was jumpy, frazzled and plainly scared. Her fear unnerved Bodine, but he fought the urge to show it and make Jenny even more panicked.

"Jenny. *I repeat*, you're safe here. The lights are on. The doors are locked. My 9-millimeter is loaded, and it is a three-second thumbprint away from my hand. It's broad daylight in Brambleton; nothing is going down in this house. OK? Let's move into the back room, if that'll make you feel better."

Bodine watched her as she headed down the foyer to his family room. He couldn't help but notice that even this new, frantic, nervous version of Jenny Jensen looked every bit as amazing as the confident woman who had been in his house and on his deck drinking wine three dozen times in the past two years. Even fearing for her life, nothing could shake the remarkable beauty of Jenny Jensen.

"Alan, I need a divorce," she blurted out.

"Whoa, Jenny — slow down. I can help you with anything, but I don't get involved with divorces when I know both parties. I not only *know* both parties, we have broken bread together in my house. That's bad lawyering and ethically improper, in my opinion."

"Oh, great, the guy who drinks wine and talks about sex with other women, in front of his wife, all of a sudden has ethics," she charged. "Didn't you once offer to '*bang me*' on the kitchen table and let the kids and Caylee watch?"

68

"I think a great deal of wine was had that night," Alan said calmly. "I was joking, and if I recall, that was contingent upon Caylee's approval. She was there too," he said, trying to inject a bit of levity into the tense moment. "Now, let's get serious." Bodine stated more pointedly.

"I am serious. Jack is a psycho, and he wants me dead. I'm afraid to sleep next to him."

"OK, I want to tell you right now, because I'm ethically bound to do so. I will treat this conversation as attorney-client privileged. I'll help you find divorce counsel, and I'll help you stay safe. What I won't do is act as your divorce lawyer. I will refer you to someone I would trust to handle my own divorce," Bodine said in the tone of an old friend and trusted counselor.

"But ...," she started to question him.

"There is no 'but' to this, Jenny. My advice is free, and I'm bound by the ethical rules to keep these communications related to your legal problems confidential. However, I'm not taking you as a divorce client. I will, however, counsel you on steps you can take to find a good lawyer and stay safe if there is a *safety issue*. Are we clear?"

Bodine's voice could not have been firmer and more commanding. Likewise, Jenny understood what he was saying, and why.

"Yes, I get it. You can't help me get divorced."

"Correct. Now let's discuss this safety concern." Bodine probed.

"This isn't a safety concern; someone is following me. They're fucking stalking me. My life is in danger. This isn't a fucking seat-belt issue. OK? Stop saying 'safety concern,'" she yelled, making quote marks with her fingers. "This is fucking life or death."

"OK, Jenny, tell me what you know. That is, give me the facts. Do you understand? I don't want to hear your fears, speculation or conclusions. Let's start with hard facts so I know how to help you."

"It started about three weeks ago," she began.

"What do you mean by 'it'?" Bodine pounced in full lawyer mode.

"Alan are you a loyal friend?" she posed to him directly in a soft, surrendering tone.

"Jenny, I am always faithful to my friends. On top of that, I have legal, ethical obligations of loyalty to you as a client. If you need help, you need to tell me everything. *Every … thing!*" he punctuated with a pause.

"OK, here it goes," she began tentatively.

****

"*No, no and no! Daaad!*" Reagan Fitzgerald bellowed as she seemingly sang the last word with the utter contempt of a teenage high schooler.

Reagan Fitzgerald was 18 going on 28. She had her mother's temper, her father's athleticism and a double shot of their proven, Irish stubbornness. At 5-foot-8, she was the tallest of the Fitzgerald brigade, as Fitz called his daughters. She was a soccer player, recently earning the starting spot on the National Olympic Development Team as its striker, and had committed to UVA on a full athletic scholarship the previous year. She didn't have an ounce of fat on her. If she had been someone else's daughter, it would have struck Fitz that she should have been a supermodel or maybe an American ninja.

Reagan had strawberry blonde hair. The hint of strawberry may have been an illusion, but in the right lighting, Fitz was sure he saw it. The highlights of her face were large blue eyes, surrounded helplessly and completely by thick lashes. She had the skin tone and color of a Northern Italian woman who was accidently shipwrecked in Ireland. The look of contempt and DNA-imprinted, Fitzgerald skepticism didn't diminish her pure beauty, but it did give her an air of maturity that sometimes was quickly derailed by parental interactions.

"It's an ambush, and I won't be a part of it, Dad. Sorry, not this time," she fired off with contempt.

Abby Fitzgerald knew she should have melted into the morning dawn, still not quite awake in the family dining room. She just couldn't do it. She sipped her coffee as she leaned against the doorframe hoping to watch this father/daughter interaction but trying to remain expressionless. She wasn't very good at it.

Still, Abby wanted to see Fitz and his female mini-me do battle. Honestly, she wasn't at all sure who would win this fight. That's how stubborn Reagan was, and that is how completely wrapped around her finger she had the mighty chief homicide detective of Loudoun County. War hero or not, Abby knew that the greatest weakness of her husband was his youngest daughter, who was young enough to be his grandchild.

Abby's mind harkened back to a night when Reagan was about five years old. Abby had woken up and found Fitz gone from her side. That was unusual, save a bathroom run. In all their years together, they did whatever they could to sleep in the same bed. That ritual came from their early years of separation when Fitz was in the service. Even if Fitz got called into work, he never left without telling Abby. That night, Abby sat up and thought, "Fitz must be in the bathroom." She turned over to get comfortable and waited for him to slip back in beside her. Then she waited some more.

Usually, she would roll right over and go back to sleep. She did this with confidence, knowing that he would pour himself up against her, wrapping his right arm around her and interlocking his right leg with hers. It was an effortless fit. Truthfully, even though they had a huge bed, they used damn little of it. Fitz once announced at the dinner table in a discussion about sleeping, "The Fitzgeralds come from a long line of snugglers."

Abby waited that night for her husband to return to bed. When he didn't, she sat up, almost panicked. As she headed out of the room to check for her husband, she moved down the hallway and saw the door to the baby's room open. Then, saw Fitz's silhouette standing over Reagan's bed. She tiptoed in and nervously asked him, "Is she sick? Is everything OK?" He turned and looked at her with a tear in his eye and simply said, "I love her so much … I could watch her sleep all night."

He did.

Now Abby thought, as that memory faded from the moment, "We are not about to witness any peace."

Fitz grabbed the controller and pointed it at the receiver over the kitchen cabinets. The music began to play, and it played the Fitzgerald way — loudly.

Detective Fitzgerald couldn't sing a lick, but that didn't stop him from belting out every word of the Travis Tritt country hit that he and his daughter loved so much:

As we sat on the front porch
Of that old gray house where I was born and raised
Staring at the dusty fields
Where my daddy worked hard everyday

I think it kinda hurt him when I said,
"Daddy there's a lot that I don't know
But don't you ever dream about a life
Where corn don't grow?"

...

They sang every verse. When that song finished, of course Reagan was singing along too. She loved Travis Tritt, and unlike either of her tone-deaf parents, the talented Reagan could sing.

"Reagan, I know this whole world is turning slowly," Fitz began repeating a line from the song. "At your age, a missed opportunity is like the end of the world — a chance you never get back," He began.

"Dad, I am joining the Marines, and I don't care how slow or fast the world turns. Don't try to talk me out of it," she said with conviction, cutting him off and seemingly trying to draw him into a fight.

"Well, the Marines are a remarkable organization, and you are a remarkable young woman. It's a perfect fit." Fitz said, stunning both women.

"Your grandfather was a Marine. He dropped out of high school to fight in World War II. You know this story, right?" Fitz began with an eerie sense of calm.

"Exactly," she said with confidence. "Then he went back during Korea. And — and you — you were at the top of your class, a scholarship athlete, and you joined the Marines and went and fought for our country. That's what I am going to do," she declared again as she recounted the fighting Fitzgerald history, seemingly a Ph.D. in it.

Fitz took a long draw on his Yeti, secretly wishing it were a Marlboro Red. He hadn't smoked since Vietnam, but some days he could still feel the pull of nicotine off the end of a cigarette. More than four decades later, sometimes he was sure he needed one. This morning, coffee would have to do.

"It's completely true. We fought for our country and bled for her too. Grandpa was so determined to join the Marines, he got a note from home at 17 to do it. When they rejected him for being underweight, he went back four weeks later, and at 6-foot-1, made the 132-pound minimum — barely."

"And you," she said. "You fought with him to join, and ultimately you did join and go over his objections," she again reminded him.

"Well, that's true too. I refer you to the great Travis Tritt, 'I was only 17 back then but I thought that I knew more than I know now.'" Fitz smiled at her.

"Here it comes," she said aloud.

"That is to say, if this 69-year-old Fitz could have advised the 17-year-old Fitz, he would have told him not to go," Fitz continued.

"*Suurrrre ... riiiight, Dad.* He would tell his younger self to listen to his father. I bet." Reagan bit back with dripping sarcasm, the type designed to deflect the anticipated argument while inviting her father to perhaps lose his patience.

The younger Fitz had no idea how calm her father could be if being calm and thoughtful would help him win this battle. His girl might be a Marine someday, he thought, but it wouldn't be any day soon. He couldn't fail like his father had.

"I could tell you dozens of stories of war to try to influence your decision. I could take you to the grave markers of young friends cut down brutally in the jungle, a few merely a year or two older than

74

you. I could lecture, yell and set out a series of rational reasons why you should reconsider, but you are a Fitzgerald. You would see it only as a challenge or dare," Fitz said with nothing but that soothing, loving, fatherly voice Reagan knew so well.

It surprised her how calm he was.

"I am at your mercy, Reagan Catherine. I am not here to tell you how wrong I think you are. I am a Marine. I am here to support you, fight for you and back you up. I am your father, which means — like the Marines say, I am *semper fidelis*."

"Yes, I know — always faithful," repeating the often-heard phrase in her house.

She looked at him intently. In the background, Abby stared too. She felt an odd betrayal. Her posture screamed, "What the hell are you doing?" Abby was standing up-right, looking like she just unexpectedly caught a bit too much wasabi on the tip of her tongue. She stepped forward purposefully but fought the urge to say something.

"My father insisted I not join the corps," Fitz continued. "He demanded it. He threatened me. He was right about it … all of it, which I accepted shortly after the first guy tried to kill me."

This was more like it, Abby thought.

"This is what I expected," Reagan began to think.

"I am not going to tell you some trite nonsense about how smart you are, Reagan. You're smart, though not as *informed* as me, which could never be your fault. You surely have more intelligence than me, but at your age, in this life, you *know* very little. Only a foolish father would stand before you and expect to make you see the light and gain the wisdom of decades of experiences you've never had," Fitz stated with the wisdom of a law professor.

Both mother and daughter studied him hard, almost with mirror-image concentration.

"I am a fool, Reagan. I am stone-cold stupid. I'm stupidly, wildly, unapologetically, and insanely in love with you," Fitz declared.

Reagan smiled instinctively, and Abby's eyes showed just a hint of excess moisture.

"Dad," Reagan said, "I love you too, but …."

"I'm not finished, Reagan."

Detective Fitzgerald steadied himself, placing his right hand on the kitchen table. He sank with precision, like a good Marine or perhaps a good Catholic instinctively dropping to the kneeler at Sunday Mass. There he was, on both knees, looking up at his youngest of seven daughters. Reagan looked at him completely puzzled and absolutely clueless about this weird and unexpected gesture.

"Reagan Catherine Elizabeth Fitzgerald, I'm asking you … I am begging you … please … with the love of your father, don't do this right now. For me, for the man who loves you, and who will always be the love of your life."

He was not joking. This was not an act. Abby stood speechless, tears rolling down her face with ferocity. She tried to fight back the audible heave of her chest that if she let slip, just a bit, might have caused her to completely lose it.

Reagan turned to her mother. "Mom, Mom — make him get up."

Chapter 7: Lawyers, Guns and Money

Jeff Handly woke up to an empty bed. He couldn't have slept more than 20 minutes all night. Somehow, in those few minutes, Janie slipped out. It wasn't even 6:30 a.m., and Janie was not an early bird.

Handly was groggy, and he couldn't really think straight. Then, with a crash of adrenaline, he sprung from his bed. He'd spent the entire night looking at the ceiling, thinking a million thoughts, worrying, bathed almost entirely in his own shame. He barely moved all night, not wanting to let Janie know he was awake. God, he didn't want to talk about it — or set her off on another crying spell.

He thought he had considered every scenario in this mess until this morning. He bolted upright with an awful thought. "Is Janie OK? What if she did something crazy?"

Janie wasn't naturally impulsive, but it occurred to him that this type of grief was unpredictable. He took off down the steps. The lights were on in the kitchen, but nowhere in the house could he find a sign of his wife.

Her car was there. Then he realized that Jackson's car was gone from its usual spot on the cul-de-sac. Jeff retreated to the kitchen relieved. He decided that Janie likely could not sleep and headed to the grocery store to get her mind off events. Perhaps she was getting food to make for Jack and the boys.

As the panic subsided, Jeff found a note on the table at his normal morning spot. His mug was out, as were his favorite Danish. The note read, "Let's start this day better. I am stopping at the church to say a prayer, and then going to the grocery store. xo Janie."

Jeff took a long, deep breath. "Thank God. Where is the coffee?" was all he could think.

****

"Brad, I am not fucking around here. If you screw me over on this, I'll make you and the Tank pay," Peggy Felts announced matter-of-factly through the receiver. She knew Brad well, and he had always kept his word. Peggy, however, didn't trust that "candy-ass phony" Tankersley. Peggy Felts agreed to sit on the brutal details of the murder until she got the "go" from Brad. In return, Brad promised her a one-on-one with Tankersley and Fitz for all investigation updates.

Being considerably smarter than Brad, she also made him agree to give her Fitzgerald's location as soon as he had it. She knew Tank would give her political schmaltz. She also knew that if she were going to learn anything, it would be from sticking close to the formidable Detective Fitzgerald.

****

"Daddy! Quit it," Reagan said, half-embarrassed and shocked.

"I will never quit on you — ever, Reagan," Fitz replied, still on his knees. "I want to make you a promise, Reagan. Can I do that?"

"If it will get you off the floor, Dad," she quipped, still studying him.

"I made you a promise when you were born, and I have never broken it, not once. But it occurs to me, you wouldn't remember that one. I want to renew my vow to you," Fitz said in earnest, his knees starting to ache.

"What was that promise?"

"I promised that at every opportunity, I would put your interest before my own. I swore I would protect you with my life and

78

with my sacred honor. I held that damn piece of tin the Marines gave me over your head, blessed you and promised to be a *real* hero for you," Fitz continued, his voice cracking as he fixed his eyes on his youngest daughter without blinking. "I would never break that promise, you know that."

"You are one tough Marine, Dad. We all love and admire that. You made this family."

"Literally," Fitz jumped back in with a smile.

"Hey, I was there too," Abby cried out, her eyes still streaming involuntary tears of pride.

They all enjoyed a brief chuckle at Abby's well-placed interference in the moment.

"If serving in the Marines were in your best interest right now, I would get up, pack your bag and drive you to Parris Island in my dress blues. I'd knock on the damn door of the base XO and tell him I was delivering a surefire, *gen-u-ine* Marine."

"*Daaaad,*" she sang again.

"It's not your time, baby. It just isn't. It's not because you aren't ready. And it's not because I am not ready to let you go. I could be strong enough for that — for you. I swear."

Fitz rose up to the seat beside him. He did so because his damned knee hurt and because he wanted to invite his daughter into a more comfortable setting to receive his coming speech.

"Sit with me, and let me tell you about the United States Marines," he started.

****

The day after the murder, Fitz had just completed his one-mile run. He decided one mile was good enough that morning. First, he had a murder to solve, and second, his left knee was still stiff from getting on the floor to beg his baby not to join the Marines. He headed to the basement for his pushups and a quick shower when he made the mistake of checking his phone.

Fitz never ran with his phone. Abby hated that he went dark. She wanted him to be able to call if he had a problem or answer if she had one. Fitz said, "I run with my gun, which resolves any problem I may have. If you have a problem, call 911." He laughed just thinking about how many times he used that line.

Truthfully though, Fitz hated being tied to the phone, and his run was the only time it was not on his hip. For him, that phone-free time was essential. Once back home, however, he had it with him. Today it was backed up with a series of missed calls, phone messages and dozens of texts. "Not a damn one of these is fucking necessary," he thought to himself.

Message from Tank. Delete.

Message from fucking Brad. Delete.

Message from Peggy Felts. Save for later.

Message from Sully. Play.

"Fitz. Sully here. I have some preliminary results. Call me at your convenience."

"Now, that's how you leave a goddamn message," Fitz thought. "It has the essential information and invites me to retrieve it from him personally. No bullshit. How much do you want to bet that message from Tankersley was 5 minutes long and got cut off? Christ, I despise voice messages." Fitz said to himself.

Fitz was about to assume the position for his warmup set of pushups, the kind where he went slow and only about halfway down just to "make sure something doesn't snap off." As he put the phone down, he got a text from an odd number. That caught Fritz's attention. He looked at it with no recognition of the number. The text said simply, "It's DeMatha."

"That DeMatha," he thought, "never uses the same damn phone."

"Fitz, I'm out walking. Hit me back. I have something for you."

Joe DeMatha — Fitz liked that guy, "even if he lives in Brambleton," Fitz thought. "First, DeMatha is old school. Second, he was raised right, and he raises his kids right. Third, he doesn't waste my time with bullshit calls and texts. The guy is a straight fucking shooter, and if he 'has something' for me, I know it's good stuff. It's real, it's likely important and it's tied to this case." Fitz smiled as his thought continued, "I love that one short text from one credible guy lets me know my time won't be wasted."

Fitz texted DeMatha back.

"What road?"

Fitz texted with his daughters and literally no one else except DeMatha. Not even his partner, Parker, got a text back from Fitz.

DeMatha shot back, "Belmont."

"Give me 25," Fitz wrote.

"Headed to firehouse, same side."

"I'll bring Seger."

"Zevon, if you have it," came back the message.

"Done," Fitz sent.

"Abby! Coffee to go. Up in three minutes," Fitz yelled from the bottom of the basement steps.

Fitz hated to skip the pushups, but he was damn sure DeMatha had something useful, and even if it didn't pan out, it would be interesting. He fired up the shower and hit the water a few seconds before it was warm. This would be like a basic training shower, fast and cold.

In three minutes he was up the steps, and Abby completed the handoff of his key and Yeti in stride.

"Love ya baby … gotta run. I am seeing DeMatha."

She laughed, "Oh brother, look out, Loudoun."

Joe DeMatha was 59 years old. His description was meaningless, really. That is to say, the magic of DeMatha was that he was any man. He had no distinguishing characteristics. He could be a farmhand, an accountant, a librarian, a mason, or nearly any profession. He wasn't one bit threatening and even less memorable.

In a mock simulation during training for one of his numerous undercover operations, an entire FBI class of cadets failed to describe him among the group of 15 they were surveilling when drill's planned explosion took place. Simply put, the man didn't stand out. He was the functional equivalent of invisible, making him the perfect undercover resource. On top of that, he was the smartest guy in nearly any room and had absolutely no fear.

DeMatha spent his entire career in undercover ops with the Department of Fish and Wildlife. That guy bought more wild, exotic, illegal animals than any man on earth, and in every sting no one saw him coming. He had an impeccable eye for detail, read people easily and just blended in.

Fitz had met him 20 years before at some federal agency training program for detectives. Fitz thought the entire week was a waste of time and money until he met DeMatha. They had been friends ever since. While they didn't hang out and do "fake macho bullshit," as each would call it, Fitz was at DeMatha's Christmas party yearly, and they occasionally had coffee when Fitz spotted DeMatha out for a walk.

Joe DeMatha, the man who never stood out, was now the man everyone in Brambleton knew. He was the guy who walked about five miles a day around his neighborhood bouncing some kind of ball. Fitz once said of him, "Fucking DeMatha picked the one ball not designed to bounce and said fuck it, I'll bounce this one."

Joe DeMatha went nowhere without his lacrosse ball — unless he was undercover.

****

Jenny began to tell her story to Bodine. "I was with a friend three weeks ago today. After chatting with her for a while at a practice, I headed to …."

Bodine cut Jenny off. God, he thought, laypeople are insufferably inexact.

"Jenny, I need details. Times, locations and names."

"Alan, there are parts of this story I can't yet tell. So, no, I can't give you names or precise locations. But I *will* give you more details," Jenny said as she looked him in the eye.

The look told Bodine he wasn't going to get more than she thought was necessary. That concerned him, Bodine thought, "once again the critical part of any analysis in the law is often the who and where."

"Jenny, if your life is in danger, it's hard to imagine how we leave anything out. It may be the littlest detail that unearths what is happening. It may help me decide if there is real danger."

"I was with a friend, a female friend, in Brambleton. OK. It was a regular night, really. I left the friend around 6:30 p.m. I decided to hustle across town to Wegmans. I did a little late shopping, got my groceries and headed home. At the light at Waxpool and Loudoun County Parkway, I noticed a car following me."

"What makes you think it was following you, and what made you notice it?"

"I made an illegal right on red at the merge on Waxpool coming from Wegmans. I then sped up and cut across two lanes to get over to the left and beat the light. I looked up, and the car in my mirror at the light when I pulled out had done the *exact same thing*," she said in slow motion and with passion.

"OK, but ...."

"Alan, I ran the second red. So, to follow me that car really ran the second red, too. My first instinct was that it was an undercover cop, and I was getting a ticket. But it wasn't."

"Was it riding on your tail aggressively? Is it possible you cut the car off when you did the illegal right on red at the first light?"

"No. Again, that car was behind me coming from Wegmans. We were at the light when I decided to make the dash because damn it, the light was taking too long there."

"OK ... so, the car behind you copied you," Bodine said, trying to get the story back on track.

"Yes. So, after I went through the light at Broderick, I sailed up the left lane, and the car followed at normal distance. Then it began to close. I figured it was about to put its light on the dashboard and pull me over. So I decided to go straight through the LCP. But the light was red," she continued, recognizing that he would completely follow the setup of that infamous intersection.

"Right ... did you get a look at the car?"

"Alan, it was dark. It was some kind of dark SUV, nondescript," she said anxiously. "I could hardly study it while

84

driving, panicking, and looking forward," she stated to him that which she thought should have been obvious.

"Here's where it gets weird. The two left-turn lanes were open, and the green arrow signal came on. I decided to bolt from the left straight lane into those turn lanes. I floored it across the line from the left straight lane and took off making a left on Waxpool as I originally planned. Sure enough, the car followed. Then I thought, crap, it has to be a cop."

"But it never pulled you over, right?"

"Exactly! It followed me all the way to Brambleton. Here's the thing, though, I took it on a wild ride. I went places no one would purposely go heading back here, and the *fucking car* followed me," she said as if reliving the moment.

"You never saw the driver or the car or the license plate?"

"The front license plate was missing!"

"That's allowed in some states," Bodine said matter-of-factly.

"I didn't want to go home, afraid the person would find where I lived. I called Jack about five times. Eventually he picked up, and I told him what was up."

"What did he tell you to do?"

"He told me to drive twice around Conquest Circle and then back toward Minerva. Once at Minerva, make a left and come back around on Explorer."

"OK … and did —"

She cut Bodine off, because now she was hitting her stride. "Yes, I did exactly what he said, and then, like magic, after following me everywhere for 15 minutes, the car went straight on Minerva and didn't follow me. Isn't that strange? Right after I spoke to Jack, the car gave up."

"Was Jack home?" Bodine asked.

"Yes, he was. And he didn't even meet me in the driveway or at the front door. In his mind, this wasn't even a big deal."

"Well, maybe it —"

"Bullshit," she yelled, cutting him off again.

"— wasn't?" he continued.

"The next morning, I went out to the car to leave for a morning appointment. On my windshield, in lipstick, a message said, 'I still see you.' I almost had a heart attack."

"Wait — on your windshield? Holy shit."

"Exactly Alan, and it got worse from there."

****

"There is no finer military fighting force than the United States Marines," Fitz started as he looked at his strong-willed, youngest daughter. He called her "number seven" of the "fabulous Fitzgeralds."

"Yes, there are small groups of well-trained, elite special forces who are, well, on a Marine's off-day, maybe as good," he smirked. "Marines are special, and it is no surprise that a very special breed of person — a competitor and a patriot — like you, would want to join. It is the ultimate test of discipline. You will be a great Marine," Fitz said, not in one bit a patronizing tone.

"So, what is your objection, Dad?"

"The Marines have been fighting wars since 1775. Five hundred years from now, Marines will be fighting, serving, sacrificing and protecting. The United States of America is never going to fall, Reagan, because the Marines will never fail her," he smiled with that Marine confidence that drill instructors pound into the persona of every recruit. It sticks for life.

"This doesn't sound like a great argument for me not joining, Dad. You sound like a commercial," she laughed unexpectedly, adding, "The Few — The Proud — The Marines."

"That's just it, Reagan, I am not arguing that you shouldn't be a Marine. I am asking you not to be a Marine *right now*. I am telling you, the Marines will be there when it is a better fit for you."

"I fit right now," she said.

"No doubt. And the Marines would *love* to have you. You're smart, strong, tough, determined and ready. The Marines will take you right now," he said, leaning in to make his point.

"That's the perfect result for them. They get you, a superior candidate among a shrinking pool of superior candidates. But for you, you can be a Marine at any time, including times when it is better for you. And, guess what; they will still want and need you."

"Dad, I want to serve," she said, a bit less defiantly.

"I want you to serve. I just want you to do it as an officer. I want you to be the leader you are meant to be. I want you to have better training, greater respect, better pay, better housing and more opportunities for advancement."

"You just want me to go to college and hope I change my mind," she said skeptically.

"You disrespect me, Reagan. I am a Marine. I come from a family of Marines. I don't want you to ever lose your desire to be a Marine. I simply want you to get and give more to the corps than any Fitzgerald ever has. We gave our blood. We gave our sweat. We gave everything they asked of young grunts. I want you to give that too if asked. But what I really want is for you to give the Marines your brains and your leadership," he stared at her intently, their eyes locked.

"I want you to be an officer, Marine Fitzgerald," he declared with noticeable pride and excitement at the thought.

"I am a father, which means I want you to be better than I ever was or could be. The first test of a great Marine officer is in showing your judgment," he said with a more traditional commanding voice, shifting ever so easily from father to Marine warhorse.

"Do you have the judgment to trust a fellow Marine? Do you have the patience to give more than just your youthful zeal? Do you have the strength to make the Marines wait for the best version of Reagan Catherine Fitzgerald? And do you have the wisdom and maturity to honor my request and recognize my promise to serve your best interests?"

She stared at him for a long time, her face less skeptical, her wheels turning behind those soft but searing blue eyes.

"I will hold you to that promise, Marine," she said proudly.

Reagan grabbed her keys and walked out the back door on her way to the Catholic youth group meeting in Ashburn.

Abby ran to Fitz as the door to Reagan's car shut. "You are the master — oh, thank God. That was a remarkable performance, Fitzy," Abby gushed with a sigh of relief.

"*That, sweetheart, was the truth,*" Fitz declared as if he were Moses holding tablets on the mount.

****

Coffee in hand, with DeMatha on his mind, Fitz was flying down Route 7 rolling out of the foothills in western Loudoun. He was headed into one of the nation's worst traffic areas. The early spring morning sun would be brutal heading east. Fitz, however, took a few minutes to watch those rays illuminate and give life to the fresh, dense, green foliage out to his left. A front had passed over the mountains last night bringing a crisp northwesterly breeze and the type of rich, deep, blue sky that would be increasingly rare when spring leapt to summer and those same mountains were dressed in haze.

Fitz thought, "That poor Jensen lady has seen her last ray of earthly sun." He cranked down his window — by hand — and turned the volume to max. That simple human movement coincided with the proper application of force to the pedal on the right of his floorboard. The Chevelle lurched forward with a rumble and bolted out of the 60s to nearly 80 mph.

> Twelve hours out of Mackinaw City
> Stopped in a bar to have a brew
> Met a girl and we have a few drinks
> And I told her what I decided to do

"Fucking Bob Seger, that left-wing hippie bastard. No one writes music like this guy," Fitz smiled to himself.

As he "rolled away" east, he never broke stride. Traffic was unexpectedly light and as he fired around the bend on Route 7 just on the outskirts of Leesburg. He never even tapped the brakes. He zipped past the exit for Route 15, afraid the back roads would be filled with buses on Evergreen, a country road now out of place in suburban sprawl. He knew time was of the essence to meet with DeMatha, and he decided to suck it up and hit the Greenway.

The Greenway was a private toll road with a flat fee for the 12-mile trip that connected Western Loudoun to Western Fairfax — and dumped drone commuters onto the Dulles toll road to battle their way into the Nation's Capital, if necessary. The Greenway was literally highway robbery. Its existence is a testament to the power of the land-developing cartel in Virginia, a group that wholly owned the Virginia legislature.

On the eastern rim of Loudoun county, suburbanites fall into two categories: those who paid the fee without any regard, and those who would sit in traffic on residential roads to avoid it. Fitz didn't have the luxury to stand on principle, plus, his EZ-Pass was funded by the county, "so F'em," he thought.

As Fitz poured it on heading to the Belmont Ridge Road exit, his cellphone went off. Obviously, the old Chevelle didn't have Bluetooth, and Fitz had utter contempt for talking on the phone while driving — or talking on his cellphone while breathing. He hated these devices, and he despised and pitied those tied to them like slaves.

Like it or not, with seven kids and his career, he begrudgingly accepted the benefits of a cellphone. He simply avoided using the "damn thing" in ways too many now think common or acceptable. "Christ, next thing you know I will be wearing my slippers and pajamas at a fucking Walmart superstore talking out loud on my phone in the middle of the produce section," he thought as he decided whether to answer it.

It was Parker, and that was one call Fitz knew he had to take. Normally, he would have pulled over. Running on a tight schedule to find DeMatha, he rolled up his window, hit answer, and tapped a few times with his fat thumb trying to hit the speaker button.

"Parker, what's up?"

"Tankersley is holding a presser at 10. He wants you to back him up," Parker started.

"Yes, well, I'd like to hit the fucking Powerball. It's not going to happen."

"Fitz, you don't even fucking play the Powerball."

"Exactly, and I don't back up glory-hound schmucks either."

"I told him you were hot on a real lead and you would do your best."

"Christ, Parker, for a snot-nosed paisan from Jersey, you're not a lost cause," Fitz grunted with a smile.

"I'm Irish like you," Parker protested.

"Keep telling yourself that," Fitz snorted. "You are not like me. What did the big Tank say when you told him I was hot on a lead and likely wouldn't make it?"

"He told me I was a lying sack of shit, and he expected you to report personally sometime today."

"Please, God, tell me he said that."

"No. Of course not. He only talks about you to Brad. He said thanks and asked you to update him at your earliest convenience."

"OK, progress. Look, I might have something. I am meeting DeMatha in about 7 minutes. I think he has something for us on this case."

"No shit, fucking DeMatha probably solved this case walking around the block bouncing that fucking ball. I love that guy," Parker said with enthusiasm of a sailor on payday.

"Well, I doubt he solved it, but he is not one to waste time. He certainly didn't call me into Brambleton to hold his johnson while he watered the day lilies."

"Chief, you are completely fucked, you know that, right?"

"I see you have been talking to Abby again," Fitz chuckled.

"OK, anything else I need to know?"

"Yes, listen, I am just the messenger here — so don't shoot me."

"Oh, shit. You've been fucking buttering me up?"

"Tankersley wants us to head down to FBI headquarters for a 4 p.m. meeting on the seventh floor. It's an update on the still missing Jack Jensen."

Fitz blew through the toll plaza, nearly taking out the gated arm. He floored it out of the no-yield zone and nearly cut off a minivan as he hit Belmont Ridge doing 60. The limit on the ramp was 25.

"Listen — very — carefully," he said, as if spooning out instructions to a six-year-old.

"Tell Tank these exact words. Use quotes to protect yourself and be prepared to do lots of ass-kissing and apologizing," Fitz grunted in his most sincere Marine voice.

"Jesus Christ and all his disciples can't make me drive to *D* ... *Fucking* ... *C* for a 4 p.m. meeting with God himself. All those A-holes live out here, and we are in the middle of a murder investigation. Their fucking yahoo is the prime suspect. Even if they were delivering Jack Jensen to me, I wouldn't go," Fitz declared, not one bit unexpectedly.

"'The Tank is not going to —'"

"Screw the Tank, that A-hole," Fitz growled as he cut off Parker. "Tell him I said I will meet the FBI for 10 minutes, at Joe's Café on Church Street in Sterling in the back booth. At 4:11, I'll be gone."

"Boss, I don't know if I can —"

"End of message, Parker. I ain't blaming you, and I ain't saying you have to buck orders. But I will be at Joe's. Everyone else can meet in Tank's private bathroom for a hot oil massage for all I care. Got it?"

"I'll let them know," Parker said dutifully, resigned to the reality that Fitz was never going to concede and surely was not driving to DC.

"Tank will fold like a cheap suit," Parker thought as he hung up.

Fitz took Belmont Ridge Road until it turned into Northstar, just by the new baseball complex on the right in Brambleton. Riding through, he was constantly surprised by the building in Brambleton, with more $700,000 townhouses going up on the right as he raced past the back of Fox Theaters. "Someone is trying to turn this into the George Fucking Jefferson version of Centreville," he thought to himself, amused.

Centreville, Virginia is on the Southern end of Fairfax County, the second wealthiest county in America, and the immediate neighbor to Loudoun County. The general feeling in Loudoun county among its many new residents is that Fairfax is exactly what they don't want Loudoun to become, a sea of soul-sucking, vanilla suburbia, whose primary characteristic is an ocean of townhomes, most insufferably indistinguishable from each other. So say recent transplants to Loudoun, which is about 80 percent of the population of a county that is not only wealthy, but among America's fastest growing counties in each of the last ten years.

"Why the hell would anyone buy a *Townhouse* for that much money 34 miles from the nation's capital? The world has gone mad," he muttered, thinking the generation behind him to clearly be fools, as each subsequent generation has sworn about those who followed.

Fitz banged a left at the end of Northstar, which dumped him out at the new firehouse. As he approached it, he popped out the Seger mix taped and deftly pushed in in another homemade cassette.

Sure enough, there was DeMatha, international man of mystery, bouncing his fucking ball.

I went home with the waitress
The way I always do
How was I to know
She was with the Russians too

Warren Zevon's classic "Lawyers, Guns and Money" began blaring as Fitz rolled the Chevelle up to within 3 feet of a grinning Joe DeMatha.

"Now, that's fucking music," DeMatha yelled as he jumped into the passenger seat. "Let me guess, you were playing Seger all the way here?"

"I'd appreciate if you would say that hippie fuck's name with a bit more reverence," Fitz deadpanned.

"It could be worse," DeMatha countered. "If Parker were here, we would be treated to some bullshit version of 'The Ghost of Tom Joad' from that Springsteen schmuck, that liberal putz who lost his voice in 1978."

"He's not bad …," Fitz said halfheartedly. "At least he was born in the U.S. and not as an anchor baby."

These two old warhorses had a good laugh at their predictable, caustic exchange of aging machismo. They loved classic rock, even if they didn't love every classic rocker.

"So, what do you have that caused me to charge my Greenway trip to the fine taxpayers of this great county?" Fitz asked.

"I think I have a blood sample from the road in front of the Jensen house. I just stumbled on it, really."

"Of course you did," Fitz responded incredulously.

"Did you guys recover anything from that site? I see the house is taped and locked off, but this spot was clearly outside the custody and control of your current investigation."

"I don't think the team collected anything from the street, so this would be an add to our investigation," Fitz said dryly, before exploding with curiosity. "How the fuck did you find this?"

"Dude, it's all about the ball," DeMatha laughed.

Chapter 8: Lights, Camera, Inaction

At 10:05 a.m., Sherriff Tankersley stepped to the microphone. The setting in front of the old Loudoun County Courthouse was perfect. The sun was pouring down, filtered expertly by a canopy of trees that had seen thousands of mornings like this one. The breeze was light, as was the traffic just 50 yards away. The old courthouse had an air of history about it, with the unmistakable message of law, order and justice as the backdrop. Brad could not have ordered a better set on which to stage the Tank.

Ironically, while the "old" courthouse was old, it was really the third iteration of "old" courthouses on the grounds in historic Leesburg. The first two were long gone, as were the bodies from a shootout between Yankee and Confederate troops once held on the lawn where the press corps was now gathered.

Brad knew how to set the sheriff up for success. The DC press corps would have ample time to get out to Loudoun without a rush. The sun at 10 a.m. would be burning off the crisp morning air, and its angle would perfectly accent Tank in his uniform, with all his expertly arranged medals. In the background sat the quintessential symbol of law, majestically painted in both elegance and tradition. The morning weather … that was just luck.

Of course, before the sheriff spoke, Brad would hit the mic promptly at 10 a.m. to address some of the more mundane details, set the ground rules, warm up the press pool and properly introduce the sheriff. This was also designed to make sure late arrivals could grab some B-roll and still be situated in time to hear the sheriff.

At 10:05 a.m., the Tank strolled up to the microphone with confidence, bathed in brass and wearing his sincere but in-charge face. The words precisely arranged by Brad and repeatedly practiced by Tankersley fell off his lips effortlessly. This was the easy part.

"A mother, wife, community volunteer and small business owner was killed in her home last night. We have no reason to believe that it was a random act. Chief Homicide Detective Ronald Fitzgerald is leading the investigation. The home is secure, and there is no threat to the greater community. Because not all of the kin have been notified, we are not yet prepared to release the name of the individual. Likewise, because the victim has young children, we prefer not to identify, and we ask *you* not to identify her by name or the pinpoint location of the crime at this time.

"We do have multiple leads, and we have a person of interest to whom we would like to speak. I can't identify that person yet, either. The manner of her death was not by gunfire, but rather the victim was hit by an object causing blunt force trauma. Those are all the details we can share at this time. I will take a few questions."

"Sheriff Tankersley, Peggy Felts. Was there anything unusual about the manner of death?"

"A homicide in Loudoun County itself is unusual, Ms. Felts. For that statistic, we are grateful. Still, this very sad and tragic loss of life affects us all, and we are looking at every angle of this case to determine if any facts might lead us more quickly to a suspect, an arrest and ultimately prosecution."

This was Tank at his best. The man who made everyone feel creepy in simple social settings seemingly had a PR go switch. Put on a camera; give him good lighting, a nice script and time to prepare; and he took tough questions and turned them into sincere, feel-good speeches devoid of substance, much like the collection of meaningless ribbons that magically appeared on his chest after election day.

The Tankersley presser was done in less than just 15 minutes. And Brad's wrap-up sent the press out quickly, except for a few extra minutes for a couple of hand selected members of the media.

****

The house phone rang early at Tank's. He skipped the morning workout to go over the statement and planning for his presser at 10 a.m. Caller ID showed a blocked number, and Tankersley instinctively let it ring through. "Ridiculous," he thought, "these automated calls were hitting people all around the clock now." It rang again, three minutes later. Tank looked at it and thought about picking it up and reaming out the salesperson on the other end. He ignored it. Five minutes later, his cellphone rang. It was Brad.

"Brad, what's going on?" Tankersley asked, clearly irritated by the barrage of early morning calls.

"The FBI is looking for you. They tried you at home, but no answer. I assumed you let it ring through because it was probably blocked," Brad explained.

"FBI?" Tank asked, "What do they want?"

"They won't talk to me. The man on the other end told me the director was looking for you."

"The director of the FBI?" Tank said as he froze in nervous excitement. "What on earth does the director of the FBI want? I would think Mr. Wray is a bit busy these days."

"Whatever he wants, he will only talk to you. They told me they would call you back in about 15 minutes. His assistant said your line was not secure, so it would be a quick, logistical call."

"You don't say ... interesting," Tank replied.

"Tank, the FBI director doesn't dial up local sheriffs at 7 in the morning for nearly any reason. If he is calling, the message is loud and clear; this is a national issue."

"Well, maybe he heard we have fucking Trump working as our chief homicide detective," Tank roared at his own poke at Fitzgerald. "Seriously, I will hear him out and reconvene immediately with you."

"Yes, assuming this call doesn't pre-empt us," Brad said.

"I didn't think about that, but let's see. I gotta run, still digesting the script."

The house phone rang, and again the blocked number came up. Tankersley grabbed it like he was winning a free basket of steroids and gay porn. It never occurred to him not to appear desperate, eager and ready to impress.

"Is this Sheriff Tankersley?" the pleasant and authoritative voice asked.

"Mr. Direc—" Tankersley began before being cut off.

"Please hold for the FBI director, Christopher Wray," the voice continued unfazed.

"Sheriff Tankersley?" the commanding but professional voice asked.

"Mr. Director, how can I help you, sir?" Tankersley asked as he slid immediately into political mode.

"Please, call me Chris," the director responded, trying to show cooperation and humanity.

"Thank you, Chris. You can call me Linden, or my friends call me Tank."

"The FBI needs your help, Tank, and we likewise think we can help your team. We can't discuss this here, but I invite you and your investigative unit to come down to FBI headquarters today for a briefing that may be relevant to your most current, high-profile case."

Tankersley thought about that phrasing and realized the director did *not* want to use the name over this line. He also realized that this was not really a request but certainly a well-oiled, politically calculated, polite demand.

"Chris, I will coordinate with my team this morning. We have a media event at 10. What time works for you?"

"Can you be here for a 4 p.m. meeting? If you arrive at the employee entrance, we will guide your team to some convenient parking and get you right upstairs. I know this is not the best location, and we will try to make it painless. We just have a series of pressing matters that don't permit us to break free."

"I understand, Chris; your plate is a lot larger than mine, and it is much fuller," Tankersley said, smiling at his quick-thinking imagery.

"We really appreciate this, Sher — ah, Tank."

"Chris, I will only say this. My chief detective, he can be hard to reach and, when reached, difficult to corral. It's possible he may miss this one."

"Detective Fitzgerald is well regarded in this office, and we certainly understand the demands on his time. I hope he can make it, but I understand that sometimes our key people need to stay on task," Wray said, not really giving a damn who came as long as Tankersley showed up and realized he must play ball.

Wray had no idea who Detective Fitzgerald was until briefed on him for two minutes before the call that morning. After the briefing Wray told his team, "I'll bet you my job that guy tells his sheriff to drop dead before he hikes down here to DC." Christopher

Wray didn't get to be the nation's chief federal law enforcement politician by being a dumbass.

"Thank you, director, we will see you at 4 p.m."

"Thank you, Tank, and I will have my assistant give your man the details on which entrance to approach for access and parking. Goodbye."

"How the hell do they know fucking Fitzgerald at the FBI? Why would he be well regarded?" Tank thought to himself, miffed that once again that Fitzgerald was taking a dump in the middle of *his* parade.

****

Joe DeMatha knew all about the murder at the Jensens' house. He actually knew Jack Jensen, and living just a few blocks away, their passing interactions over the years became more social than professional. DeMatha had many skills tucked firmly inside that nondescript frame. One of them was reading people. You don't do 300 undercover operations without knowing how to read people. It's a skill that saved lives, usually his own.

"Jack Jensen was one cool customer, and his FBI unit and the multiagency task force to which he was assigned was top flight. They don't air-drop you into Syria to have tea and crumpets with a bunch of knuckle-dragging, 11th-century death cultists unless you are one smart, mentally tough, no bullshit pro," DeMatha reasoned as he thought it through. DeMatha couldn't completely rule out the idea that Jensen snapped, but in his opinion, this may not have been a simple domestic murder.

DeMatha wondered early the next morning if Jack Jensen's job might not be related to this case. He told his wife, "I don't want to press alarm buttons here, but Jensen has been all over the world lately. Something hot is happening, and I wonder if the people whose lives he's been making miserable might not be involved in an operation against his unit in the homeland."

Fanny DeMatha didn't like that speculation much. Her head turned on a swivel. "You think this could've been a hit or terrorism?" she asked, alarmed but titillated.

"I think that's as likely, or more likely, than Jack Jensen killing Jenny," he said with his famous serious tone.

"Who would ever kill that poor, sweet, beautiful woman?" Fanny asked aloud.

"Probably any one of the men she was fucking," DeMatha thought. No sense sullying her name to Fanny at this point. He poured his Grape-Nuts and lowered his head as if to be reading the back of the cereal box.

****

Bodine was wondering why he ever agreed to cooperate tonight. "Cops," he thought, "can't help but be dicks. And this Parker, he's a dumb-as-dirt dick."

Parker's abrupt, pointed tone caught Bodine by surprise. So did his recitation of the facts about what Jason told the responding officers. Bodine shifted in his chair and looked up at Fitz's partner, his glare now fixed on the imposing Parker.

People sometimes mistakenly overlooked Jack Michael Parker in the partnership of Fitz and Parker. It's hard to imagine why. Parker was an impressive specimen, nearly 25 years Fitz's junior. The 6-foot-3 Parker was a triathlete and a CrossFit devotee. Parker was a native of Monmouth County, New Jersey, and he traced his Irish lineage back through Ellis Island and across the great pond to County Cork, Ireland. The New Jersey branch of the Parker family migrated from Newark, where Parker's father and grandfather were both police officers.

Parker followed his passion for baseball to George Mason University, which is how he became one of only a handful of "his people" to leave the Garden State. Like most New Jersey expats, Parker spoke with an inexplicable pride and reverence for his home state while admitting that he wouldn't move back there for $100 million.

Parker prayed at the altar of Bruce Springsteen, as they were from the same hometown. He also thought Jon Bon Jovi represented the armpit of both rock 'n' roll and New Jersey. Parker claimed he once saw Bon Jovi and his entourage run out of a strip joint on the Asbury Circle by bouncers who didn't think the rock star or his group were the right clientele for a titty bar. When pressed, Parker couldn't really explain why he was there, too, but he remembered that Bon Jovi's entourage that night couldn't produce IDs, and when the bouncers denied them entry, he swore he saw a wild-eyed Bon Jovi screaming at them: "Hey, I'm fucking *Jon Bon Jovi.*" Parker told the story convincingly.

Parker too was a cop's cop, and he was raised on the code among police. Working with Fitzgerald was no fun task as a junior officer, but he had earned the respect of the legend. Fitz also knew that Parker's famous Irish temper sometimes had a great and unexpected effect on witnesses, who often viewed him as the second fiddle.

Bodine hadn't given a moment's thought to Parker, either. He had been playing this game of cat and mouse with Fitz, and Parker's presence was much like cheap wall art from Target. It was there, he'd seen it, but it was unworthy of comment, criticism or even consideration.

Parker stared back at Bodine. His glare was neither menacing nor provocative, simply confident. He had just throat punched the bombastic Bodine and showed him that he wasn't some water boy lackey for the legend. Parker's look said, "Yes, now you have to contend with two of us, and we know facts you need to explain."

Bodine's response was measured, and the longer-than-normal pause clearly reflected the training of a trial pugilist who knew that it was better to process rather than merely react. Bodine was smart and calculating, even if at times he could seem unhinged or reactionary.

"Detective Parker," Bodine said in a sharp, smooth, completely confident tone, "I thought you were just the secretary in this relationship. Look at you trying to come to the big boys' table. Take a seat, son, and remember not to break the china now that you are sitting with the adults."

Parker's blood pressure ticked up about 25 millimeters. His fair Irish skin betrayed his inward effort at restraint as the vein in his forehead edged into prominence. His neck and cheeks turned a decided pink.

Fitz jumped in.

"Alan, stay focused. We need to understand what the young man told us and how it fits into the unusual circumstances of the night."

"First, I assume you understand that you have no business interviewing that minor in the absence of a guardian who has given consent," Bodine stated, sharply and unapologetically.

"Hey, slap-dick, this isn't our first investigation. Just because you prey on cheaters and scum to make a living doesn't mean you know a fucking thing about real law, obviously," Parker spit back at him like a hairball.

"The kid volunteered the information to the responding officer. We didn't question him or fucking waterboard him, so let's get to the part where you make an explanation," Parker said, his voice reverberating off the paper-thin walls coated in builder's beige.

"This is a dizzying game of good cop, bad cop and wannabe good cop, and I am not interested in playing," Bodine stated firmly, looking at Fitz as he suddenly decided to treat Parker like that piece of cheap wall art.

"Alan, why would the young man say that? And please, let's stop the needless dance. Fill in the details of which you are aware. We have a murder to solve," Fitz said, trying to restore a sense of calm to the room.

"My client was convinced she was being stalked," Bodine said in a more measured tone, still looking only at Fitz. "Over a 3-week period, she had become paranoid, and seemingly for good reason."

Bodine may not have realized it, or perhaps it was a conscious decision, but his answer clearly was more cooperative and open-ended than had been the case the entire previous interview. Parker let just a small smile unpurse his lips, recognizing that he had cracked open the door.

"Alan, tell me in detail, why did she believe she was being stalked and by whom?" Fitz pushed gently.

"First, let me say, she was certain it was orchestrated by her husband. When I say 'orchestrated' it is because several of the factual incidences I will lay out here clearly indicate that the events of concern could not have been the actions of Jack Jensen himself, as the facts prove him to be verifiably in a different location when the stalking took place. Still, Ms. Jensen was certain he was behind it all."

Parker was now seated again, and he was writing furiously.

"Please, Alan, give me every detail you have. I certainly don't need to explain to you how critical the precise details and timing are for us."

"It's quite a story, and based upon the facts she described that I could reasonably conclude to be accurate, I became convinced she was being stalked. I was just never convinced it was Jack Jensen."

"Alan, your judgment will be much appreciated. You know the woman. You evaluated her personally against both the story she told and what you knew of her. We are going to give faith and credit to you for those observations based on your expertise. However, before we get to what you *think,* can you systematically work us through what you *know* — and what of those facts you found to be correct, accurate or, as you noted, verifiable?"

"Of course, detective. In fact, when she first came to me, I had a very difficult time breaking down her story from what she thought and speculated about to actual, concrete events.

"Before I go one step further, I want to make clear an important fact. Jenny Jensen was terrified for her life, and the Jenny Jensen I have always known was afraid of nothing. When you hear these details, you will understand why."

Parker couldn't resist jumping in, which Fitz was nonplussed about given the sudden change in the cooperation.

"Why didn't she go to the police if she was so terrified?"

Bodine completely ignored Parker. Staring at Fitz with a new intensity, he said, "She did."

****

Peggy Felts must have been part bloodhound. Indeed, she was without a doubt the "best in show." In the early morning hours just after dawn, she was back out at the Jensens' house putting all her reporting skills to work. She was doggedly and deftly manipulating the sheriff's deputies protecting the crime scene for anything she could. Under the guise of shooting B-roll and updating and changing her takes for the morning news hits on and after the 7 a.m. news cycle, she was really there to gather information by any means possible.

Using that famous charm, she singled out two deputies, one in his late 40s and one fresh recruit. She figured she might use her wares to ply them for information. She'd played this game a million times, and in her mind, the men with guns were simply no match for a professional reporter with guile, great looks and the biggest set of balls on the scene.

She approached the older deputy first with the full knowledge that he might not be an easy mark for her, given his experience. Still, she was going to play both the older man and the father cards. That is, she assumed he was a father and that if he were, it might give her an opening. For Felts, she just loved getting information from those whose sole job was to give her none.

"Deputy Pike, how are you this morning?"

"Ms. Felts, I am fine, but I can't talk to you."

"It's a beautiful spring morning deputy; surely we can exchange pleasantries over the weather or lament our early-morning assignments without running afoul of Fitz's order," she said with a flirtatious smile.

"This comes straight from the top, ma'am."

Strike one. "Look how easy that was," she thought. "The gag order on this investigation comes directly from the Tank, who would normally never be involved directly in the nitty-gritty. That's interesting." She began to wonder if Fitz had even talked to the Tank yet, the thought of which amused her.

"See, I knew Fitz wouldn't be so rigid. He and I go way back."

"Yes, ma'am, I recall."

"You know, Detective Pike, we could have gone to high school together, you and me."

"Excuse me, ma'am? I don't think we went to school together, I would have remembered," he replied somewhat awkwardly.

"No, of course you are right — I merely mean we are close in age, detective, and when you call me ma'am, well, it makes me worry the lines on my face are getting more pronounced."

"Ms. Felts, you don't have any lines on your face," he said with a smile.

"Middle-aged men," she thought, "Christ, are they suckers for a blonde in a tight dress. Really, they are suckers for any woman who shows interest and has a pulse."

"This is one sad and crazy case. That woman was so young and beautiful," she said unprompted.

"Ms. Felts, I see what you are doing here," Pike smiled.

"Jiminy Cricket, Pike, I'm not pumping you for information, I am merely making an observation. I mean, I already have an agreement with Brad and the sheriff on this exclusive. I don't really need information from you. I am out here shooting some crime scene shots we call B-roll to support the different segments we will run on this story. I'm just trying to make conversation while I nail down the must-do list," she said quite convincingly.

Felts leaned in to Pike, "That's some crazy shit someone did to that gal, sticking a Swiffer in her ass."

Pike was shocked Felts knew this detail. He just found that out this morning from one of the evidence-collection techs, and when he did, he read the veteran off for sharing info with people outside the approved circle, including him. He thought, "Man, I can't believe she got read in on this by Brad and the sheriff. But, how else could she know?"

Pike replied, "Not the last photo any of us would want, Ms. Felts," he said with a chuckle.

Felts now had a second confirmed source on the Swiffer, and she had Pike thinking she was authorized to gain access and info on the investigation. "Lordy, this is easy," she thought.

"Pike, if I don't see you, enjoy the rest of the day. It's supposed to be beautiful. I have to head out soon for the presser. Tank is going to fill me in on the father."

"They found the father?" he asked.

"Bingo ... holy shit. They haven't found the fucking father yet. I didn't even have to work for that little cookie," she thought, patting herself silently on the back.

"Tank says this is juicy — I can't wait find out what that means," she whispered to him.

"Must be, we had a BOLO out, and the fucking FBI has even been dodging our inquiries to find the guy, given his hotshot job with them," Pike whispered back, suddenly becoming a one-man TMZ.

"They don't know where the dad is, and the FBI is stonewalling the investigation. Fuck me," she thought, "I hit the motherload here."

"It's going to be a hell of a story," she said with a big grin.

****

Fitz looked at DeMatha, who was sporting a shit-eating grin. "How much time do we have?"

"I'm retired, Fitz, I am along for the ride as long as the music is good," he said with sincerity.

Fitz peeled out, making the left onto Belmont Ridge and slightly fishtailing it right out in front of the workforce housing on the right. Places like Brambleton don't have 'low income' housing. In Loudoun, they have 'workforce housing' — which is a new name for — 'low income' housing.

"You do know the new Dunkin' Donuts is just around the corner by the new Walmart," DeMatha pointed out.

"No drive-through at that damn place. Plus, it's some kind of organized groupie hang out for people with antique cars. I like the cars, but the last thing I want is a bunch of fucktards putting their prints on my car while I am stuck standing in line with two-thirds of the great country of India," Fitz announced as if gospel.

DeMatha tapped the dashboard, as if hitting a hidden microphone. "Testing. Is this thing on?" He roared laughing. "Have you ever considered what would happen if some tape emerged of your backward-ass, misogynistic, ethnocentric, racist rants? That would be the end of the Fitzgerald bill," DeMatha joked, hoping for a rise from Fitz.

Fitz smiled. "Look, I don't have many vices other than political incorrectness and an unabridged penchant for truthfulness. People have been trying to kill me for years — with bullets. If they want to use my own words to get me, have at it. America could stand a bit more truth and a crapload more political *in*-correctness," Fitz declared with a very Southern emphasis on the "in" before "correctness" — much the way Southerners exaggerate the "in" that begins "*in*-surance."

"What does that money-changer say in his bullshit ads, 'not a sermon, just a thought,' " DeMatha stated firmly, recognizing that Fitz wouldn't be writing speeches for Mitt Romney any time soon.

"Oh, and that Fitzgerald bill is the biggest load of crap I ever heard of. I'll give that fucking politician credit, he's a slick son-of-a-bitch using my impending forced retirement to breathe life back into my career for his own political purposes."

"Seriously, Fitz, if they pass that bill letting you waive mandatory retirement, are you going keep working?" DeMatha probed.

"Abby said she wants me to decide when my career is over. For now, it's over in four months and 28 days according to the law. Tank already has my retirement party planned."

"I bet that fucking poseur is down in the holy city of Richmond once a week trying to make sure your bill dies," DeMatha laughed.

"No doubt," Fitz smiled, secretly wondering whether it was all really going to end. "Since I am still working cases, and you did call me about a lead, how the hell do you have evidence in my case after my damn evidence techs have been working around the clock?"

"I don't know if it is evidence, but I do know I saw what was unmistakably two to three indications of blood in the road just in front of the house. They were about 14 or 15 feet from just before the mouth of the driveway in the middle of the damn road."

"So it's outside the tape and clearly outside the range of a parked car?" Fitz asked.

"Yep. In fact, if you are heading to the house from Minerva, it's just before the mouth of the driveway on the same side of the street."

"How the fuck did you see that?" Fitz asked, shocked.

"Pure luck, and I had to play it carefully because your girl Felts was out there snooping around, probably waiting for you to show up. I am not shitting you, her news van was parked about 11 feet from it. It wouldn't surprise me if she got a sample of it herself."

"How the hell did you get this without someone stopping you or noticing you?" Fitz inquired more out of disbelief than the need to know.

"I was looping around on my walk the opposite way on Conquest, mostly to be curious. I knew if I came from that direction, I would be across the street and I could walk by knowing nothing was roped off. Ironically, most of the time I start that loop walking from the Minerva direction. Thanks to all the LEOs, I feared that side of the street would be completely closed off to pedestrian traffic," he described with precision to Fitz.

"When I came around from the east instead, I was walking, bouncing my ball and getting a rhythm. I saw the street was accessible, and other than three sheriff's cruisers and the collection van on the same side as the house, the road was wide open. I decided to cross the street in front of the house on an angle so that by the time I got to the Jensen driveway, I would be as close as possible to the scene. Honestly, I thought I might catch you there," he explained with an investigator's precision.

"As I'm bouncing the ball, the morning sun behind me picks up a shade in the form of three distinct, dark spots out in the street in front of the driveway. As I get closer, I think this is something in the road. Then I see Felts, and she is working some deputy like a $3 whore. The good news is, she has him distracted. The bad news is, she is there and sees me."

"She doesn't know you, right?" Fitz interjects.

"Nobody knows me," he laughs. "But now I am wondering how I am going to stop, bend down in front of them and start picking at these spots without Felts and your boy wondering what the old guy with the ball is doing."

"Please, tell me how you blended in. Let me guess, you pretended to be a manhole cover," Fitz laughed as they roared down Truro Parish.

"No, you stupid old dick. I stood there like a goofy, nosy, old retired neighbor and bounced my ball in front of the house, looking at it curiously like 'Wow, man, what happened at the Jensens'?'

"After about three or four minutes of bouncing with some occasional glances down to keep my eye on the ball, I was pretty damn confident I found three distinct blood spots in that road."

"No shit … sitting there fucking exposed to traffic?" Fitz noted with a slice of concern in his voice.

"Exactly. So I decided to do another circle around Conquest, which you know conveniently is a circle. I went home and got a few quick evidence-collection tools and two bags. I then did two more laps around, mostly to establish that I was a weird old dude on his fitness routine.

On the fourth lap, I 'accidently' bounced my ball on my foot, and it went under one of your cruisers. So, I bent over on my knees to find it. While there, I took six swabs of the three spots and deposited them each in separate bags, which fit nicely in my basketball shorts. Thank God everyone wears those knee-high shorts that look stupid and have 12-inch pockets."

"Are you fucking kidding me? You are telling me you were on your hands and knees in front of my crime scene collecting evidence and not one bastard thought to ask you what the hell you were doing?" Fitz said with his voice clearly lost between irritated and amazed.

"No, sir, they knew what I was doing. I was looking for the damned ball."

"Where was Felts? She would have sniffed you out."

"She was gone after the third lap, which was why I made the run at it," he said matter-of-factly.

"The young deputy came toward me as I was finishing, and I let out a huge groan as I feigned trouble standing up. I told him I had bounced the damn ball off my foot and couldn't find it. I explained my walking routine, and sure enough he was able to help me find the ball right under the cruiser. He was nice enough to bend down and get it for me."

"That's was mighty nice of him," Fitz growled.

"I offered to give him my name and address if he needed to make an official report. He said no, but he did suggest I change my route until the investigation was over."

"For fuck's sakes," Fitz exclaimed, exasperated.

"I took the six samples back to the house and quickly tested them with my old kit to establish simply if there was human blood present. Each tested positive for human blood. I kept those segregated, and I have them in this pocket and their matching, untested counterparts in this pocket."

Fitz looked at him, amazed. "Well, I suppose that left no room for money in your pocket for fucking coffee then?"

Fitz barked his usual command for coffee and added an extra-large, black, no-sugar for DeMatha.

"Didn't you drink black coffee in Vietnam? Why the hell do you load it up with all that crap?" he asked.

"I did, dumbass. I also shot people in the head, and on at least one occasion gutted some barefoot commie at close range with a knife. That doesn't mean I liked those things, that's just the way it had to be at that time."

"What the hell is the matter with you?" he asked as they both laughed.

"We have to get this to Sully, and somehow, we need Sully's team to get out there and make a collection of its own since your ball-bouncing ass is outside the chain of custody. Mostly, we need to understand whose blood this is, and if it is Jenny Jensen's, what the hell was doing in the middle of the street?"

Fitz grabbed his coffee, pulled over in the lot and dialed up the medical examiner. "Sully, it's Fitz. Listen, I have an emergency. First, I am going to hand-deliver samples. You need to match these — if they *are* a match — immediately to Jensen's blood. Can you do that in some insanely quick timeframe?"

"Fitz, we can't do a DNA match in any time faster than 36 hours, even with a presidential order. I am not Horatio Caine, and this is not the set of *CSI: Miami. But*, if the blood is not the same type, we can know that almost immediately. Does that help?"

"Immeasurably. Sully, this is a handoff, me to you and you back to me with results immediately. Got it?"

"You may stand over my shoulder and get the results in 10 minutes if you so desire," Sully replied.

"Can we do it somewhere so that not everyone knows I am there waiting on a hit from you?" Fitz inquired.

"I am the chief ME, and you are, well, Fitz. We can handle this without anyone else, and my people will be on task in the lab. I can do this in my private space," he assured Fitz.

"We will see you in 22 minutes. I have a guest. I want him to see the results."

"That will corrupt the chain of —"

Fitz cut off the doctor. "I know that, Sully, but if this does match, we have to haul ass out and collect a new sample anyway, as my friend here is the one who collected these."

"From my crime scene?" the doctor asked, shocked.

"No, doc, from 20 feet outside *our* crime scene in the middle of an open fucking road."

"That's truly unusual, detective, and hence the strange protocol. We should get out there immediately and —"

"No, we need to match now and if need be make a plan to collect quickly and without any additional fanfare. I am on the blower to create a diversion with the evidence truck that will block the road and stop anyone else who hasn't done so already from running over our evidence."

"That's why you are the chief detective, Fitz. See you shortly, and I am most intrigued to meet your curious evidence-collecting friend."

"It's just DeMatha."

"Jesus H. Christ — of course it is.," Sully said repeating one of Fitz's favorite lines.

Abby was no too fond of taking the lord's name in vain, but Fitz always reminded her that that this wasn't "Jesus Christ," it was some poor bastard with the same name and different middle initial, hence no mortal sin.

Chapter 9: Face to Face

When Jenny's lover climbed on her, she was already lost in a passion that she couldn't really comprehend. "This is crazy," she thought. "I have done some reckless and wild things in my life, but this is no cheap thrill."

Jenny Jensen had a yearning that beguiled her. It was an obsession. The first time the two were together, she was left nearly paralyzed and speechless. This … this passion … this aroma, this euphoria had consumed her. Since that lifechanging surge of sexuality lit the flint in her cold heart, she hadn't thought about nearly anything else. She simply wanted to get back to that moment. She was love sick — stupid, crazy, insanely lovesick.

She'd been in this particular position before, more times than nice ladies should divulge. But this fit, it was right. The weight, the feel, the touch, the power. It worked like her mad new lover was the missing beverage in a life of thirst. The sex was uninhibited. But it was more than merely reckless or even primal.

You simply couldn't have lovemaking like this — without love. Every move worked, every touch titillated. Every tease increased anticipation, and every warm breath across her skin was like a contagion for a desire she didn't even want to combat.

"Where has this been my whole life?" Jenny Jensen wondered.

As her lover worked down the nape of her neck, over her left shoulder and to her breasts, pausing only slightly to give them the attention they demanded, Jenny heard herself moan — not for effect but from affect. The magical mystery tour continued, to her navel, then her hip bone, where the touch and caress were so soft yet so powerful.

She felt herself being gently turned and flipped. As she gave into the movement without hesitation, she was face down and breathing hard. She's pretty sure no one ever thought to put a tongue *there* before — but she was mighty happy about this adventurous maneuver. She buried her head in the pillow and gushed with pleasure previously unknown to her.

****

Reagan Fitzgerald was already running behind. Her high school Catholic youth group retreat was down in Ashburn. After yesterday's drama at home made her late on the first day, the train wreck that was her wardrobe had conspired to make her late again. When her phone rang, she nearly picked it up instinctively before remembering her father's admonition that she should never answer the phone while driving. Fortunately, she was Bluetooth and hands-free enabled.

She hit the phone symbol on her steering wheel, and on the other side of the cellular signal was the oldest of her sisters, Kelley Fitzgerald.

"How did it go?"

"You owe me, big time. It was crazy, Kelley. Mom nearly had a stroke, and Dad, well, he made me cry."

"Dad yelled at you?" she shouted through the phone in disbelief.

"No, of course he didn't yell. You know Dad."

"I know Dad all right, and you are his favorite little Reagan Catherine," she teased.

"No, Kelley, you are Daddy's favorite, which is why I completely don't understand this entire ruse. Just tell him. For crying out loud, you're 48 years old. You're a lawyer, a prosecutor and a marathoner. Just tell the man."

"He is going to be so mad, and frankly, I just don't want to disappoint him."

The brakes screeched as Reagan pulled into the parking spot at St. Theresa's. "Damn," she thought, "are we in the church today or the school?"

"You OK there, Reagan?"

"Yes, just parking. I am running behind for the A-Team meeting and retreat."

Reagan had always embraced the Catholic faith. Her best friend was devout, too, and the pair had been very active in a dynamic teen youth group run by the diocese. As a senior, she was now a leader in the movement and one of the girls the group called the A-Team.

Abby had raised all the girls in the Catholic Church, and Detective Fitzgerald complied ruthlessly with Abby's demands, but he was a self-described "cafeteria Catholic," picking and choosing his beliefs. His principle belief was that it was an absurdity to go to church every Sunday and pretend that "those cats have any damn special communication channel to the Lord that requires my donation."

Fitz didn't share his more cynical side with his girls, but his noticeable absence made clear he was not devout. As he once explained to the girls, "It is your choice to follow a faith and my obligation to respect it. I am a spiritual man, and many of my moral beliefs are in line with Catholic teaching. I am just not a church guy."

Reagan was a church girl, and she loved it. Fitz admired her passion and wondered if someday, before lying on his deathbed, he might make a better relationship with God. He just didn't want it to be phony.

"OK, I am headed over to the school now. Listen, you just need to tell Daddy. I don't know why you underestimate him. You know he is going to say all the right things," Reagan schooled her sister, a woman old enough to be her mother — by 10-plus years, no less.

"I know Dad. He will say all the right things, and then look at me differently the rest of my life," Kelley lamented.

"Then you don't know Dad," Reagan shot back.

"He's amazi— holy crap! Wow. Damn, lady. What the hell?"

"Are you OK, Reagan?" Kelley asked. What happened?"

"Talk about a distracted driver; some lady nearly made me a hood ornament. I was looking right at her, and it was like she was looking through me."

"Wow, are you sure you're OK? Did she stop or wave or something?"

"No, she just kept on going."

"Did you get the license plate or a description of the car?"

"Jesus, Kelley, you're such a prosecutor. She was just a distracted driver. I'm fine."

"So can you describe the car?"

"Let's stay on point. If you don't tell Dad soon, he's going to find out. The man knows a pregnant lady when he sees one." Reagan laughed. "Maybe you can convince Mom to have another with you?"

"No one likes smart-ass teenagers, Reagan," Kelley hissed.

"Seriously, Jake died nearly five years ago. You're in love. You didn't plan this, but it happened. Dad is going to be thrilled, not disappointed. Besides, after you made me pull this Marine Corps story out, they are both ready to hear anything now."

"That was the point. I do owe you for sure, this news will be a little less insane after that one. I can't wait to hear what mom said, let alone dad."

"Wow, Dad is more amazing then we knew — and you should already know that. Trust him, Kelley."

"I have four kids, ages 23 to 17, and I'm having the love child of a married man. No dad is *that* amazing."

"Love child? What is this, the 1950s? The married man's wife left him three years ago; they just never got divorced. Kelley, it's 2018. You did hear about the election, right?"

"Funny kid. I love you. I will call Dad as soon as this new case settles a bit. Thanks, honey — and don't talk on the phone while you cross the street."

"No kidding. It looks like that lady has already hit something else."

****

"I can tell you, detective, with the highest degree of medical certainty, that this blood is a completely different blood type than that of your victim, the unfortunate Mrs. Jensen," Sully began.

"Mrs. Jensen is AB negative, and this blood is O positive. Ironically, these two blood types couldn't be more different. That is to say, O positive is by far the most common, and AB negative is remarkably rare," the ME explained in his unpreachy yet completely professorial tone.

"We need to know Jack Jensen's blood type immediately," DeMatha blurted out.

"Sir, we need to get a sample of this blood collected from the source, using the proper procedures and chain of custody. I suspect

121

that need is just as immediate so we can find a DNA profile," Sully declared.

"What we need is to find out what the FBI knows and isn't telling us," Fitz stated affirmatively. "And I am sure as shit not driving to DC now to go through that fire drill. DeMatha, I need to drop you in Leesburg for 15 minutes while I speak to my fearless leader and explain to him how this is going down."

As Fitz and DeMatha jumped in the car, they looked at each other and said the same thing: "I think we are looking for another body."

"Fitz, seriously, it is possible that this is a terror operation," DeMatha said with some measure of concern.

"You have no idea, DeMatha. This just got real."

"The wife told her personal lawyer — America's biggest A-hole — that she had been stalked for what would be about four weeks now. She thought it was the husband. Apparently, our victim liked to have sex, preferably often and with other people's husbands."

"Well, Christ, everyone in Brambleton knows that," DeMatha stated, as if it were common knowledge in the community.

"Actually, I don't think this was an open secret, according to my interview of her lawyer. At least, she didn't think it was an open secret."

"Fair enough, but I have seen that one around this dysfunctional, sleepy little exurb for years, and I always suspected she was sleeping around. But I had no proof of it."

"You were right. What we don't know is what Jack Jensen knew, and we also don't know the identity of her lover — who, according to her lawyer, she was going to leave her family to be with."

"Any chance this fellow's name was Mohammad? Isn't she part Middle Eastern?" DeMatha asked.

"Look at you, DeMatha, you racist, profiling motherfucker."

"Tell me, if this is terror, how do you see this going down?" Fitz asked as he screeched up in front of the courthouse and headed to the commonwealth attorney's office to meet his boss, who confirmed his location by text.

"It looks like the press has beat feet. You can sit tight or head to the diner. Think about the terror scenario you propose. I will be back very shortly."

****

"Jill, it's Janie."

"Hey, Janie, I saw your text. I am sorry I didn't get back to you earlier, I have been swamped with work. I can take Jeremy, CK and Matt to CCD. It's no problem. I just have to get Rich to take Maddie to soccer and then swing back and get Sean to his SAT prep course."

"Oh great. I don't know what car I will have, so I don't think everyone will fit," Janie said monotonally.

"Oh my gosh, Janie, it's no problem. I can't believe you were even coming out tonight. Are you OK?"

"I just can't talk about it, Jill. You know. It's not real to me. I cried all night, and I have no crying left to do. But — it's like a dream, a sick, weird dream, and I have been pretending all day that it didn't happen."

"You let us know what we can do. I will drive and pick up, it's not a problem. Rich and I are really sorry to hear about Jenny. I

123

know how close you too were. Just let us know if we can do anything to help you and Jeff — or Jack and the boys."

"Thanks, Jill. You're so sweet."

Janie was relieved to reach Jill, who was always willing to help with every mom duty. Her boys had been playing baseball together since they were 4 years old on the Loudoun South Little League T-Ball Cubs, where her husband, Jeff, and Jill's husband, Rich, coached together.

"Jill Brown, that's one squared-away mom who doesn't try to get in anyone's business," Janie thought. "Everyone else in this neighborhood would have pumped me for gossip."

****

The main entrance of the prosecutor's office in Loudoun County, Virginia, is anything but inviting. The building sits on the corner of the courthouse complex, and when you enter it, you immediately descend three or four short steps on a darkened staircase and come face to face with a glass window — much like a prison visitation room. The foyer is cramped, unwelcoming and not designed for people to hang around. It's a waiting room for one or two at best.

Of course, prosecutors have carded access granting them passage in either direction from the window or, if they please, by another door. The only good thing about the building is that for working prosecutors, the office is just steps from the courthouse.

Fitz hadn't hit the first step when he was immediately greeted by Brad, who was there with one of the deputy prosecutors to ensure instant access to the building and hurry Fitz to his meeting with *the* sheriff.

Upstairs, Tankersley was exchanging pleasantries with the elected commonwealth's attorney. They were members of the same party. Tankersley was acting as if he knew all about the murder, and the commonwealth's attorney, or CA as they are known in Virginia, was acting as if he believed him, which he didn't.

When the CA's assistant buzzed him to let him know Fitz was in the building, his face took on a less pained, visible sign of relief: "Please, show the sheriff to the secure conference room." It was a meeting the CA was delighted not to be in, but happy to host in his building.

Loudoun County is purportedly America's wealthiest county on a median-income basis. You would not guess that by the look of the inside of the CA's primary, Grade-A conference room. The chairs were 40 years old, the window treatments were shabby, the table was banged up and scarred, and the room looked like an emergency conference room at a Motel 6.

The Tank positioned himself at the head of the conference room table, leaving the chair to his right open for his able assistant. When Fitz walked through the door, Tankersley remained seated.

"Detective Fitzgerald, what is the sudden emergency? I had hoped I would've heard from you last night or earlier this morning."

"Good for you," Fitz thought. "If you're going to run this county and its damn fine department of real officers, you should show some balls and take charge when meeting with a subordinate."

"Sheriff, I have been quite busy, and I left the communications to Parker to keep you informed. If he has not done so, I shall have him drawn and quartered — after we solve the two murders, of course."

Tankersley was so "nakedly incompetent with respect to investigative details that remarkably the reference to 'two murders' soared right past him," Fitz thought.

He was still laser-focused on Fitz not kissing his ring, staying in contact and showing up for his presser as well as having Parker relay that insubordinate message about the FBI meeting.

"No one wants to go to DC, Fitz, but to DC we are going at the not-so-subtle request of the director of the FBI. We must play ball with these guys. They have assets that can help us, and their guy is a high-level player."

Fitz was both delighted that Tankersley decided to grow a pair today and thoroughly irritated that he had to put up with it.

"Sheriff, based on the facts we have now, it's a damn good guess that 'their guy' is dead. That's why I said, *two murders.* We need immediate information from that office, and we need their cooperation, in Loudoun County, today. So no, I am not going to DC, and I strongly recommend that you not go either."

Tankersley looked like someone just handed him the wrong script at a presser.

"Jack Jensen is dead?" Tankersley partly asked and partly exclaimed. "When was someone going to tell the sheriff of this county? I just finished a press conference assuring the people of Loudoun that they were safe." Tankersley snorted as he considered the possible political ramifications of having falsely assured the public it was out of danger.

"We just confirmed 10 minutes ago that a significant amount of blood was found outside our crime scene that does *not* match the victim. Jensen is missing. The FBI wants a meeting, which tells me they don't know where Jack Jensen is either. My best guess is that the blood belongs to him, and that he's either dead or being held hostage. I'm guessing dead."

"Wait — you just said he *was* dead? Do you have his body, or are you just speculating here?" Tankersley demanded as he rose from his seat.

"I have no body. He's dead or captured is my working theory. My gut tells me he is dead, but I don't have all the facts yet. We need the FBI to confirm his blood type, and then we'll at least know if he is the other injured party."

"That's all the more reason to make our meeting and find out what's happening. If you're correct, we'll have to turn jurisdiction of this case over to them anyway."

"Ahh … no."

"No what, detective?"

"No to all of it. First, we have one body, a civilian. We have no evidence of a federal crime at this time. Perhaps when they confirm he is missing, and the blood type is his, we can and should run a joint investigation. I think that's correct. Until then, this is our investigation. Also, we need that info now, and we can't have our resources pulled into DC. FBI has 35,000 employees. We don't. We need to stay on the ground in Loudoun working this case, and they need to deploy assets out this way immediately, I suspect. So, call the director and tell him to meet us at Joe's. We should bump it up to 2 p.m."

"Let me get this straight. You want me to call the director of the FBI — a presidential appointee — and tell him to meet my subordinate at a café in Sterling if he wants to be briefed on his missing man?" Tankersley asked, incredulously.

"I wouldn't sell it like that, but yes, I'd like to meet him sooner, and do it in Loudoun outside the watchful eye of the press or any other entities or groups," Fitz said dispassionately.

"I *am not* calling Director Wray. And *I am* ordering you and Parker to be at that meeting at 4 p.m."

Brad looked up from his notes, as even he was surprised by the tone of Tankersley's voice and his shocking decision to draw a red line in the sand with Fitz.

"Sheriff, you're the boss. That means you can fire me. While you process that paperwork, I'lll call Wray myself. And I'll bet you my pension against that chest full of phony fucking tin you have that he shows up at Joe's at the fucking appointed time. Do you know why he will? Because he's not fucking stupid. You let Parker know when the paperwork is complete with the county. That's when you can have my gun and badge." Fitz turned and headed for the door, moving with a renewed sense of purpose.

"You've crossed a line here, Fitzgerald. You don't run this damned department, I do," Tankersley yelled, trying to convince someone other than himself of the truth of his assertion.

As Fitz exited the door he never looked back, but he shouted loudly enough for the entire building to hear him, "Then man up, Tank, and run the damn department. I'm going to work to solve these murders until you replace me."

Just as Fitz made it to the elevator, he was intercepted by another deputy CA, Kelley Fitzgerald, his "number one" daughter.

"Working on your diplomacy skills again, detective?" she smiled at him.

"Diplomacy, dear, is for people with ambitions. Will we see you for dinner on Sunday?"

"Of course, Dad. Seriously, don't get too far out on that limb. He's not worth it," she said leaning in closely toward her father.

"No, he's not. But those victims are worth it," he said in a distinct blend of cop, Marine and fatherly tones.

Fitz had one more stop to make; it was going to get serious fast. He hit the door of Detective Henry 'Hank' Butler and walked right in without knocking. A startled Butler looked up ready to pounce until he saw Fitz.

"Butler, did you take a stalking complaint from my victim?"

"What?"

"Jenny Jensen, the nice dead lady who was brutally murdered and then whose dead body was barbarized? *Jensen, J-E-N-S-E-N*, does that ring a goddamn bell?" Fitz roared.

"Ah, no … I mean, I don't think so."

"No? You're going to tell me *no?*" he asked, with a rare rise in the tone of his voice with a deputy.

"Sir, I think —"

"Butler, I have a copy of statement made to you in this system by Jenny Jensen, and she claims she was being stalked by her husband and she feared for her life. Are you saying that happens so often in your office that you didn't connect her name with the murder in my case?

"No, I —"

"You what? You didn't think it was relevant? You thought I should hear about from another witness?"

"Sir, I just —"

"You what? Just fucked up? I see nothing in this file, Butler. Nothing. You did not one damn thing to investigate this complaint made weeks ago."

"Well, sir, I just —"

"Butler, when a person in your care shows the courage to come forward and make a complaint, the only thing you should *just* do is investigate the hell out of it. That's what you do. Unless you have an order from a superior to sit on it and say, fuck this shit, you investigate it. And, if someone *ever* tells you to slow the investigation of a complaint of possible violence against a citizen, a woman, you come see me, and I'll get them fired."

Butler was mortified.

"This woman is dead, Butler — *D-E-A-D* — *dead.* No one I know comes back from that, no matter what damn book you read in what damn church. For all I know, I have to tell her kids that's she's dead because you were busy playing fucking solitaire on your computer, and taking her statement while alive was not a priority," Fitz continued manically.

"Butler, this job isn't for everyone. You hear me? This is tough work, and it takes tough people committed to protect and serve at any cost. *That's — not — you.*"

"Sir, I —"

"Sir nothing, Butler. I'm going to solve this case without delay. When I do, I'm coming back to this office. You better not be in it. Do you understand me, son?" Fitz glared right through him.

"Should I contact my rep?" Butler asked meekly.

"Butler, if I have to bring you up on charges to get you fired, your next job will be super-sizing French fries in another state. You want me to file that charge? Or would you prefer to give your notice and go find another line of work?"

"But, sir, I —"

"Butler — there is no line, thin or thick, of any color, that protects people who fail their duty to protect my citizens. Take my advice, don't be here when I return."

****

Brad Smith looked at the sheriff. Tankersley was fuming.

"Process it right now, Brad. You hear me. I want his fucking badge, and you make sure this happens today, in the next fucking hour."

"Boss, let's talk to the deputies and check with legal," Brad offered.

"Legal?" he asked as if more irritated. "Fuck legal. They are going to give me some mumbo-jumbo. They're all in the bag for Detective Trump anyway. This is straightforward insubordination, and I can fire him for cause. Let him sue the department."

"Tank, you're the boss. I am just here for strategic communications and political strategy. That's it. You fire this guy without checking every box, and you do it in the middle of a huge investigation of a high-profile murder or murders, and this could have real political blowback. Also, your own damn party is trying to pass a bill before his mandatory retirement to keep him on the job. No one is going to like this — no one."

"I can't have this guy running my department. I'm the sheriff."

"Right now, the only people who know about this blowup were in the room. You fire him, and this will be in every newspaper, including the *Post*. And Felts, she will be on this like a drunk, naked prom queen."

"OK, strategy man, you get with legal, and *you* develop a strategy for getting him out — no matter what it takes, in the best and fastest way possible — for the betterment of this office."

Tankersley stormed out of the room, but Brad was hot on his trail.

131

"Sheriff, we need to reach the FBI director before Fitzgerald."

"Why the hell is that?"

"First, we want to let him know that Fitz has something hot and that he will be calling. This will make us look less like schmucks out of the loop. Second, let me call Fitz and tell him to hold his call to the FBI until we reach them."

"Jesus, who do you work for, Brad?"

"You, sir. If we let him reach Wray first, lord knows what he will say. And if we don't give Wray a heads up, he will think this whole department is incompetent and you're weak."

"Fuck a duck! You make sure you get this squared away."

Brad frantically dialed Fitz, who hadn't even hopped in his illegally parked car yet. In fact, thanks to the diligence of the City of Leesburg, Fitz found himself face to face with a parking enforcement officer who was just writing down his license plate.
Fitzgerald pulled out his badge and politely offered it to the ticket hound.

"You're illegally parked, officer, and this is not an official vehicle," she said, unimpressed and not really paying too close attention to him or his badge.

"Ma'am, we all have a job to do. I'm not angry at you. I thought you might give me a professional courtesy, but I'll gladly take the penalty. Here's my ID to make it easier." His commanding voice gently tugged her head from the pad causing her to take a look at him.

The officer then looked at the ID and the impressive badge with the Chief Detective inscription. She had heard this name a million times. "Holy crap, *this* is *the* detective Fitzgerald," she thought. She honestly wondered if he might shoot her rather than take the ticket.

"Detective Fitzgerald, my apologies. I had no idea this was *your* vehicle."

"Please, don't apologize. I was wrong to slot the car in here, and frankly, you were right to identify the vehicle and ticket it. Nothing here gives me carte blanche. You're just doing your job. I had important information to give to the sheriff on a pressing case, and I didn't want to hunt for parking."

"Of course, detective. Have a nice day. It was an honor to meet you, sir."

"That's kind, officer. I appreciate your discretion."

"I almost gave a ticket to God almighty," she thought. "Man, that guy couldn't have been classier if he tried. How the hell is that guy nearly 70 years old? What a hunk."

Fitz's phone went off, and it was Brad. Fitz knew it was damage control, or at least he hoped. Leaning against his car, he took the call soaking in the warm sun on his face.

"So, do I have to duck Parker all day so he can't collect my badge and gun?" Fitz said answering without a hello.

"Detective, I just want to put this all back together for everyone, and I am instructed to do so," Brad started.

"I guess that makes one or both of us Humpty Dumpty," Fitz snorted.

"The sheriff will call the director and let him know you have an urgent message, to expect your call, and that you have a suggestion based on new information. Does that work?"

"So, he is showing deference to the lead detective and letting me try to talk the director down from his perch. If I fail, I assume you folks will go to DC?"

"Don't fail, because then it looks like we're not all on the same page, which will be bad for the department, you, Tank and, frankly, any cooperation you hope to get from the FBI."

"Christ, Brad, you really are the brains of the operation. I'll wait 25 minutes before I call FBI. Do you have a number for me?"

"Yes, I will text it to you. It'll get you to his assistant, obviously, not the director. He apparently doesn't even dial his own calls."

"If I were a presidential appointee, I might not dial a call either," Fitz laughed. "Thanks, Brad, and no matter what you do, don't waste your time and his capital on trying to fire me."

"Sage advice, detective."

Chapter 10: The Real McCoy

Alan Bodine had written a few thousand "team" emails in his day to his many Little League and travel baseball teams. This one, he thought, would require some wordsmithing. The email was just about done, he thought: "I will send it out under the header, 'Practice and Prayers.'"

Dear Friends:

While we thought about keeping some sense of normalcy for the kids today with baseball, the more correct conclusion was that our boys need to be together, with their families in this tough time. There is nothing normal about these events.

The Jensens need your prayers, your fellowship and your support. Likewise, your boys will need your guidance on how best to handle this situation. I am happy to counsel you on how you might discuss this matter. That hard decision falls, however, firmly in the hands of each family.

Today, we kept our boys home from school so we could talk to them about Jenny's passing. We elected to leave out the details, noting only that she has died at home and that her death was under investigation. It may be that we have to tell them more later. They are working on a card and package for their teammate. We told them that if they choose to text him, please send a short note of simple support and not ask questions or spread rumors.

Our Sunday games remain scheduled, but we will decide if it is in the best interest of the boys and community for those games to be played.

We are all brokenhearted today. Please, help each other and let us draw on our collective strength to help the Jensens.

Regards,
Coach Bodine

Alan was catastrophically concerned about the rumor mill. He wisely counseled Jason not to talk about the death or anything he saw online or by text. He knew, however, it was merely a matter of time before details got out and the neighborhood gossip spread like a bush fire. Death of any kind is a tough subject at any age. Describing death to a 10-year-old living in a suburban bubble inside of America was even more difficult. Most kids, thankfully, have no concept at that age that their parents can or will die. Certainly, no one expects that to happen to young, vibrant parents in their early 40s. It goes without saying that murder and the heinous torture of a loving mother are just not a conversation a child should hear.

The worst part of Alan's concern was his recognition that that he kicked off the rumor mill himself last night when he called Caylee. As for Caylee, she was sick about the death and even more upset that she called Janie. She just didn't know how she could keep that from her. Caylee, after all, had a reputation of being a "carrier" rather than a transmitter of gossip. Most people spoke to Caylee about things they heard because they knew she had no compelling desire to share. Gossip wasn't her thing. She was the full measure of decent.

"Honey, you must be exhausted," Caylee said to Alan as he hit the send button.

"It was a long night, and there are more ahead," he said quite solemnly. "I just need a nap, maybe an hour. Then we need to talk about everything."

"Can you at least tell me about the boys, where they are?"

"Jack and Jason?" he asked, referring to the Jensen children.

"Yes, my god, are they OK," Caylee began to cry as she pressed her husband.

"Caylee, they are safe with Jenny's parents right now. I will give you details later. As for Jason, I don't know if he will ever be OK … really. But physically safe, yes. They are with family and now out of the Brambleton echo chamber."

****

After narrowly escaping the parking ticket, Fitz thought it unseemly to bang an illegal U-turn in front of the courthouse too. He took the long series of lefts around and back onto King Street. He pulled up in front of the old Leesburg Diner, and there was DeMatha, the invisible man, bouncing his ball and smiling like the cat who caught the canary.

"So, did you get me some special credentials? Maybe you got old Tank to deputize me?" he laughed.

"Well, there may be an opening in homicide. I think I just got myself fired just less than 5 months short of retirement."

"I knew you should've brought me with you," DeMatha insisted.

"Yes, you would've been there pulling some Jedi mind trick, I'm sure. By the way, do you have a phone on you?"

"You know I don't carry my own phone," DeMatha said, looking at him in surprise.

"Oh, I know that, because you fucking text me from a different damn phone every week."

"I don't like to be tracked," DeMatha stated matter-of-factly. "This phone is my youngest's. She had it taken away for getting a B."

"You took Annie's phone away for a fucking B? I know you spent a lot of time undercover in the Pacific, but I didn't know you were any part Asian."

"Ahh, yes, a B, the Asian F. Listen, getting into a Virginia college is hard enough. The kid has one job, that's it. It's called student. You fail at it, you lose rewards. None of this stuff is theirs, you know; It's is all ours."

"Jesus, you're a complete dick. You know she will go to college, rebel and fuck everyone on campus, then pose for 'Girls of the Mid-Atlantic' — holding a sign that says, 'Hi, Dad.,'" Fitz roared in laughter.

"Perhaps, but at least she will do it at William and Mary and not fucking ODU or that giant terror cell, George Mason." DeMatha howled at his own joke.

"That's twice today, Joe, twice you got down on Middle Easterners. Just because Mason has a strong population of Muslims doesn't mean the campus is a terror cell. It's a fine, diverse university run by a nitwit."

"Yes, they have a broad collection of left-wing crackpots. I remember a few years back going to a graduation where some anti-Semites were encouraged by the president to protest at the graduation. That guy is an idiot," DeMatha declared.

"Well, I can't disagree with you on Cabrera. The guy is an open advocate for illegal immigration and sanctuary colleges, which means he is, *per se,* a moron."

"Don't get me started on illegal immigration," DeMatha begged.

"Fair enough. I need that phone to call the director of the FBI."

"What?"

"Yes, I just got the go text from Brad. I'm inviting Wray out to Joe's for a pow-wow. You want to meet the FBI director?"

"You are going to call the director of the FBI and invite him to Joe's for some corned-beef hash and to share a milkshake?"

"Watch," he laughed. "And I don't share my hash with anyone."

Fitz punched the numbers in and heard the ringing on the other side. After four rings, he knew he was not getting through. "You have reached the assistant to Director Wray. Please leave your name, number and a brief message, and I will return your call."

"This is Detective Fitzgerald with the Loudoun sheriff's office. Please have Director Wray return my call to this number. Please have him confirm the blood type of his guy and move his schedule for a meeting in Loudoun at 2 p.m. Thanks."

"I have a case of some goddamn American beer versus your sissy red Zinfandel that says neither Wray nor his assistant calls you back," DeMatha roared.

"You're on. Just because I don't have a magic bouncing ball, son, doesn't mean I can't still pull a rabbit out of a hat. Hold this phone while I call Parker.

"Parker. I got DeMatha here with me on the speaker. We may need to dump you for another call — if it goes click, don't take offense. DeMatha likes you; he just hates Springsteen."

"Hey, Parker — I was just listening to "Brilliant Disguise"; seems your Boss was OK without the E Street Band," DeMatha chuckled.

"That's just heresy, DeMatha," Parker yelled, not one bit joking.

"Listen, we're headed to make a stop in Sterling. I can't get anywhere near Brambleton yet or that Felts lady will fucking tackle me," Fitz began. "Did we draw those samples from the road, and are they secure?"

"All set, boss, no visible fanfare. We pulled that off on the sly. Backed the van up out of the driveway, used three squad cars to cover like we were loading gear, and we grabbed the samples during the on-load. I am sure we drew no additional attention. We dug a few holes in the road, per the precise order of Sully. He wanted to be sure we didn't just swab it," Parker explained.

"Great. Sully always has his reasons. Listen carefully. We are looking for a second body, and we are looking for any evidence of a team or a wet crew. You need to expand your exterior perimeter — carefully. Track anything that looks suspicious. But don't send a whole team out there like we are looking for a lost toddler."

"No sweat, boss, I'll do it myself."

"This is important: We are now nearly 14 hours past this event, and we don't know where the hell this woman was before her murder or who she was with."

"Right, the little kid had no idea, and the second kid thought she was out with a 'group of moms,' but he didn't know with whom or where."

"Both the older boy — what was his name Jack Jr. and Bodine speculated that we start by asking some woman named Janie Handly. According to both, it's likely they were together or that Ms. Handly might know," Fitz continued.

"I don't want to send this whole community into a panic, and the last thing I want to do is interview a bunch of wine-drinking, chatty Cathys, who will then set the neighborhood on fire with rumors and innuendo. But for fuck's sake, we need to nail down who saw her last to complete the timeline and to tell us critical facts, like her state of mind when last seen or whether they observed anything different about her."

"Didn't we determine last night that neither of the Jensens' cars were in use, boss?" Parker piped up.

"We sure did, and that was critical because based on Bodine's story, there is no way this woman was walking around in the dark. She thought someone was trying to kill her. We know this; someone dropped Jenny Jensen off at home, and I think it's a damn big deal that whoever that was hasn't stepped up to give a statement," Fitz added.

"Great point," DeMatha chimed in.

"It looks like it is going to be ladies' night at the station," Fitz said.

The phone rang in DeMatha's hands, and the message read "Blocked number."

"Parker, we have to roll. Fitz out."

****

Director Wray had the strangest look on his face. No fewer than seven FBI senior agents from the executive wing were in the room with him for the initial briefing on the double phone calls from Loudoun County. The first call, from Tank, received about three minutes of analysis and innocuous discussion, ending with the conclusion that events were outpacing the small department, it was in over its head and the chief had no idea what was really happening. It was the voicemail from the chief detective that had everyone gathered around.

Truthfully, after it played the first time, Wray sent for the research team and told them to find every fact they could on

Fitzgerald. He wanted more than what he had heard that morning, which was cursory. He gave them 10 minutes to find something real about the curious voice on the message belonging to Detective Fitzgerald.

"Play that message again," Wray commanded. This would now be the seventh time they'd heard it.

> This is Detective Fitzgerald with the Loudoun sheriff's office. Please have Director Wray return my call to this number. Please have him confirm the blood type of his guy and move his schedule for a meeting in Loudoun at 2 p.m. Thanks.

Wray's chief deputy blurted out what most were thinking. "Does this guy think the FBI director is going to call and chat him up and then come out to Loudoun for lunch?" The room broke into a small chuckle.

"First, I can't believe that damn stupid sheriff gave out the bat phone to an underling. Second, this guy must be living too long as a huge fish in a really small pond to phone the EMT team, demand we clear the director's schedule, and then have a meeting in his favorite lunch spot … which apparently is next to a place with a sign that simply reads, 'Massage.' "

"Jim, what's your take?" Wray asked James Gannon, the chief of the famed FBI profiler unit who was part of the meeting by conference call. Gannon had nothing more than what he heard on the phone, the morning two-minute briefing on Fitz and the voicemail message from Fitz sent to him earlier. Gannon used his own time online to dig deeper during the collective meeting.

"Honestly, this can go two ways. This guy is either some old sheriff who thinks he invented law enforcement, and he is now yanking the FBI's chain in the final draw-down of his career …."

"*Or* —" Wray jumped in.

"Or this is one seriously squared-away cop who is sitting on something he thinks you need to know now, and he isn't wasting your time or his own."

"Your take, Jim — which one is it?"

"With the information I have, the eight minutes I spent online and fact that this guy has a Silver Star and seven daughters — and the Virginia legislature has a bill with his name on it to extend his service — I am going with the latter, Mr. Director."

The brief team came through the door, and Wray immediately put them on the spot. "Tell us something we don't know about this guy, and give me your personal assessment: Is Fitzgerald the real McCoy or a pretender?"

Wray had three guys on his briefing team, and he trusted those agents and their judgment. They worked with and for him previously, and they had proven their chops in sizing up politicians, diplomats, reporters and even lowly LEOs.

"The guy writes poetry and has a library in his house with 10,000 books. Real McCoy," Agent Malone declared.

"Three local sheriffs swear to me he walks on water. Not that he *thinks* he walks on water — *they* think he walks on water. Real McCoy," Agent McIntire declared.

"The guy competed in the Murphy challenge in Falls Church last year and placed eighth overall. Not eighth in his age group, but the then-68-year-old finished eighth among all competitors. Real McCoy," nearly yelled Agent Kauffman.

"Well, gentlemen, my take from his tone was authoritative and confident, not arrogant. Plus, it appears if I don't call him back, he might come here and beat the crap out of me — or outsmart me

— or as a god, damn me to hell," the director said in a rare moment of levity.

The talent assembled in that room was not there to stroke the director's ego. The FBI had a crisis. They had no idea where their man was, and given where he was supposed to be, they were gravely concerned.

Jensen had been scheduled to depart with his team at 0500. He should have been assembled with the team by 4:15 a.m. He wasn't. No one had heard from him, and everyone knew the gravity of missing the flight to Kandahar.

Chapter 11: Corned-Beef Hash

Jenny Jensen collapsed in her lover's arms. She needed the strength. She needed that touch. She needed to be held. Many lovers had held Jenny, but not in that special way her partner had that had changed her whole life so quickly. She was drunk and dizzy from the feeling of desperation. Whatever first love was, this was it on crack.

Jenny spent the last few weeks on an emotional rollercoaster. This new love, this magic-carpet ride kept her thirsty all day. Her days were no different from her nights. It was one fanciful dream that ended in ecstasy. She didn't fear the shaking and trembling that came with the lovemaking; her body ached for it.

Still, into this crazy, insane love was now interjected this stalker. It had to be Jack, who was, effectively, a spy. Worse than that, he read people, he didn't believe a damn word they said and his profession and expertise drove his suspicion.

"He knows. He knows about this affair," she feared. And she thought again to herself, "if he knew about this, then he had ripped the scab off all the other stupid, meaningless, rush-driven, restless fucks she had had.

Jenny looked into her partner's eyes. "I found you — I found you before he ruined my life," she whispered to the love who held her so strongly. "He's going to kill me. I know it. Oh my god, he's going to kill you," she blurted out.

"We will be forever safe. He has no idea about us. Soon, it will be just you and me. Now … let me taste you."

Jenny fell back on the sofa, and in seconds she was back from the nightmare and riding that rollercoaster to the finish line.

****

Jeff Handly had finally settled down. He decided he was working from home on this Friday. The events were so surreal, and he was worried about Janie. He was also worried about that dark secret he held about his time with Jenny. Mostly, he was tired from the sleepless night and both sick and guilty about his happiness that he would never see Jenny again. He just kept telling himself, "The secret is buried with her." Now, he wondered, "Can I keep it together until she is in the ground so that Janie doesn't see right through me?"

Jeff was wading through his garage. On the far side was his sons' sports equipment. The Handly garage looked like what one might image would be a Dick's Sporting Goods store, if Dick's had an entire section of used equipment. He'd been meaning to go through "this crap" since Jackson left for college last year. Now, with Jeremy playing travel baseball for the Clowns Red, 14U team, he knew most of this old gear was nothing but yard-sale fodder.

Still, Jeff had reluctantly agreed to let Jeremy play for the middle school team. They needed a few team bats, and he had promised Coach Rich he would find a few BBCOR bats that the coach's son could try out. Jeremy was now hitting the new model Ghost, and if Jeff didn't find those other team bats, the coach's son would be using puppy dog eyes to let him borrow it. "No one hits with the Ghost," he thought. "The f'ing thing was $400." Mostly, Jeff was trying to keep busy, and he had been promising Janie he would clean this mess up and make room for one more car. "Today is as good a day as any to get the job done," he surmised.

The Handly house phone went off, and the creepy voice-messaging system kept repeating the same thing: "LOU-DOWN SHARE-EEF." After the third time, Handly realized it was saying,

"Loudoun sheriff." A bolt of adrenaline hit him in the form of pure panic. He fumbled for the receiver and hit "talk."

"Is Mrs. Jane Handly home, please," the voice asked in a surprisingly pleasant tone.

"She is not. May I ask who is calling?" he stuttered.

"This is Detective Parker with the Loudoun County sheriff's office. Do you know when she will return or how I may reach her?"

Handly pulled the phone from his mouth. He held it out from his body, scrunched his face in pain, then drew a long, deep breath, exhaling for what seemed like too long a time.

"Hello?" Parker chimed from his end, as if asking whether someone were still there.

"Yes, I am sorry, detective. I don't know when she will return. She is running errands and grocery shopping."

"I understand," Parker said. "Is this her husband?"

"Ahh, yes, it is. How can I help you?"

"Is that Mr. Handly?"

"Of course," Jeff said, surprised, his tone almost irritated.

"Sorry, Mr. Handly, I found long ago that just because a couple is married, they may not share the same last name, particularly in Ashburn."

"Oh, of course; we know people like that too. Janie is probably at Wegmans, but she was gone early today, so I expect her back pretty soon. Is she in trouble or something?"

"No sir — gosh, I wouldn't think so," Parker said in his best "aw shucks, you don't have to fear the cops" voice. "I am part of the team investigating a crime in your neighborhood. We are talking to nearly everyone in the community who may know the family. We are told that your wife and Ms. Jensen were great friends. We just need to ask a few questions and see if she can help fill in some details for us."

147

"Of course, Detective Parker. We were devastated by the news. Janie hardly slept last night, and I think she was out early today to try to get and stay busy."

"Well, Mr. Handly, I am sorry. What is your first name?"

"It's Jeff, Jeff Handly. Please, call me Jeff. You keep saying Mr., and I feel like you are asking for my dad."

"I understand, Jeff."

"I don't want to take up too much of your time, sir, as we have many people to speak with. I do, however, want to try to reach her closest friends today."

"Janie will absolutely want to cooperate. Do you have a number where she can reach you? When she gets home, I'll have her call."

"I'm right around the corner. Do you mind if I come by in a about a half hour to see if she is home?"

Jeff paused for a minute, but thought, what's the harm? "No problem, our son is at school, so that is fine."

"Great Mr., I mean Jeff. If she is not home, I will drop my card and contact with you."

"Perfect, officer, thanks."

Handly hung up and let out the rest of that long breath that must have been trapped, like his heart, in the top of his throat. Wow, he thought, "they don't even know my fucking name. That's good. I wonder if he is playing me." As his hands shook, his mind wandered.

"Fuck, Janie may not be ready for this, but I could look guilty by telling him he couldn't come here."

He picked up the cellphone and dialed Janie. It went straight to voicemail, an event that under normal circumstances would be a great excuse to leave a message. Now he thought, "Shit, she better get this message."

"Janie. Hope you are OK, sweetheart. Give me a ring *before* you get home. The sheriff wants to come by and ask some routine questions about Jenny. I want to make sure you are ready. I love you; bye."

****

"Let me answer this fucking thing. I'll be your secretary," DeMatha joked as he looked at the blocked number.

Fitz grabbed the phone, looked at DeMatha before hitting talk and said, "I like a nice Zinfandel, dumbass. Get me something from Tom Seaver's winery at GTS vineyards." As DeMatha rolled his eyes, Fitz fumbled for the speaker button on the unfamiliar phone of his friend's teenage daughter, thinking, "This is always how I thought I would talk to the director of the FBI."

"Is this Detective Ronald Fitzgerald?" the voice asked with authority through the speaker.

"Yes, sir," Fitz declared.

"Please hold for the director of the FBI, Christopher Wray." Fitz smiled as he looked at DeMatha, making the thumb-to-his-lips universal signal for tilting back a beverage.

"Detective, are we on a secure line?" Wray warned, more than asked.

"No sir, but it is the cellphone of a 16-year-old girl unrelated to me by blood or marriage. So, fire away."

Wray's team looked at each other half quizzically and somewhat amused. McIntire leaned over to his research colleagues and whispered, "He's fucking MacGyver, too."

Wray smiled to himself, recognizing that our nation's enemies were unlikely to be listening to the phone of an anonymous 16-year-old girl. He opened the file before him on Jack Jensen, though he already knew the contents. He read it again.

"Detective, I can confirm a match on our mutual friend."

"Sir, I very much appreciate the courtesy of your time. I am mindful of the entirely unusual request I have made, and I am damn sorry if your team has wasted one minute of time trying to figure out if I am nuts or not. I assure you, whatever degree of nuttery I may have, it does not affect my law-enforcement judgment."

"We recognize your record of accomplishment, and we are happy to rework this meeting trusting your judgment, detective."

"Sir, the sheriff gave you a great spot for us. Can you and your team make that at 2 p.m.? I recognize too that moving your schedule was a big ask, and when you arrive, I promise you will concur it was necessary."

"We will be there. Low profile, but we will send an advance."

"My guy will welcome that team, and the store will close if necessary for the time needed for our teams to host this private party. I will send you some details for your team's benefit."

"I can honestly say, detective, I look forward to meeting you."

"Thank you, sir, and thank your team for me. I am sure they were inconvenienced."

"I will, detective. Good bye."

Wray turned to his team and asked, "Well?"

"Well," McIntire said, "I heard the corned-beef hash is terrific there."

"Great, the director of the FBI is meeting in a coffee shop in Sterling on no notice about his missing chief interrogator with a sheriff who may be cooler than Clint Eastwood and John Wayne — or he may be crazy," his deputy blurted out.

"Live a little, will you," Gannon said through the speaker. "I bet this is useful."

****

Fitz pulled into the lot off Church Street just over the east side of 28 in Sterling. Joe's Café was a little diner/coffee shop straight out of a North Jersey hamlet. It seats about 55 people, and on most mornings, 15 people are waiting in line for one of those seats. The décor is authentic diner drab. It's not a chain. Of course, it isn't owned by some guy named Joe, either. It's owned by Rami, and it's operated by Rami and a staff of waitresses like "Chica" who know your order, refill your coffee and give service with a playful and genuine smile. The food is great, it's cheap and Rami makes you feel like you're a guest at his mother's house for breakfast.

"The place has real food and real fucking people," Fitz says to DeMatha. "I like real fucking food, and I love real fucking people. Well, some of them. If I could just get Rami to make some real coffee, we'd be OK." Detective Fitzgerald was famous for bringing his own coffee which he got from Dunkin' Donuts. But Fitz had too much class to bring it in there in a Dunkin' container, so he put it in his Yeti, which kept it extra hot.

Joe's Café was also like Cheers for cops. The place was crawling with detectives and law enforcement. If Rami ever got held up, some poor bastard would have to be Shop-Vacced up thanks to all the holes. If you were in Joe's and you were not carrying, you'd be the only one. Fitz loved it. DeMatha, on the other hand, was not so sure he liked everybody carrying.

151

When Fitz walked in with DeMatha, Rami greeted them like a brother he hasn't seen since Thanksgiving ... if Rami actually celebrated Thanksgiving.

"Hey, Fitz! You are shutting me down today, maybe — I hear?"

"Just giving a few new customers a tour. Is that OK?"

"Any chance it's a gaggle of bikini models?"

"If any of these guys are wearing bikinis, I'll shoot them myself," DeMatha roared.

"The lunch crowd will be light at that time, but then you knew that. Do I really need to lock up?"

"Let's play that by ear, Rami. I hope not."

"This is a group of high-profile friends, and their security will be tight. I don't have the final say, but they will trust our judgment. I expect a detail out back and two located strategically in the lot."

"No shit?"

"No shit. We have to keep things quiet, you can't use this as promo — got it? Please, no *Real husbands of Loudoun County,* OK?"

"No sweat. We'll take care of your boys."

"I will have a few of my guys at the front table, two at the counter and one guy in the booth in front of the back two booths. So we are taking four of your tables."

"Make us a bill for 25 of your biggest lunches and leave it with me. The boys will order what they really want. I'll pay you in cash when the party is over. Sorry for the fire drill and inconvenience, but we have a serious need to meet, in private, out here — outside the eye of too many busybodies."

"Sounds good, Fitz. We will take care of your people. If something changes on the fly, let me know? No sweat."

"Come to think of it, you might want to make me 12 club

sandwiches to go, too. Have some bags of fries and sodas ready. If we need to close this, just give any of the workers who show up a freebie for the inconvenience, and lunch will be on me. I'll take the leftovers back to the scene; our team should be finishing up at that location."

"You think we will have to turn customers away?"

"I think my friends would feel better if some of your possible work-crew crowd gets a nice handshake and a free lunch rather than have them pour in and make my buddies nervous about who they are."

"I got it … good thinking."

"Just tell them you have a store emergency and for the inconvenience the lunch is on you. Again, if necessary."

"Done."

Rami loved to shoot the shit, and he loved hearing all the gossip. But he knew there was a big difference between getting bits of funny local color from detectives and asking Fitz anything about a serious situation. He also knew that taking care of Fitz, no questions asked, would be a net profit on the day and an invaluable favor for local cops who already considered his store their home.

"We will see you shortly."

"2 p.m., right?" Rami confirmed.

"Butts in the chairs at 2. The advance boys will start filing in at 1:30. *You* are the point of contact."

"Great, we'll be ready."

"DeMatha, let's go see if we can make Ms. Felts orgasm," Fitz laughed.

"I'll go first, old man," DeMatha snapped without blinking.

"That should be quick."

153

****

Janie Handly knew she couldn't make the trip all the way to Pittsburgh and back that day and get the damn grocery shopping done, too. She was pretty sure she wouldn't hear from Jeff all day, and that was completely fine with her. She had told Jeff two weeks ago that her car needed work, and that usually meant she was going to take the opportunity to visit her parents on the Southeast side of Pittsburgh. Janie's dad had been taking care of Janie's cars since she first learned to drive the old four-on-the-floor in high school.

Tinkering with cars was more of a hobby now for her dad. For Janie, having the work done by Dad was often an excuse to visit her parents and her hometown. She also loved taking her cars to someone she could trust, even if it meant listening to her father complain about the Jap cars and computers. He still could handle most major maintenance and any bodywork. Plus, he always had something cool to drive in the interim if she needed it.

Driving up to see her dad would be the right tonic to settle her nerves. In times of crisis, nothing beats the feeling of family and home. Her other home was downright dysfunctional lately, and she couldn't deal with a needy husband when she had needs of her own. Mom would make her lunch, and Dad would handle the car issues. Her problem was, she couldn't make that whole trip on this day. But this car situation, particularly now, absolutely had to be handled. Jackson needed the car when he returned from college, and he certainly couldn't drive it like it was now.

Her dad was a downright saint, and as he had done more than once over the years, he agreed to meet her at the Phantom Fireworks in Breezewood, Pennsylvania, right off I-70. There he would switch out her car for a loaner. She was just happy she reached him on such short notice.

For Janie, her dad's saintliness converted a three-hour, 45-minute trip one way into one hour and 40 minutes. That made the trip more relaxing. It would let her drive with her favorite playlist and try to flush the events of the last few days down the drain. It also gave her time to prepare for the inevitable.

Of course, when Janie pulled into Phantom's parking lot, her father, Buford Mackey, was already there. He popped out of his car with two bags. One was filled with fireworks for the boys, and the other was a care package from "your mother" as he always referred to his wife.

"Dad, you didn't have to do this."

"Janie, first, the boys love these fireworks. Tell Jeff not to try to blow his damned hand off again this year," a reference to a nearly 20-year-old incident where the man who stole away his little girl got careless and nearly blew off his hand on the Fourth of July. Buford always called her husband "Jeff not-so-Handly." It was neither a joke nor a compliment.

"Second, young lady, you don't sit in the lot of another man's business without buying some of the goods — it's bad form."

"I brought you the 4Runner. I just tuned her up. She should get you and the boys around as much as you need it. You do realize this will require a visit all the way home to return it and visit with your mother, right?"

"Of course, Daddy."

Buford took the keys for the Pilot from her and asked, "What do I need to know?"

"It needs brakes for sure, probably front and back. It's squeaking on the passenger side in the front."

"That's probably a belt or a tensioner, I hope," he interjected.

"It may need a tune-up, plugs and all," she volunteered.

Buford looked at the front end. "Is this from the incident?" he asked, referring to Jackson's last-summer fender-bender.

"Who knows," she said coolly. "I think he uses the grille and bumpers as parking finders."

"That's some pretty bad damage there, young lady. Are you protecting that boy or your husband?"

"I am protecting no one," she said defensively, in a tone that caught her father's ear.

"If you taught that boy the value of hard work and sacrifice instead of giving him the damn car, he might not abuse the privileges," her dad said in his chastising voice.

"Daddy, you gave me every car I ever had," she demurred.

"That's different, Janie, you're my little girl," he smiled.

For the first time since the last time she saw him, Janie felt a sense of normalcy and serenity. She really wished she could stay.

"OK, Dad ... tell Mom thanks for the package. And thank you for taking care of Jackson's car. He really appreciates it."

"Sure, he does," Buford said cynically. "Oh, and tell your man not-so-Handly to stop spoiling these kids and dreaming they are going to the major leagues. Tell him to spend some time with his damn wife."

"Dad, we are not doing this today," she said.

"It's your burden," he said somewhat coldly as he slammed the door.

Janie opened up the 4Runner and found the seat already set to her size by her father. She smiled as she thought, "Burden? You have no idea, Daddy."

****

"Brad, it's Fitz."

"Yes, detective."

"The meeting with Wray is a go at 2 p.m. at Joe's. I assume the sheriff would like to attend and run the meeting."

"That's quite gracious of you, Fitz, but I think this is your baby. What does he need to know about that meeting, though?"

"I will brief Parker and have Parker brief you. I am pulling up on the crime scene now. And, Brad, do you have Felts' contact if she is not already here?"

"Peggy Felts?"

"Yes, I am going to chat with her, mostly to get her off my ass."

"Detective, you should know —"

"Oh, I know. You guys promised her something, or she would already be on the hood of my damn car."

"We did, but we have also not told her your whereabouts, so we are trying to keep you free. But my guess is she already decided we might be slow-rolling her."

"Well, I will show up and give her some love and make clear that the sheriff told me to pledge my full support to her and give her some guidance. If that can buy me enough time to meet our new contact, without her showing up as the fucking waitress, it will be worth it. Besides, I somewhat like Ms. Felts."

"I know she respects you, and I know she now knows how smart you are. I am guessing, however, she is still looking to pee in your punchbowl as payback," Brad warned.

"I have no idea why she needs payback. I gave her the best feature of her life and the slam-dunk line of her career. Are you saying she's just mad because people didn't hate me?"

157

"You stole her moment, Fitz."

"No, I shared her moment. I'll remind her."

"Oh Christ, don't do that."

"She'll be president of the Fitz fan club after today; watch. I think I have an idea how to both inform her and maybe use her for our own needs. Heck, I think I am going to invite her to Joe's.

"What?"

"Well, if I screw this up, Brad, I'll have you for damage control. Or I'll have Tank expediting my paperwork."

"Everyone knows there is no paperwork, detective. I know you're not a fan of what I do, but the truth is what you do is what is best for our sheriff."

"Twice today, Brad. Twice now I have come to think highly of you. Of course, it's barely past noon. Let's see how the day plays out," Fitz laughed. "I'm here, and Miss Red Dress USA is right out front. She's made me. Got to roll."

****

"Wray is coming to Loudoun for 2 p.m.," Brad said strategically, sticking his head only halfway in Tankersley's door.

"Really. So, the fucking director of the FBI is coming to Loudoun County so Detective Trump can have his favorite corned-beef hash? This country is completely fucked."

"Fitz offered you lead at the meeting, and right now he is briefing Felts at our request, boss."

"I am the lead? He said that?"

"Yes."

"And you told him to give love to Felts, and he is doing it?" the genuinely surprised Tankersley asked.

158

"You bet, boss."

"Well, look at that, he must really be worried about that damn line he crossed. We may buck this bronco yet, Brad."

"Well, we sure seem to have a saddle on him," Brad said, laying it on thick.

"Make sure I get a full brief before this damn meeting. And let's put a hold on his paperwork until we see how this plays out."

"Yes, sir, I beat-feet to the county attorney with that right after the blowout; I will see if I can walk it back," he said to his boss, lying through his teeth.

"Yes, do that 'til we know for sure how this all comes out. I rather like Fitz being made to play ball."

"I thought you would, boss."

"Remind me to order the corned-beef hash first today, just to make Fitz look like the copycat. That fucking Trump-wannabe."

"Well, I told him you weren't going to the meeting."

"What? Why the hell would you do that?"

"The meeting is fraught with political peril, and if it blows up, I'd rather have you here, running the investigation from the war room while Fitz is screwing up the diplomacy. It keeps you clean, and it keeps you in the spotlight running this investigation."

"I get that, but I think you might want to consult with me on these decisions first, OK, Brad?"

"Yes, sir," Brad barked.

Bradley Smith didn't have any doubt of the success of the meeting. He just didn't want his guy sitting next to Fitz. That juxtaposition was not good for his boss — ever. It was like putting a new $900 fake oriental rug next to a $100,000 antique. It was obvious which one anyone would prefer when laid side-by-side in a room. Alone, in the right light, with proper staging, Tankersley looked the part. Next to the real McCoy, he screamed cheap knockoff. Brad thought, "I see no upside making you look stupid, Tank."

****

"Peggy! You moved out here to Loudoun County?" Fitz asked in a big, friendly, clearly joking voice.

"Detective, you should stop chasing criminals and become one. You are very hard to find," she laughed.

Felts really wanted to hate Detective Fitzgerald, but she couldn't. Her jovial reply revealed an authentic, whimsical nature as well as a hint of respect for the man she once underestimated on national TV.

"I've never heard of a man who didn't want to be seen by you, Peggy. How can I help you on this case?"

"You're too kind, detective. As you probably know — or who really knows with Brad and Tank — they promised me access to you for updates and an interview in order to hold off on certain details I have on the case."

"This sounds like a Brad special," he said, without the same jovial manner.

"It was. I immediately assumed he didn't consult you. But then, here you are. And I don't suspect you showed up here without some idea that I would be here. So, basically, now I'm completely confused," she laughed.

"Actually, I was aware from Brad that he'd told you I would help out on this. Needless to say, the deal was cut without my input. *But*, I know you'll do an honest job, and frankly, I'd rather be helping you than having you think I am not. So I thought I would stop by, talk to my team and, if lucky, run into you."

"Great!"

"Can I just shoot straight with you and get to the hot takes?" she asked him in a serious but still friendly tone.

"Of course. As much as I enjoy the company, I'd prefer to get at it, too. We have a great deal going on in this case, as I suspect you have ferreted out."

"I know the husband is missing," she said cutting to the quick.

"Any chance you know where he is?" Fitz asked playfully.

"Is the FBI involved in this case?"

"The investigation into the death of Ms. Jensen is exclusively being handled by the Loudoun County sheriff's office," he answered robotically.

"Yes, but has the office been in touch with the FBI?"

"Of course. As you noted, we have not yet located Mr. Jensen, and he is a person of interest. So, we made the customary inquires to his employer regarding his whereabouts."

"And —"

"Mr. Jensen has a high-profile position with the bureau, so before they can give us details, there is a bit of box-checking to be done on their end."

"Box-checking?" she repeated, as if the term were from another language.

"The FBI doesn't answer to a lowly Loudoun detective, nor should it. I am told this particular matter is working quickly through the chain and we should hear something this afternoon. We could not be happier with the level of cooperation by the FBI — which is the gold standard in law enforcement."

"You missed your calling, detective. You should've been a politician or a diplomat," she smiled as a nod to his obvious attempt to paint the FBI as nothing but awesome and helpful.

"Politician or diplomat?" he asked wryly. "You insult me twice in one sentence."

"My sources tell me Mr. Jensen is the lead interrogator with the FBI's HIG group, so he is essentially a spook."

"No need to use such racist terms," Fitz said with a slight smile.

"What?" she said, truly looking completely confused.

"It was a bad joke, forget about it. Technically, the HIG is not an FBI group. It is a multiagency intel group to which members of the FBI may be attached. Your info is correct; he's attached to that unit, though I'm in no position to say his role or seniority. All of that we're waiting to hear about."

"How do you know this guy isn't on a plane to the Mideast with a bag full of cash and identities?"

"I don't."

"Well —" she began before the detective pulled her close.

"You want a story?"

"That's why I am —" she again couldn't finish.

"I will give you the story you always wanted, but I want you to look me in the eyes and tell me you won't fuck me over. Got it? Tell me you want the goods and you'll play ball to get them."

Felts felt the authority and seriousness in his voice. She knew he was neither joking nor stalling. If she were going to make a deal and trust a source, it would be with this guy ... every day.

"Detective, give me something I can have that others can't, and I will gladly repay the favor."

"Good. Now listen but do *not* write this down."

Felts stood within a breath's distance, staring intently at Fitz. From a distance she looked more like a lover or perhaps an adoring daughter than a reporter. Whatever he was saying to her, she didn't even blink once.

"No fucking way," she said when he finished.

"*Way*," he said, feeling like the nearly decade-old response made him somehow hip. As usual, the line that would have fallen flat for mere mortals hit the button.

"That's 2:12 p.m. — and don't fuck this up."

"I'm trusting you, detective."

"And I you, Ms. Felts."

Fitz rolled out of the scene and back to the car. He hit the gas and took off up Conquest. As he left, DeMatha waved to Felts.

Felts looked quizzically at the car thinking, "Who the hell is that guy? I've never seen him before in my life."

"Why are you waving at Felts?" Fitz asked.

"Don't sweat it; she has no idea who I am," he roared.

"No doubt."

Fitz leaned back. "Felts doesn't know it yet, but she's about to help me solve this damn case."

"Do tell?"

"In due time, my friend, *in due time*."

Fitz pushed in the tape, and out blared the opening to "Lodi" by Creedence Clearwater Revival.

"Back when rock was great," Fitz declared.

"No shit, brother," agreed DeMatha.

Chapter 12: Road Cake

Jenny melted into the sofa. She moaned audibly, surprising herself more than her lover who was at the working end of the love zone. She peeled off her own shirt and instinctively ran her hands across her breasts and down through her lover's hair. She cradled the nape of the neck, and with a gentle tug she took the lead. Their eyes met — and no words were necessary.

They had catapulted past the raw, energetic, consuming, sexual part of this encounter. They were focused on each other with a look of human hunger. It was nourishment for the heart and soul and not merely the needs of the body.

Jenny somehow became lost in those deep blue eyes. Like an ocean, they enveloped her, transfixed her, and in them alone she was held captive, riding a wave of emotions she never knew she could tap. These feelings of needing and wanting — from the heart — they were unknown to her. If she ever had them with her husband, she didn't remember it — not like this.

Jenny craned her neck down to meet her lover's upward advance. Before their eyes closed like synchronized swimmers as their lips met, they paused for a long moment. They were caught in a dueling, transfixed stare. There they sat at the intersection of unbridled passion and new love. It was moments like this that branded lovers to each other's souls. Jenny was certain it was her first, real love, and it would be her last. Of course, Jenny had no way of knowing that it would be, in fact, her last love.

It began as a long, slow, soft kiss. Jenny poured in the passion, and the two were tongue-tied, nearly drooling on each other as it became animated. They drank in the lust. They were like college lovers drunk on hormones and not one bit inhibited. They were naked in moments, tumbling and spread out on the floor … neither with a care or a thought about who might walk through the front door.

Jenny surrendered and pulled her lover on top, neither gave a thought about the time of day, the open windows or their proximity to being spotted, if only by the letter carrier. In the throes of new love, the universe was put on hold.

Neither of the star-crossed lovers was checking her watch, turning off lights, pulling down shades or worrying about beds or blankets. They were drinking in life, and it was pouring off their faces like it was coming at them from a fire hose.

It is no wonder neither heard the first knock on the front door.

****

"Sully, anything else to report to us?"

"Detective, I thought I might hold the interesting news until you decided it appropriate to phone me," Dr. Sullivan started.

"Sully, what the hell would — *wait* — you're just yanking my chain, right?"

"Detective, if I have anything definitive for you, I will hunt you down, you know that."

"What about something not so definitive?" Fitz asked as he sat out in front of DeMatha's house.

"Hold on, doc."

"DeMatha, go put on some decent clothes, you're meeting the FBI director," he shouted.

"Go ahead, Sully, what do you have on trace?"

165

"When we correctly bagged the new crime scene samples, we pick up a few trace elements. It is hard to even speculate what they might be, so please do not ask. I can tell you we have separated them and sent them for a battery of analyses."

"These are elements from the street, correct?"

"Yes, so they could be related or not. However, they were embedded in the larger sample we pulled. My analysis indicates the sample and trace were mixed."

"Explain, sir," Fitz asked, not fully following the doctor.

"First, we removed large samples from three distinct areas. Rather than merely swab, we did our best to actually remove the entire samples, to include some road surface area. As you can imagine, the blood sits on top of a host of particulates, all of which are somewhat predictable. They include dirt, sand, traces of salt, some broken particles of road materials, pollen etc. The blood sample should sit on top of those materials, and then dry that way.

"The two small trace pieces we found were not below the blood but rather mixed in it, which to me indicates the traces found in this instance arrived with the blood and not before. Are you following, detective?"

"Yes, it's like you have a road layer cake, and you expect the crust to be on the bottom. Lo and behold, you have some crust in the middle of the cake, correct?"

"Remarkably, that is an astute analogy."

"Doc, how do we know that —"

Sully cut him off and finished his thought: "— that the sample wasn't run over and the cake now mixed together?"

"Exactly."

"First, we have no tread marks. Second, the position of the samples lies clearly outside the normal driving patterns of vehicles adhering to their side of the road. Third, only these trace elements appear to be mixed. If something like a vehicle had corrupted the sample, rather than our interesting little friend DeMatha, all the ingredients would look like a frozen stew and not your more orderly and aptly described road cake."

"And you have no theory on what these ingredients in the cake could be?"

"Theories abound, detective, but I get paid to tell you what the science says, not what the scientists thinks the science might say before it says anything."

"Fair enough, Sully, but we need this in record time," Fitz said, hoping for a better answer.

"You always do. I can tell you, the amount of blood is consistent with a significant injury. In addition, in at least one of the sites, it appears as if the sample was smeared, or maybe wiped, based on the pattern. If you give me about 30 to 45 minutes, I should be able to tell you something definitive on some of the particulates."

"Thanks, doc, and that timeline is right up against a meeting I am having. I'd sure like to be armed with more information rather than less."

"Indeed, detective. But hurried science is sloppy science."

"Doc — one more thing. I think you'll like this."

"Yes, detective, *tha-rill me*," he said with some dripping sarcasm.

"In about 10 minutes, you should have in hand, by special courier, a DNA sample to match against your harvested blood sample from the road."

"You don't say. *My, my, detective*, I do have a Chris Matthews-style tingle running up my leg," he chuckled, knowing Fitz's penchant for politics.

167

"You probably peed your pants, Sully. Try the new adult diapers."

"You are forever 17 years old, detective, the one reliable personality trait you have other than loyalty."

"Thanks, Sully, both have served me well."

****

Detective Parker knocked on the Handlys' front door. He then rang the doorbell. He noticed two cars in the driveway, and he was a tad excited that he had caught both Jeff and Janie Handly at home, just as Jeff surmised his wife might return. "Maybe they're putting away groceries?" he thought.

He gave the doorbell another try. The door suddenly flew open to the sight of a large, mid-40s, balding man. He was tall, reasonably fit and clearly sporting some bags under his eyes. Parker decided they were likely less a regular feature of the man's appearance and rather more a function of a recent loss of sleep.

Jeff Handly was a sports nut, and even at his age appeared in much better than average shape. At 6-foot-3, roughly 220 pounds, Handly had long legs, a slight, abnormally small trunk but broad, full shoulders. His hair was short-cropped but only because growing it out would accent his loss of follicles. He had Midwestern features such that his skin clearly had a fair German hue to it. He was, despite the darker hair, a clearly white man, in every sense of the word.

"Mr. Handly?" announced more than guessed the man on the stoop. "I am Detective Parker, sir; we spoke on the phone."

"Yes, hello, detective. I hope you haven't been waiting long. I was doing some cleanup in the garage."

"Cleanup? Everything all right?"

168

"Oh, yes. I am trying to organize a decade's worth of sports gear and make room in the garage to fit one of our cars in there."

"I see. I thought maybe you and your wife were putting away the groceries."

"No, she hasn't come home yet."

"Oh, neither of those is her car?"

"Oh — no. Gosh. That's why I am making room. We have three cars, and my wife is using my son's car. Hmm — not sure why that is, honestly. She doesn't like that car."

"What kind of car is it?" Parker asked in his "Hey, I'm not really questioning you, just making conversation" voice.

"That's the old Honda Pilot. Once it got too many miles, we gave it to our son. He's not allowed to keep a car on campus as a freshman. He should be home soon, and I promised Jane I would clean this garage out and make a spot for at least one car, probably hers."

"Boy's off to college, huh? Was that a big step?"

"Well, we have one at home and one playing baseball down at Radford."

"A college ballplayer? Wow, that's impressive."

"Thanks, he made it further than Dad," Handly said with a self-deprecating laugh.

"So, no luck finding your wife yet?"

"I haven't really been looking, but no luck reaching her by phone. I called to let her know you were coming. If I know her, she is buried in Wegmans trying to decide what type of fish to buy and grilling the counterman for recommendations."

"No doubt."

"Do you have time for a few questions? It might help me get some clarity on a few issues."

169

"Sure, officer, I'm happy to help," Handly heard himself say as he really wished he hadn't answered the door.

"Great. Can you tell me if your wife spent any time yesterday or last evening with Jenny Jensen?"

"I'm not entirely sure. I think they might have been together for a girl's night out with some other baseball moms."

"Really? Do you know where they were and who was with them?"

"I'm not even sure they *were* together, and I could only guess who else was there. I do know that she mentioned earlier in the day that she and the ladies all *might* be going to the Feeleys'."

"The Feeleys'?" Parker interjected to slow down the machine-gun-style train of thought.

"I'm not 100 percent sure if Janie went." Handly continued.

"You did see your wife last night, right?"

"Oh, yes. I was watching the K-State game, and I spoke to her during the game. It had to be around 11:15 or so."

"When you say you spoke to her — you mean in person, at your home?"

"Yes, that's right. I think she was out and had come back … I … I think? I was hunkered down in front of the TV. I only know that she had been talking about a happy hour at the Feeleys', which is not uncommon for that group."

"You never confirmed that she was there or who she was with?"

"Nope. I was watching a game."

"Once I got the call about Jenny, I told her, and, well, she cried all night. Honestly, we didn't even speak, she was so upset."

"So, you can't confirm she was at that location or who was with her?"

170

"Right."

"Who do you think would've been there, and let's start with who are the Feeleys?" Parker asked with a spark of familiarity.

"Andy and Kate Feeley — they're baseball royalty in this part of Loudoun. Andy's a longtime baseball coach and former college catcher. The baseball moms in this neighborhood tend to get together often and rotate between our house, the Browns, the Jensens, the Bodines and the Feeleys."

Parker cut off the high-speed information dump to clarify, "Andy Feeley — from George Mason?"

"Yes, that's him."

"You don't say? He was a few years ahead of me; I *know him*. We played together."

"No kidding?" Jeff Handly said quite surprised.

"The guy was nicknamed 'Feels.' I loved him. He was an intense player," Parker added.

"Well, it's a *small world*," Handly said, feeling a bit relieved.

"Not at Feeley's house," Parker laughed.

"What?" Handly asked, completely not following the reference.

"Oh, it's kind of a Mason legend. Let's just say Andy didn't hit really well, but he sure swung a *big* piece of lumber," Parker chuckled.

"And here I thought he spread that rumor," Jeff, roared, letting down his guard.

"You say they live around here?"

"They live right in Brambleton, just around the corner. He's still with Kate, obviously. They have the Bram baseball moms over often. Sometimes the moms from the South Riding side come over, but I have no idea if any of them were there last night."

171

"OK, let's walk through the names and contact information for all of the 'regular' baseball moms. Is that OK?"

"Oh, I can do that, I suppose," Jeff said with a little hesitation as he realized he'd just agreed to send the sheriff to a bunch of neighbors' houses.

"Great, let's start with Andy. Maybe I'll swing by and surprise him, too."

****

DeMatha hopped into the car, looking like he had been a middle-aged model for Old Navy.

"Christ, DeMatha, why the fuck does the world's most vanilla dude break out essentially a khaki suit? It's like you're goddamn invisible!"

"This is as good as it gets, trust me. If I show up naked, they still won't remember me," he joked.

"Now, walk me through your terrorism scenario, because that is all the feds will care about," said Fitz. "I don't want to dump this on them willy-nilly, and I suspect they have already run these scenarios. In addition, I have some relevant facts you may not. Still, I want to hear how you see this happening."

"Obviously, if he's dead, which we can't confirm, you have a double murder. You have a pre-murder stalking. You have a high-profile murder of a high-profile intelligence interrogator and the brutal defiling or postmortem desecration of her body. You have one body on full display and the intel source missing, which could be to torture and gain more information."

"OK, but why not brutally murder all of them? Why leave the kid alive? Also, why so sloppy? Knock on the door, double-tap to the chest, bam," Fitz countered.

"Maybe they missed the kid?"

"If the kid was killed and the mother tortured, predeath, my concern level about terror would be higher," Fitz deduced.

"How about this: Terrorists attempt a snatch and grab of Jack while the two are outside. A fight ensues. They knock out Jensen and follow his screaming wife into the house, smash her from behind, and then stage it to look like a sex killing so they can have time to torture Jack Jensen for more targets," DeMatha theorized.

"Here's what you don't know. The killer took Mrs. Jensen's pants and presumably undergarments with him," Fitz explained.

"What?" DeMatha exclaimed. "That's weird shit."

"No, that's smart shit, or at least an attempt at smart shit."

"Wait ... let me see if I am tracking before you explain this to me. You think the killer offed Jenny Jensen, and then, to hide his identity, he took the pants and underwear. You think he raped her and didn't want to leave behind a DNA sample?"

"I think that's possible," Fitz offered. "Then, of course, that would mean the killer had some reason to think he would be in the system and identifiable."

"Well, some of these terrorists are in the system," DeMatha said, halfheartedly. "I don't suppose a terrorist hitman takes time out for a quickie rape before a murder. Plus, a rape would cause more pre-death violence than the scene supports."

"That's why I don't think it's a rape. I think there could've been some consensual sex before something went really wrong. Of course, if he had sex with her, chances are he left something behind not in her panties. He would have to have a pretty adept knowledge

173

of sex crimes to understand that taking the panties probably didn't help — if he climaxed in or on her."

"Did Sully rule that in or out?"

"He didn't think it was a lover's tryst, but he does that analysis as a matter of course. I didn't speak to him on that point directly, but he often gives that update if there's semen present. Let's call him." Fitz did.

"Sully, I forgot to ask you this."

"No."

"No what?"

"No, there is no sign of semen or any indication of forcible sex."

"How did you know —"

"Because I forgot to close that loop with you; my apologies. Let me add, however, that based upon a thorough examination, it is more likely than not that the victim engaged in sexual activity pretty soon before her death. I make that finding based on a host of physical characteristics associated with my examination. I would say with a high degree of medical certainty that she engaged in sexual activity within an hour or so before her death."

DeMatha looked at Fitz: "He caught her red-handed and flipped out."

"What's that, Fitz?" asked Sully, unsure if the DeMatha comment was to him.

"That's just DeMatha here having his own orgasm, doc. Sorry. Let me ask you this, now that you've had her on the table, can you pinpoint for me your best medical hypothesis on a precise time of death, and then work backward for me on the probability of a sexual encounter? I want to make a timeline for our team and investigators tonight."

"I put her death at around 10:15, plus or minus maybe 7-10 minutes. So, she was likely killed between 10:08 and 10:25 p.m. Now Fitz, I tell you *that* based on years of experience, but know this, such precision is not commonly accepted as reliable."

"Is the hour-before-death guess on the sex firm?" Fitz asked nicely.

"I don't guess, Fitz; I hypothesize based on medical evidence and many, many years on the job."

"And how is the medical evidence at pinpointing the quality of your hypothesizing?" he laughed.

"I think it is safe to say the sexual activity likely occurred between 9:15 and 9:40."

"Thanks, doc. And, you say there was sexual activity, but no sign of semen?"

"Yes detective, please don't make me run through all the reasons why that's possible. Let's just say, this isn't TV. We don't always get the semen."

"OK Sully, got it."

"It's a jealous rage by Jack Jensen," DeMatha declared.

"Go fish," Fitz bellowed. "For that to happen, he would have had to catch her in the act somewhere outside the home, follow her, kill her in his own house and do so in a struggle where there were *no* defensive wounds, he was badly injured and bled out, but only in the street?"

"That doesn't work," DeMatha agreed, after replaying that in his head a few times.

"The person who killed Ms. Jensen was not her husband," Fitz stated as if fact.

"So we're back to terrorists?" DeMatha asked, more than a little exasperated.

"Let's first eliminate people before we start including people. Jack Jensen isn't doing that to his wife in the living room where his kids live. He isn't taking her pants, either. Something else happened here, and we're missing some pieces of the puzzle."

"My first thought was he couldn't have done this, either, but I am having a hard time linking the physical evidence to a set of facts that make sense."

"Well, you're about to meet the director of the FBI, so let's not speak to him with terror theories before we can rule out more concrete facts."

"Agreed."

Chapter 13: Party of Five

Jenny didn't hear that first knock on the door. She was sweating, her heart palpitating, and every muscle in her body was twitching from the strain of pleasure. Her neck off the carpet, head craning, she peeked down to watch her lover devour her. And there was no way Jenny's paramour heard a damn thing from down there.

Jenny heard the second knock and barely flinched in reaction to it. Every fiber of her physical being was tied up in absorbing pleasure. "Oh god ... oh Christ ... finish me," she howled, probably loud enough for someone knocking on her neighbor's door to hear.

Jenny gushed with pleasure, and her body went limp as her head hit the carpet, the sweat rolling down her cheek, past her ear and to her neck. The third knock was like an injection of adrenaline. "Holy shit, they are not going away," she thought. At that same time, she realized that a curious outside guest might even be able to glimpse her — or them — from the narrow side window that decorated both sides of her faux-wood front door.

"Fuck, I hope they didn't see us," she said as she leaped like a ballerina into a standing position and darted for her clothes. "Relax, baby, they wouldn't still be knocking if they saw that — unless they wanted some, too." Jenny smiled at the innuendo and was briefly comforted by the reality that if anyone had seen them, they likely would have run off the porch embarrassed. "That would be a bigger problem," she realized, "than getting dressed, answering the door and not looking like I was just gang-banged in a porn fantasy."

She hadn't seen two people dress that quickly since her dad came home when she was 17 and she and her boyfriend were naked as jaybirds in the basement. The memory amused her, thinking she still could be so passionate and impetuous a lover decades later — as an adult on the floor of her own living room.

Jenny ran her hands through her hair twice as she fast-shuffled the last steps to the door. Her unexpected visitor greeted her as if it were any other day, and Jenny replied casually, "Hey … what brings you by? Have you been knocking long?"

Jenny wondered as she spoke if her lover were safely up the back staircase. If not, there would be no easy way to explain the situation.

****

The FBI advance team was in the lot at Joes Café at 1:29 p.m. It was a single, nondescript vehicle. It carried three agents, not one of whom looked the prototypical part. In fact, the group looked like three guys on a late lunch from Orbital or some other close-by office. The vehicle circled around the back of the rundown strip mall. It found the rear entrance and let one agent out, as the rear of the building had some parking but no activity. Likewise, none of the stores had public entrances through the back. To enter the café, one needed to go through the front door.

The back of the building had all the charm of unkept masonry, potholes and trash dumpsters. Agent Chance thought to himself, "This is a great place to dump a body." Still, it was clear that no one could get to the building by vehicle or path from the back without coming around from the front on one narrow road to the left of the building, facing it from the street. While that might make emergency exiting difficult, it gave the team a much better plan to defend from an attack, which would have to come from only one direction.

As Chance and Stanton drove back around the front playing the role of lost locals looking for better parking, Stanton noted his displeasure with the proximity to a major road where a drive-by attack could pin the group down and endanger the director: "I don't like unknown risks and unknown turf."

Chance reminded him that this plan worked only because they had an FBI chopper fueled and running that was literally three minutes out, and it could put down in the bare, flat field, just behind the back lot. Chance also told the nervous and irritated Stanton that the three "work vans pulling in would serve as cover in the front of the lot from a direct-fire assault on the glass-store front."

"I've been doing this a long time, and Im telling you, a last-minute, unplanned frolic and detour with the director is not a good idea. It's the way we lose a protectee," Stanton declared.

"The director signed off on this, and we've taken every possible precaution. I just hope this fucking yokel hasn't wasted our time," Chance stated, reiterating what everyone on the detail already knew but Stanton didn't want to accept.

The on-site, advance team didn't get the full brief on the man they were deridedly calling, "Captain America," Detective Fitzgerald. So the team's trepidation and lack of confidence was rooted more in the FBI's traditional lack of respect for local LEOs.

Chance opened the door to the café and was greeted immediately by the proprietor, Rami. Of course, Rami had no way of knowing for sure if these were the guys on whom he was waiting, and he immediately asked for a name and how many in the party.

"We're with Fitz," Chance exclaimed, using the settled-upon phrase that would let Rami know the team had arrived.

"Great, let me take you to your table."

The café had about 17 customers. Five people were at the counter. It looked like two pairs of men and one older gentleman on the end sipping his coffee. Nothing looked amiss. Two of the men had matching uniform shirts from a local HVAC company. Their truck was identified and cataloged on the way in. Agent Miller was merely standing outside the back door of the café; he was also running down every plate in the place.

Stanton felt sure the two were textbook legitimate. He made a mental note of the condition of their work boots, the lack of creases in their Dickies, and the disheveled and worked-in appearance of their blue-collar man-blouses. "Two down, 15 to go," he thought to himself. Stanton would not rest until all in the room were properly identified and accounted for.

Rami showed Chance and Stanton to the back table, a spot normally reserved for his regular crew. If Rami put you at the back table, his normal customers knew you were friends of the family or Rami compatriots. You didn't just walk into Joe's Café and get the back table.

Stanton was immediately relieved, as he estimated that no shooter could hit the back table from the street for numerous reasons, including the pitch of the property and the very useful separation wall just inside the front door. The wall was probably designed to keep waiting customers from leering over the booth at diners, and it served to block the wind from freezing out customers each time the door opened. Today, it would serve as a hedge against sniper activity.

The FBI director wasn't under any known or reported threat, but he never moved without careful preparation to protect him. That included the type of advance work that considered every scenario, including the possibility that he was tracked regularly by enemies looking for an opportunity to take him out. This was the state of the world in post-9/11 times. Security operations and advance team were already considering plausible foul-play scenarios related to Jensen's disappearance, and one included an agent gone rogue.

"Excuse me, sir," Chance inquired of Rami, "can you show me where the restrooms are?"

"Of course, sir, they're right back here. Follow me."

Chance followed Rami down the narrow hallway in the back. Once out of sight of the dining area, Chance headed straight for the back door to check in with Miller.

"Every car in the lot is accounted for, sir," Miller told the senior agent.

"OK. Can you hear us on coms?"

"Yes, I heard every word, no dead spots."

"When I get back in, I'll give you the signal, and you answer back," he told Miller. "We'll know then everyone is being heard."

"Check."

Agent Stanton watched a table of five, including a grandmother and two small children, check out. He liked that the number in house dropped to 12. Rami verified the three remaining people at the counter, which really left only seven souls in the café whose backgrounds were unverified — two tables of two, and one group of three. One table looked like a miserly couple in their late 70s seeking an early-bird special. Stanton deemed them no threat. One table looked like a late-teen couple drinking milkshakes and sharing YouTube videos. Stanton figured they cut class. That left one table of two, stout, serious-looking men. These, Stanton assumed, were plants from the local sheriff.

Stanton walked by the two men and said, "Christ, I can't imagine it will rain tonight." One man looked up and said, "No shot of that tonight, pal."

Check, those were Fitz's men, positioned exactly as Stanton had been told they would be. "OK, these guys pass the easy test," he thought.

Chance came back through the hallway and seated himself at the table in front of the back table. He was quickly joined by Stanton, when he suddenly heard through his earpiece, "Do you think the rain will hurt the rhubarb?

"Can you believe this damn forecast for rain?" he said, directed at Stanton.

"No shot of that," replied Stanton.

Both men then heard over the coms, "check."

At 1:55, the used Range Rover pulled into the plaza and parked in the last spot on the far end. It was facing the rear of the building such that with one turn of the wheel, a driver could go down the left path on the side and around the back.

Four men emerged, two at a time. Nothing about them overtly screamed "feds." They moved at a casual pace down the sidewalk under the overhang of the seven-store, nondescript strip mall headed toward Joe's. It was about an 80-foot walk from the car, taking them past the new, not yet opened Hispanic deli, and the storefront that merely read, "Massage."

The director opened the door and took the lead, heading in first. These moves were carefully choreographed to ensure that nothing about this party of four looked like a federal agent operation or that there was any particular hierarchy among the men.

The three work vans had backed into the street-side parking spots blocking out Joe's front windows approximately five minutes before the director arrived. At 1:58 p.m., the three men sitting in the '78 Cutlass for 20 minutes poured in behind the new party and took up positions at the front table. Each placed his own Yeti on the table, a sign to the feds in the back that they were the additional sheriff's team ordered in by Fitz.

At 1:59 p.m. on the button, Fitz's car screeched around the corner and, with a bit of fancy driving, parked abruptly about two storefronts down on the left from Joe's. Out popped Fitz and DeMatha, the ad for Old Navy.

The director was seated at the back table, flanked by his deputy on to his right, on the inside of the booth. Across from him was his personal bodyguard, sitting on the aisle facing him. James Gannon was on the inside of the booth on that same side. The table sat eight, though it was really better to have just six, no matter what Rami claimed.

Wray was barely settled in his seat when his bodyguard said, "He's just arrived," referring to the com signal that indicated Fitz had pulled in and parked.

"Gentlemen, I'm honestly a bit excited. I'm either going to be impressed or pissed. We shall find out," he smiled.

Detective Fitzgerald passed through the door and gave Rami a big smile. "Thanks," he said. "Are my friends here?" "You bet, right in the back."

"Let the fun begin, Rami — are you ready?"

"I hope so."

DeMatha followed in about 6 feet behind and broke right toward the counter. It would not have been obvious to anyone in the room that he was with Fitz. In fact, Stanton stuck his eyeball on him immediately, identifying him as the only person now in the room for whom he could not account. That made Stanton quite unhappy.

Wray sized up Fitzgerald as the detective made the 30-foot walk from storefront to the rear, heading straight for him. "There is no way this guy is nearly 70," Wray thought.

Fitz's shoulders were broad, and they sat naturally back. He had not even the hint of slump in his posture. He was wearing a black T-shirt with the very familiar Pink Floyd logo and name emblazoned on it; Fitz's chest filled out the shirt like a gym trainer's. His skin had no obvious brown spots, wrinkles or sagging. It was taut, and his veins accented his forearms and biceps like the familiar view of fit man in his 30s. His hair was thick, nearly black but decorated impressively, if not sparingly, with hints of silver. He walked with confidence, yet his relaxed manner, broad smile and physical appearance made it clear that he was not at all intimidated by the events.

As Wray studied him in that brief moment, replaying in his head both Fitz's background and this very unorthodox meeting, he couldn't help but think, "Man, I really like this guy."

Wray leaped to his feet, took a few steps forward and greeted him like an old friend, putting out his hand and exclaiming, "Fitz! Glad you made it." Like a synchronized Marine drill team, Wray's bodyguard stood up and moved off to the back and Wray tucked into his seat, which permitted Fitz to take his seat and be face to face with the director.

"Welcome to beautiful Loudoun County," Fitz began. I bring news, and I don't think it is good."

"Do tell, sheriff."

"I think your man is seriously injured or worse."

Wray's face tensed up, and his otherwise welcoming, neutral face turned sour.

"We found blood outside what we thought were the boundaries of our crime scene. The blood types match. We are running a DNA match from the information you sent, and we might know something as early as this evening."

"Yet you conclude he is likely dead or seriously injured?"

"The amount of blood is consistent with a significant injury. It is not so significant as to indicate catastrophic blood loss, but it clearly indicates significant loss of blood. In addition, he is missing and unaccounted for. Put those facts together with the location of the blood, in the middle of a residential street, and we have a significant mystery. Moreover, nothing inside the home indicates blood loss there, which appears to mean that whatever injuries he suffered were suffered outside the home. The wife, on the other hand, was killed inside the home, and nothing at the scene indicates her death or any injuries were suffered outside the home."

"This is troubling. As you might be aware, we have had no contact of any kind with Agent Jensen before the murder. Without giving you details, I can tell you that he was scheduled to leave this a.m. in support of a mission, the type of which men like him don't miss. In short, he is missing, and we had considered him, to this point, a possible fugitive. You seem to think he could be a victim?"

"We have considered the possibility that his circumstance may be related to his job, and that what we have in this case could — and I emphasize *could* — be something more than a domestic-violence incident," Fitz said, studying Director Wray.

The men at the table were transfixed by the exchange, as each studied the two leaders, all while processing the details and running, in their own minds, a series of scenarios.

Wray paused for a second longer. He then asked, "In your opinion, do you think this could be an act of terror related to his job and position?"

"I don't think so," Fitz heard himself say. "But I am not a terror expert, nor do I have any access to the intelligence or resources of your department. Likewise, and this is critical, I can't rule the theory out. However, I want to walk you through why I think it is not terror. Then you and your team can use that information and marry it to your own facts and intelligence."

"Please, fill us in precisely, because the wheels of our system must move quickly under these facts to ensure we protect the unit and other targets. *Now* I understand why you wanted to push this meeting up," he said.

"Before I give you everything I have, I want to inform you that the man who came in behind me is with me. My guess is your team is eyeballing him. He's a former undercover federal agent who has taught undercover tactics to senior-level classes at Quantico. He knows Jensen, and he's assisted me in this investigation. He was the first to raise the idea of terror, and like me, he is also convinced that Jack Jensen did not kill his wife. So, if this is *not* terror, then we need to find a theory and facts that fit the physical evidence. Nothing about the evidence, to our mind, makes the terror theory complete or likely — yet."

The deputy director whispered into the coms, "The last man in is clear."

Agent Stanton was finally satisfied.

"If I am hearing you correctly, Fitz, you think this is a double murder but not a terror event, and that conclusion is based entirely on the physical evidence?"

"It's 2:08, sir, so I need to break from the details to let you in on something critical to my investigation. I have enlisted the help of a local reporter — you may have heard of her — Peggy Felts," he said.

"Yes, Felts, she's dogged, and fortunately she isn't on our beat."

"I asked her to arrive at 2:12 to this location today. This reporter knows too much, and she is either going to gum up my investigation or I can use her to help it. If I am correct, her report will help shake free some leads, and it will let down the guard of the murderer. Perhaps I should explain more?"

"It appears you have two minutes before she arrives. I grant you all that time," he smiled.

"Great. The murderer staged this crime. Everyone agrees. The wife was beaten from behind, by surprise, with a blunt object. She was then rolled over, her pants removed, she was hogtied, and she had a Swiffer stuck up her ass."

The entire table winced.

"Forensics concludes all of the staging was postmortem. Why does the killer take the victim's pants and undergarments? That's probably not terror. Does the husband possibly confront the killer in the street and then is wounded or killed? We don't know. However, what we want the killer to think is simple; we want them to think the 'staging' has us chasing a nondomestic theory. We want Felts off our ass, and we want her to sell this like she believes it. If she does, our killer will believe we are not looking at him. If we just give her some story, this woman will smell bullshit. I want to put her in it and have the FBI at my side to make the sale."

"What if she runs with the idea but puts her own twist on it — like the idea that we think this could be a terror hit? Won't we have a panic?"

"I thought of that. My idea is that we make the missing Jensen a suspect. If this is a terror hit, maybe we flush out chatter on that end. If it is not a hit, we indicate to the real killer that we are hot on the husband, and that the staging worked. That killer, assuming he has killed Jensen too, will think he is free to plan an escape, at least until we find Jensen's body. This frees up time for our investigation to get a lead on the real killer."

Wray studied him. "Detective, there are many possible problems with this plan, and not having had the chance to analyze it, I can say I have reservations much greater than merely the obvious ones, which include a federal agency using a bulldog reporter to make a false report.

"Still, Jensen isn't just one of our guys. He is a HIG guy — that makes him one of the president's guys. We have very broad discretion in working to safeguard this unit and its members. Your ask here is remarkably high, and everything about you tells me I think I can trust this. However, if this goes south, the price is much larger for the FBI than for you, don't you agree?"

"I do. That's why I am not selling it, I am merely explaining it. I won't be one bit upset or disappointed if you say no. I'll work with you to solve these issues some other way. Of that I'm confident."

Wray looked at his deputy, then at his FBI profiler, then directly back at Fitz. Not one bit of his training nor one ounce of the politician in him thought this was a good idea. Still, he loved the improvising and saw the immediate wisdom in it. Using the press to ferret out leads and flush out suspects was a long law enforcement tradition. And wow, he loved the balls Fitz had for suggesting it.

"It's a go."

Peggy Felts had just pulled into the lot in her news van, and she was getting out with her crew and camera. She saw no obvious signs of the FBI, but she sure saw Fitz's car, right where he promised it would be. She just couldn't believe Fitz was going to give her the first interview with the FBI on this new development.

Chapter 14: Will You Brief the President?

Janie was racing back through west-central Maryland after leaving Jackson's car behind with her father. The 4Runner was a nice car, but it had old bones, lots of street noise and clearly some windows that long ago lost their pressure seal. She turned up the radio and fumbled around trying to find a decent station. She needed "some good tunes," she thought to herself, "to keep my mind from racing about the events of the past few weeks." She caught a station out of Frederick that had just cued up the Rolling Stones' "Start Me Up." She cranked the volume to max and began to drive in rhythm, thinking of the irony of the words *"If you start me up, I'll never stop."*

Janie was overcome with emotion, and the tears welled up in her eyes as the musical distraction only keyed her obsession. "I will never stop thinking of you, Jenny," she said out loud as her chest heaved and the tears began to flow. She pulled over to collect herself. As she did, she noticed the "missed call" notification on her phone. It was Jeff, and he had called five times. "Christ, this is the last thing I want to deal with now." She decided to ignore the calls until she saw the text from Jeff too. It read simply, "911." She then realized Jeff had left her a voice message.

Janie Handly hated voice messages. If you left them for her and you were not her father, mother or Jenny Jensen, you might as well be screaming into a well in the forest. Your message would never be heard. "Fuck, fuck, fuck," she said aloud. She played the message and listened to it carefully. Then she played it again. Then again and again. She knew the police would want to speak to her, and she knew it was all closing in on her. She didn't expect it to be this fast. "Thank God I got the car up to Daddy," she thought.

Janie had this all thought through. She'd planned every detail, and she was ready to tell the complete story. Now she had about an hour to practice it before she would get home. Janie wasn't just a supermom; she was a math whiz and substitute teacher, too. She understood that the police would be looking to account for every minute that night, and her story had to fill the time, make sense and, above all else, not reveal the truth.

****

Parker left the Handly house with a fat pocket full of names, addresses and contacts. He had hoped to find Janie Handly home. Still, he had a long list of old-fashioned police tasks to complete. He needed to reach the Feeleys' first to confirm everyone who attended the party where Jenny Jensen was last seen alive.

He also needed to follow up with the cyberunit. Fitz left strict orders for Loudoun's team to immediately create a mirror image of all hard drives recovered in the house and to be sure to send copies to his outside forensic expert. Parker knew Fitz trusted his guy Trevor to find the unfindable and to follow the proper protocols. Trevor was some kind of former spook who was a part owner in a Reston-based cyberintelligence and computer forensics company.

Parker could still hear Fitz reminding him, as he had every time for the last 13 years, "Don't fuck this up and send it to those poseurs in Fairfax again. They aren't experts; they set up computers for lawyers who are luddites." Parker could laugh about it now, but it wasn't funny when he accidently followed the advice of another sheriff and sent Fitz's evidence to a Fairfax-based "forensics" company that many local lawyers used for IT services and rudimentary forensics. He still hadn't heard the end of that rookie mistake.

Parker hit the contact for Trevor, and the phone rang only once before Trevor Richland picked up with his trademark, "This is Trevor."

"Trevor, it's Parker."

"Parker, it's Trevor," he jousted back in his high-pitched, sarcastic tone.

"Richland is one strange duck," Parker thought. Still, the guy was a former counter intel field agent, and Parker knew that Richland was the go-to forensic and human intel or "humint" guy for more than a few federal agencies that liked to use outside help. He never let Fitz down on a rush job, and Richland simply put together a forensic analysis better than anyone else.

Richland liked to remind them that anyone could make a mirror image of a drive; anyone could use forensics tools to uncover deleted files that were not already written over. "That's not forensics," Richland told them once. "That's fucking monkey work."

"Do you have the drives yet?"

"Have them? Of course. Shit, I am tearing that crap up right now. Lots of monkey work here. But you can bet your ass I'll do the real work to find and piece together this lady's life. Wherever she has been on Al Gore's amazing internet, we're going on that journey."

"Great. When will you have something?" Parker asked.

"You mean something other than a shitload of messages from this lady's dozens of lovers?"

"What?"

"Your suspect list is longer than a porn star's johnson," Richland laughed. "Half of these motherfuckers have been writing her love notes and pining for one more shot at her."

"No shit?"

"The pledges of undying love are fucked. A couple of these guys sent dick pics. Who the fuck sends a dick pic in their 40s? I should get paid more for this shit."

"How many so far?"

"Dick pics — what you want them in color glossies?"

"No, you crazy bastard, how many of these forlorn ex-lovers?"

"I am at like 10 dudes so far, and one of these people might be a chick? I haven't found much on that yet, and just looking at it fast I can't really verify a sexual relationship from what I found so far. Maybe I'll find a beaver colony. I'll let you know."

"OK, listen, you have to send me what you have as you get it. I can't wait for the official report."

"I will send you these recovered hits as they come. I will put it in a file and drop them in your Dropbox."

"Perfect," Parker exclaimed. "Holy shit, this case just got crazy," he thought.

****

"Peggy, you're right on time," Fitz boomed as he greeted her at the front door of Joe's. "It's just you and no camera inside. I will give you some footage later, but not of the director."

"The director of the FBI is here?" she was almost ashen. Her mind began to race. How big was all this if the FBI director was involved?

"Yes, and he'll speak with you *very* briefly. I mean, he speaks to you, and he doesn't answer questions. You get a quote or two and a new contact. Then you get me, which was all you were really promised to begin with."

"You lived up to your part. I'll play by the rules," she answered. "I might be aggressive, but I'm not stupid, Fitz."

"I never once thought that," Fitz smiled. "Let me bring you in and give you some context, then Wray will give you a few details, and we'll get out of here."

"Hey, seriously, before we go in — how did you get the FBI to meet in Loudoun in this café?"

"They had business out this way, and the matter was pressing for everyone. We wanted to stay out of the limelight, and this place is as shadowy as one can get for that purpose. Who the hell thinks the FBI director is having coffee at Joe's Café in Sterling?"

Felts smiled, "Not to mention the super-cool 'massage' shop right next door. That's a nice touch."

"Yes, well, nothing like a good table shower after breakfast, whatever the hell that is," Fitz said feigning ignorance.

Fitz led her to the back, and like a bunch of 1950s boys at a cotillion, the agents fell over themselves trying to move out of the way, stand, give a seat and be gentlemanly.

"Ms. Felts," the director started, "thank you for making time to stop by today."

"Thank you, gentlemen, for making space for me and for giving me a peek at where this matter stands."

"Detective Fitzgerald will give you the rundown first."

Fitz methodically walked through the case and facts as they were known to him at the time. The key information was, of course, that they did not know the whereabouts of Jack Jensen, and they considered him a suspect. Fitz left out a few details, like how DeMatha cracked part of the case by finding blood in the street. Fitz did confirm that blood had been found "at the scene," just not in the street. He also said that "preliminarily" it was a match to Jensen.

Given that she had been to the scene and knew the parameters of the taped-off area, Fitz assumed she would take his "at the scene" comment to mean in the house.

"The working theory is this, Peggy: It was a domestic dispute gone awry, and Jack Jensen snapped. We think it is possible that her death was unintentional. That is, he may have struck her and, finding her dead, panicked. We think they had a knock-down, drag-out fight, and he cut himself or was injured in the fight. He tried to stage the death to look like a heinous sex crime and now has beat feet into the darkness."

Felts had a million questions, but she started with the one she wanted officially confirmed. "Can you confirm that she was hog-tied and — how do I say — mutilated with a Swiffer in her rectum?"

"That depends. Will you broadcast that description?"

"I won't report that until you say I can."

"That is correct. And we confirmed all of *that* was post-mortem."

"Thank God, I suppose. This guy is in the HIG unit. Are you worried he is already out of the country using a series of aliases?"

Director Wray stepped in, "The FBI has had no contact with Jensen. He did not arrive at a preplanned location today for a pending assignment. Without hearing from him, based on our protocol, we must conclude he has fled. We have no evidence that any federal resources were used in aid of his fleeing."

Felts had too many questions but one she needed to ask: "How do you know he isn't a victim, too?"

"Felts is no dummy," Fitz thought. God, he hoped she wouldn't push on the physical evidence or try to piece it together with questions.

"Nothing in the evidence indicates that Jensen is dead."

195

"Not even the blood?"

"No. That's the first thing we looked at. The physical evidence is consistent with a struggle, and we suspect that he was either cut while killing her or maybe had a small cut in the altercation."

Fitz then looked at her. "We think he is on the run and likely trying to leave the country."

Wray busted in: "We are combining the resources of the FBI and the sheriff's office to locate him in what we will call mutual cooperation."

"Would you say this is a joint investigation?"

"No," Fitz jumped in, refocusing her questions to him. "The FBI has a protocol for missing agents, and they are using that protocol. They are likewise sharing any information found with us. In addition, given their national footprint, they can direct resources around and outside the county. However, this remains a murder investigation over a domestic dispute, in our opinion, and that is being handled by the sheriff's office at the direction, of course, of Sheriff Tankersley."

That made Felts smile. "Of course, and why isn't the sheriff here?"

"The sheriff is leading the resources of the office in this important case, and he is personally running the coordination efforts at the request of the director," Fitz said in an Academy Award performance.

"Detective, Mr. Director, I believe every word you say except for that bullshit about Tankersley."

All the agents laughed, maybe none harder than the FBI profiler.

"I will, however, broadcast what you said so that I can rub Tankersley's little ego, making your job and mine easier.

"One last question, gentlemen, will you brief the president?"

"I want to answer this delicately," Director Wray began. "We won't be making a special report to the president. We don't consider this matter a national security issue. However, given the job held by Mr. Jensen and its importance to national security, he will have to be informed of the matter, which will be done in his next daily briefing book."

"Do you expect him to call you and ask about this?"

"I do not."

"Ms. Felts, we need to get the director and his team on the road. Can we call this a wrap on your end?" Fitz asked in his best Virginia gentlemanly tone.

"Of course, detective. May I impose upon you to see me out safely?"

Peggy Felts stood up abruptly, sensing that these men were done with her but hoping to steal a small debrief on her way out the door from Fitz. The men in the room instinctively stood as she did, working themselves out clumsily from Joe's cramped booths.

"Ms. Felts, it was a pleasure meeting you, and please reach out to my office if you'd like to follow up," Wray said, extending his hand to hers.

"Thank you, director."

"I am delighted to walk you out, Ms. Felts," Fitz said with a hint of Clint Eastwood seriousness wrapped in a Sean Connery smile.

As the two walked back down the left aisle of the café, Felts couldn't help but notice the wall to her left, which was an altar to law enforcement. Bulletin boards of law enforcement patches adorned the walls. They were placed in between tacky pictures of '50s and '60s hot rods. "This place reeks of testosterone," she thought. It normally would have turned her off, as she didn't really suffer these tough-guy displays of machismo very well. Still, there was something a bit sexy about the thought of all those handsome men in uniform.

Peggy Felts didn't just look the part of all-woman; she loved being one, too, when it suited her.

She turned to Fitz at the door, looking at him closely. "You delivered, detective. I'm impressed. I'll do my part as promised."

"I am glad you're satisfied, Ms. Felts."

"I am, but I'm hoping you will stay in touch and not make me chase you like a schoolgirl, detective. People might talk." She laughed.

"I should be so lucky to have such talk. Yes, I'll keep you apprised, and as I promised when I whispered in your ear, play this right and you'll get a front-row seat. It's good for all of us."

Before returning to the table for a wrap-up with Wray, Fitz grabbed DeMatha. "You ready to the meet the director?"

"Let's rock 'n' roll."

Chapter 15: The Dinosaur Game

Mary McDougal stepped through Jenny's front door without being asked in, as if she was looking to find someone. It did not go unnoticed by Jenny, whose heart was still racing from both the lovemaking and the adrenaline of getting dressed and answering the door.

"I was on the Bram side of town and thought I would stop by and say hello. Plus, I really wanted to return those pants we borrowed from Jack Jr."

"Well, you didn't have to make a special trip from Willowsford just for that," Jenny exclaimed, barely hiding her annoyance.

The McDougals were part of the travel baseball mafia, and Mary and her husband, Jimmy, were knee-deep in everyone's business, particularly as it related to baseball. Jimmy was always recruiting kids, pushing baseball lessons and jumping himself and his kids from team to team. If the McDougals had a business, it would be bridge-burning. Their boys were great kids, terrific ballplayers and well liked. They were like Marilyn Munster, perfectly normal kids who were the product of weird parents.

The McDougals were a volatile mix, and among the moms most likely to become unhinged and thrown out of a baseball field, the famously loud, hot-tempered Mary McDougal was a prime candidate.

"Christ, she is probably here to try to get Jack to jump from Alan's to Jimmy's team," she thought. "Or maybe she finally found out about that time I made Jimmy beg for it. What a mistake. That putz has been either penning me love letters or crying — actually crying — trying to get me to fuck him again. Worst fuck ever," she thought as she turned to Mary.

"Mary, I'd offer you something to drink, but I'm just leaving for the store."

"Oh, I thought you might have a few minutes to talk, but I understand."

"Jesus," Jenny thought, "she sounds serious. I hope she didn't bust Jimmy writing one of his sad-sap emails to me."

"Gosh, Mary, I'm sorry. Can it wait?"

Mary worked up a lot of courage before coming over, and in fact she may have even had a shot of courage or two just to do it. Mary McDougal wasn't just a member of the Jenny Jensen fan club, she was the president. She worshipped Jenny, and she spent a lot of time cozying up to her. This matter she had was one she felt couldn't wait much longer, but she sure didn't want to catch Jenny in the wrong mood. The news would be a big enough shock.

"No — no problem at all, Jenny. It can wait for sure. I don't want to get in the way of your busy day. I was just taking a chance you might be here." Mary was fighting back the urge to say what she really wanted to say — and how she really felt. She'd practiced this a long time, and she was sure this would finally be her moment. It was nearly impossible to get her away from Janie Handly long enough to say more than hello, and here she was in Jenny's house, and she still couldn't get this matter off her chest.

"I'm sorry, Mary. Why don't you text me and we'll get together later this week? Maybe you can come by and we can have a glass of wine, just the two of us," Jenny asked as she led her back toward the front door.

"I'd love that," Mary said, visibly perking up.

Jenny shut the door as she waved and smiled at her surprise guest, who trembled as she got back in her Jeep.

Mary looked at her watch and thought, I have two hours before the boys all pile through the door. She raced home.

****

The FBI director was on his way home. Quietly, the team broke down its positions, and life at Joe's Café returned to normal. Before leaving, Wray spent a few minutes with DeMatha, who regaled him with a couple of undercover stories. Meanwhile, Wray gave Fitz his direct-dial, private cell number. The two promised to coordinate directly and to keep each other in the loop on every development. Fitz told him that once he had the DNA match, he would confirm it.

Before rolling out of the lot, Fitz and DeMatha called Parker for an update. "OK, so basically, everyone with a dick in Brambleton could be a suspect? Great," Fitz blurted out after learning the forensics piece. "Where are we on talking to the people at this party that the vic went to the night she was killed?"

"By midday tomorrow, we will have spoken to all of them," said Parker. "I have statements from two, and I have three ladies who promised to speak with me tonight. They're all accounted for."

"What about this Handly woman? It seems she is the list topper."

"She is. I reached out to her, visited her house, spoke with her husband, too. She is out running errands, best he can tell, but she has not yet returned. I plan to speak to her as soon as I can, and I made that request quite plain to the husband."

"How does he do on establishing the timeline?"

"He's worthless. He is not sure she went to the event, or if she did, when she came home that night because he was quote, 'hunkered down' watching a K-State game. She answered him when he called for her, which was when Bodine's wife called to spill the news about the death. Other than that, he doesn't know if she left, with whom she might have gone or when she got home. He did give us a bunch of names of people likely there.

"So on the timeline, he gives us nothing. But on witnesses, he gave us a jackpot. The two statements I have both put Jensen and Handly at the party, and each said they arrived and left together. To me, that's a double jackpot."

"Well, well, well, that *is* big news. Talking to this Handly woman will be key to our timeline, it appears."

"Yes, and boss, they left that party well before the time of death. The best I can tell, they left at least 50 minutes to an hour before the time of Jenny Jensen's death. The question is, left for where?"

"Well, it looks like it is going to be ladies' night for us in Brambleton. We need to tie this timeline down tightly."

"Mostly, we need to hear from Ms. Handly, and I mean now," said Fitz. "Was the husband cooperative, besides spilling all these names?"

"Yes, straight as could be. I didn't sense he was hiding anything. According to him, the wife is out running errands and likely at Wegmans and not picking up her phone."

"Did you get into it with him on how she reacted to the death?"

"He said she cried all night, was very upset. You know, the type of reaction one might expect to the news."

"And now she is out keeping herself busy all day, probably trying to keep her mind off the events, I suppose?" Fitz volunteered.

"That's what it sounds like."

"Well, Mrs. Handly is now the most important person in this investigation, other than Jack Jensen, who is likely dead. Call Trevor and tell him to dig anything he can connecting Ms. Handly to Jenny Jensen from that computer — by every means he has. We need to know everything about the Jensens and the Handlys."

"Richland does say there is a hint on the computer of lots of communications between the vic and a woman and that the relationship might have been more than close friends."

"What? Is it Handly?"

"He didn't know yet."

"Parker, if Handly and Jensen, or Jensen and some other woman, are playing the dinosaur game, we need to know that yesterday."

"Yes, I know — I get it."

DeMatha busted in, "What the fuck is the dinosaur game?"

"Jesus, DeMatha, the dinosaur game? You've never heard of that?"

"Well, let's just say both sexes can play the dinosaur game … but it's probably more fun to be the 'lick-a-lot-o-puss' than it is to be the 'mega-sore-ass.' "

After a pregnant pause, DeMatha busted out laughing. "You two men are just completely fucked — you know that. Love it — the dinosaur game. Never heard that crazy shit before."

"In all seriousness," Fitz breaks in, "if Jenny Jensen is a lesbian or has had a lesbian tryst, the field of suspects has broken open even wider." "Parker, this information, if true, needs to be held closely, as in just you and me. I don't want this crap leaking out to the team and finding its way where it might not belong. Joke as we may, but being a lesbian isn't illegal, and it certainly doesn't make one a killer. It would, *however,* lead us to more possible people with whom we may have to speak. We can't go on innuendo here, so let's see what Trevor finds before we go off, pardon the expression, half-cocked — or not cocked."

"Let me get with Trevor and see where he is and let him know the new priority search terms," Parker said as if to wrap the call.

"Great. I have a message here from Sully, and hopefully he can give us more information on the DNA or the trace evidence. Fitz out."

****

Janie pulled the 4Runner into the driveway and saw Jeff still working in the garage. "Christ, he really must feel like shit if he is actually finally doing that project," she thought. She was now ready to face him, and face the detective, her story completely bulletproof. It kept racing through her mind, "No one will ever know — can ever know — the truth."

Jeff approached the vehicle cautiously, not wanting to push any panic buttons or ask too many questions. As Janie got out, he asked, "Hey, how are you doing?"

"I'm OK. Really. I am sad, sick still, but we will be OK," she said, with the emphasis on *we.* "I just had so much to do, and I thought the drive would help, so I kept my appointment to run Jackson's car up to Dad and have him get it into shape."

"Holy crap — you got all the way up there and back this quickly?"

"No, he met me more than halfway. He was very helpful. He asked to send his regards to you too," she said unconvincingly.

"Well, now I know you are putting on a front, Jane," he said with that broad smile she remembered so well on a younger face at a much happier time.

"All right, you still aren't his favorite — but you're mine. Now come give me a hand because I stopped at Wegmans for a few quick items on my way back."

"Did you get my message?" he asked hesitantly.

"I did. I am happy to tell them what I know. They sure won't crack the case on my testimony," she said with a chuckle.

Jeff took a long look at Janie and he could see the life back in her after last night's dreadful events. He prayed this was all behind them and that once this case was solved; he and Janie could move forward.

"I will call that officer right now, get dinner going and then meet him at his convenience to give a statement. I can't imagine that will take long."

"Do you think you should have counsel with you?" Jeff heard himself ask.

"A lawyer?" she said, surprised. "Why on earth would I need a lawyer? Did the officer say anything that makes you think I am the chief suspect?" she asked with a smile.

"Of course not. He was here, and he really wanted to establish a timeline and clear up details."

"He was here?" she asked.

"Yes, he called, then he came by. He seemed anxious to speak with anyone at the Feeleys'. I told him I didn't even know if you went there."

Janie wanted to press Jeff for details on what else he asked, noticed or observed. She really wanted to know what else Jeff might have told him.

"I am surprised he called *and* came by, but I guess they need to get statements from everyone."

"I told him you were at the grocery store, so I suspect he stopped by thinking you might have returned. Of course, I didn't know your grocery run included a trip up to Pittsburgh. He caught me midproject as I was trying to make room for the cars."

"Well, it's fine. I will tell him all he needs to know."

****

When Mary McDougal got home, she wasted no time. On her way home, she had texted Jimmy and confirmed he would not be back for nearly an hour and a half. The boys were accounted for, too. She took one more long swig from the bottle of wine she opened before going to Jenny's. She looked in the mirror and thought, "I was so close to the real thing." She kicked off her sandals and headed to her room. She locked the door just in case.

McDougal then went over to her jewelry box, opened it and used a nail file to pop the velvet bottom from the box. It was a picture of Jenny from a group beach outing about four years ago. Jenny was blowing a kiss as she posed for the picture, with her cleavage nearly pouring out of her bikini top.

Mary locked the door, with a sense of paranoia, and moved over to the bed. She took off her shorts and peeled down her panties, already damp. She lay herself on the bed. Holding Jenny's picture in one hand, she reached down between her legs, and in that moment, she closed her eyes and tilted back her head. "Soon … soon you will really be here, too," she murmured aloud to herself.

****

"Detective Fitzgerald, it's Sully," the message began. "The DNA is a match. The blood on the street is the blood of Jack Jensen. Also, I have news on the trace evidence. Put simply, we think it is paint particles from a motor vehicle. In fact, we can match it to automobile car manufacturers. Call me back."

DeMatha and Fitz looked at each other, almost with matching pained expressions. Two great analytical minds were chewing the data and processing it like modern computers. "Holy fuck, Jensen was hit by a goddamn car," DeMatha blurted out.

"Yes, that's exactly it. That explains the 'road cake,' " Fitz answered.

"Jack Jensen was hit by a car, likely injured or killed. The driver obviously intended for the accident. Rather than help Jensen, the driver loaded him in the vehicle and either finished him off, is holding him hostage or took the body to be dumped."

"DeMatha, we have to piece this together. It still doesn't make complete sense, does it?"

"No, not yet. But we now know, with some certainty, that Jensen was run down. What we have to do is figure out if that was before or after Jenny was murdered and if it was done by the same person." DeMatha's mind raced.

"Well, we now have another piece, and that piece should help narrow this search when we match paint to a car manufacturer and then compare it to prospective witnesses and suspects. It's still a long way from solved," Fitz reminded him.

DeMatha stops his curious searching through Fitz's tape selections to listen more intently.

"How do you run someone down on a residential street and no one notices? Are you kidding me? I've got to have our people recanvass this neighborhood and find anyone who heard anything that night. The first round through, we came up with nothing but zeros," Fitz declared.

"Yes, but you didn't have this info to cue witnesses to a car sound or car activity. Heck, just someone hearing the braking might help the timeline, right?"

"True, but it is a fine line between jogging a memory and planting an idea. It's a lead, and it's a good one. But we need *more* information."

****

When Felts' exclusive with Fitz and Wray was broadcasted, the story was picked up quickly across the DMV. Every station ran with the breaking news, which was that Jack Jensen was a suspect on the run and wanted for questioning in the death of his beautiful wife.

Driving down the road to Tuskies for dinner, the man most divorce lawyers in Loudoun called Mc-G-Spot nearly crashed his car. In the world of divorce, a bustling business in a wealthy county of beautiful, bored and seemingly unfaithful people, Chester McGovern, aka Mc-G-Spot, had the world's largest collection of bad boys and girls on his camera.

The fight to gain leverage in high-dollar divorces often led clients to press their lawyers to hire someone to follow an unfaithful spouse. That someone was McGovern. His nickname came from his uncanny knack at and unrelenting job of catching people at the precise moment of infidelity that left little question as to who was doing what and who was enjoying the hell out of it.

McGovern called his date for the night and gave his apologies. He told her to hold the bar at Tuskies, but he likely wouldn't make it until later that night. She would have to go home, ironically, to her husband if she wanted to get lucky. After hearing the news on his car radio, McGovern headed back to his Leesburg office and quickly dashed into the safe. He pulled the file marked "Jensen." He tapped his fingers nervously as he paged through the pictures he still had. "*That*," he thought, "was some of the steamiest sex he ever shot," all for a client now apparently a murder suspect.

Kelley Fitzgerald looked at the caller ID and thought, "Can this day get any worse?" It was a name she knew well. One of Loudoun's busiest private PIs, a man whose photo collection included a lot of men and women in sexual exploits with people not their spouses. "Christ," she thought, "he probably has me and the commonwealth's attorney on that damn camera. Why the hell is he calling me after hours on a Friday?"

"Chester McGovern, to what do I owe the pleasure," she asked in a sarcastic and commanding voice, reminiscent of her father's famous tone.

"Kelley, I have something damned serious, and you're the only prosecutor I trust."

"Is it Donald Trump and a Russian hooker, Chester, because it is Friday, after 6, and I've had a rough week."

"Kelley, I have pictures of Mrs. Jenny Jensen having sex in a parked car on the night she was murdered. In fact, I have a file full of other pictures related to the case spread out over nearly two months."

"And after this woman was murdered, you held these back from the investigators because — why?"

"Listen, you can jam me up, or you can help me, and I'll help your dad. There is much more to the story, and I want to talk to your father. I also want an assurance that I am not going to get fucked for this."

"Chester, I ain't giving you jackshit until the lead investigator tells me to cut you some slack. Got it?"

"But —"

"But nothing, Mc-G-Spot. If Fitz clears you, I'll clear you. Right now, I'll put you in touch with him and hold off on charging you until he says so. That's what you get."

"I'll bring the file in to meet with him, but I am bringing my own counsel, and I want you there."

"Ha. You're bringing a lawyer with you to meet my father? And you think that'll help you? Christ, you're an idiot, Chester."

"Listen, Kelley, I ain't asking you to date me, but there was a time that I did you more than one solid when you were working sex crimes. All I am asking for is a little consideration."

"My debts are paid to you on that, but I'll tell you this again, if the chief investigator says you are clear, then you will be clear. I wouldn't bring some dick lawyer with you. That's my payback to you. OK, just to be ethical, I will remind you that you have a right to bring counsel. Just to be fair about my father, I'll tell you that unless you are bringing my sister Quinn, he's going to destroy your lawyer."

"What's her number? That's a joke."

"What time and where?

"That's your call, Kelley."

"Let me find the lead detective."

"Sully, what is the car we are looking for?" Fitz asked before Sully could even say hello.

"Detective, it's a paint particle, not a VIN number."

"Fine, of course. But can you narrow this down for us?"

"The paint is used by three car manufacturers, fascinatingly enough. Two foreign car companies and one domestic. Both Honda and Kia use it. This includes vehicles manufactured here and abroad. Oddly enough, the paint is also used on Jeep and Chrysler products."

"That's great. So basically, dozens of possible car models and millions of cars? Any chance it is some puke green or roasted rust bullshit color? I think mint green, like *My Cousin Vinny*?"

"No detective, this is a gray vehicle. You are looking at either a painted plastic bumper or a grille. We are analyzing the material to see if we can find properties that will exclude one or more manufacturers. That's going to take us more time."

"Right now, 100 percent, you're telling me and the team we're looking for a gray vehicle with some damage on the car, and likely front or rear bumper, grille or hood?"

"Yes."

"Well, we will alert body shops from here to the Mississippi for anything that has come in since the night of the murder. It's a start."

****

"Richland, what have you found, my man," Parker blurted out as he picked up the call from Trevor.

"Your girl Jensen was a sex machine."

"Anything on the dinosaur angle?"

"OK, that's where this gets interesting. I found a series of communications from a Gmail address to Jensen. It appears Jensen first ignored the communications, which were saucy as shit. Later, she tried to stop them. In the end, the communications got a lot more aggressive."

"Threatening-like aggressive?"

"Not really. They started off with some sexy talk wrapped around a pledge of love. In the end, it was beaver shots and masturbation with a promise to love Jensen forever. I thought I might find a video, but no luck."

"What's the address, and can you track it or find an IP address?"

"So, I figured this was some star-crossed lesbian stalker from the neighborhood. And it may be. But this person masked the email address and used a series of proxy servers. I am not giving up on tracking it, I am merely saying right now I can't nail it down. It's a pretty sophisticated move for a run-of-the-mill secret lover."

"Package those up and send."

"They are already in your box, pardon the pun. By the way, I will leave this to your detective skills, but there are some identifying characteristics on this body and around that woman's genitalia. How you get the neighborhood to let you inspect, you let me know."

"Tell me quickly about the second set."

"Oh, this is much more interesting. This is pretty much out in the open. That is, while dozens of these emails were deleted, many were not. That Gmail account lists the person's name right in it. It's your girl Handly."

"What?"

"Handly. Most are signed Janie."

"Do they talk about sex and share pics?"

"I haven't read them all, but the last three or four weeks they clearly talk about love, lovemaking and all kinds of deep, forever feelings. They don't trade any pictures or video, but you read a few of those threads and there is no doubt that those two have been snorkeling up each other's thighs. This stuff is like a Harlequin novel."

"No kidding — it's that obvious?"

"I don't give a shit who you are, you read the exchanges I sent you and you will read a love story — between two hot, 40-something, suburban moms."

"OK, you, sir, have nailed this."

"Listen, I am just an old intelligence officer and geeky computer guy, but I will be shocked if you can prove that the one lady writing these emails — Handly — murdered that woman. She might have killed for her, but there is no way she killed her."

"Love does some crazy things," Parker interjected.

"Also, based on my analysis, everything in these emails that gets outside the friend zone is found in the deleted slack space. In short, they were trying to hide this stuff the old-fashioned way, by hitting delete. You look at what's left in the inbox, and you can tell they are close, and maybe flirty, but nothing steps over the line. It's all packaged up for you — and I am still sifting through the forensics. I expect to find more from everyone."

****

Janie Handly picked up the phone and called the detective's number on the card. Parker looked down and saw the number come up as Handly, J. "Holy shit, this is really falling in my lap."

"Mrs. Handly?"

"Yes, this is Jane Handly. Is this Detective Parker?"

"It is indeed, Mrs. Handly, and thank you for calling me back. First let me say, my condolences on the loss of your dear friend."

"Thank you, detective, I appreciate that. She was indeed a dear and remarkably close friend."

"I'm sure. Mrs. Handly. I appreciate the call tonight. We have had a few developments in the case, and I am being pulled in two directions. Do you have time to meet tomorrow?"

"I can make time, detective, but I must work around my family."

"Oh yes, Mrs. Handly, family first, I understand your priority. Can you suggest a time?"

"How is 11:30 a.m.?"

"I can make that work. We are working out of a war room here; may I impose on you to come to us? It might be nicer than putting another cruiser in your already shell-shocked neighborhood."

"That's no problem at all. Just tell me the address and where to go, and I will be there in plenty of time for 11:30."

"Great. I have your cell number, so I will text you the information. Thanks again."

"I am happy to help."

Parker hung up the phone and opened the first file in his Dropbox. It was marked "M&MGirlforyou." He clicked on the last file in time, an email just 20 hours before the murder. It was from the anonymous stalker. "*Jees-us Christmas,*" he said out loud. Then he thought, "There was a time you couldn't pay for porn like this."

Hogan walked in, looked at Parker and asked, "What's up?"

"Oh, just another long night of looking at lesbian, lovesick, Loudoun County housewife porn. Want to help?"

"I think I can clear my schedule …. First, is she hot?"

"Hot, a-bothered and — possibly a killer."

Chapter 16: The Mc-G-Spot

Fitz was fired up, and he was headed back to the station to let Parker know about the trace evidence and the DNA match. He had pulled over first to give Wray a call and let him know about the Jensen DNA match, too. Wray was concerned about the car angle, and he and his team were now increasingly antsy that this might have been a terror attack and a snatch-and-grab of Jensen. Fitz worried too, anew, about that possible angle. It was now easier to make out that scenario to fit the physical evidence.

Fitz just didn't see how Jensen was running in the street after his wife was murdered by terrorists only then to be run down by the getaway car. At FBI headquarters, the camps were split on which way to go, and protocol demanded they consider the worst.

Fitz's phone rang, and it was his "number one," as he called his oldest daughter, Kelley. Fitz pulled in quickly to the parking lot of Heritage High School and hit the talk button.

"How's my number one tonight?"

"Dad, I'm doing OK. Unfortunately, this is a business call."

"Really, you're calling me as a deputy commonwealth's attorney?"

"Yes, and you're going to be very happy, in part, and very *unhappy* in part."

"Make me happy first, honey; maybe it will stick."

"That was my plan. Do you remember that scum-sucking private eye everyone calls Mc-G-Spot?"

"Loudoun's finest, yes."

"He claims he has pictures of your victim having sex in a car on the night she was killed. He took them for his client, Jack Jensen."

"Lovely. Did he take them first to a scrapbooking class to pretty them up before disclosing them to authorities in a goddamn murder investigation?"

"Detective, he asked me to clear him from holding this evidence, and I refused to do so until he met with you, and you agreed to give him the all-clear."

"Well, if he has useful information, is completely truthful, and he lets me throat-punch him, I see no reason why we can't work it out."

"Detective, please, no throat punching."

"Where is this bottom-feeding, five-pound bag of dogshit? He's probably selling naked pictures of his own mother, I suspect."

"No doubt, but right now he is asking to meet with you at the time and location of your choosing. Oh, and he was thinking about bringing a lawyer."

"I might shoot him, you should be so advised."

"I recommend against it, detective; the commonwealth's counsel here is pretty solid."

"Yes, well, she comes from good stock."

"I was ethically bound to advise him of his right to counsel, but I also told him that wouldn't help him with you. So we won't know how smart he is until he shows up."

"Tell him 7:30 p.m. at my office … are you coming?"

"I will be there, of course."

"Excellent."

"Man, the developments in this case are fast and furious, Fitz," DeMatha blurted out. "I was just out walking with my damn ball, and now I am putting in a 14-hour day."

"I can run you home to Fanny if you would rather watch the Hallmark Channel and have a glass of Ensure."

"Fuck you, old man."

The two laughed uproariously as Fitz punched in some classic rock for the short trip to the war room down Evergreen to Route 15 and right into downtown Leesburg.

Lord, I was born a ramblin' man
Tryin' to make a livin' and doin' the best I can
And when it's time for leavin'
I hope you'll understand
That I was born a ramblin' man ....

****

Fitz and DeMatha blew past the war room to find Parker. When Fitz opened the door, he saw a room full of deputies all leering over Parker's shoulder.

"Please tell me your cousin in New Jersey isn't sending you nudes again, Parker." The room snapped to attention as Parker, DeMatha and Fitz let out a chuckle.

"Men, I bet you didn't know that New Jersey, an erstwhile, urbane and sophisticated center of liberalism and diversity, still permits first cousins to marry. Seriously, you can look it up. Parker has a bunch of first cousins, and in fairness to the man, he is looking to increase his dating pool while cutting down on his wedding guest list for the right woman."

"That's pure bullshit," Parker declares.

"Actually, the part about Parker having a naked cousin you would look at is bullshit, but both New Jersey and Virginia permit you to marry your first cousin. But just 20 miles from here, in the great state of West Virginia, such tomfoolery is outlawed by statute."

218

"Really?" asked Hogan.

"Yes, really. It seems in West Virginia, siblings don't like the competition from cousins," Fitz said hardly holding back his own girlish giggle.

"Ba-dump-dump, and Detective Fitzgerald will be here all week, folks, don't forget to tip your waiter," Kelley Fitzgerald barked from the door opening behind her father.

"OK, boys," said Fitz, "now that I am in serious trouble, let's move to an update, which might, hopefully, start with why you are all in here."

"Fitz, Jane Handly and Jenny Jensen were having a love affair," Parker blurted out.

"No shit. I mean — please, detective, tell me what you found. And, please tell me my daughter is not still behind me."

"Oh, the deputy commonwealth's attorney is still there, and I do have more — much more. Jenney Jensen had at least 13 lovers in the last five years. Only one woman. However, a second person was a stalker, and we don't know the identity or gender yet. But we think the stalker is a woman. As far as we can tell, her identity was unknown to Jensen, and her advances were clearly unwanted or unwelcomed."

"Really? Continue."

"We are examining a series of emails from the stalker, a person who covered his or her identity and masked his or her IP address. The pictures include graphic pictures of sex and sex acts, all with just one woman. Assuming the woman in the pictures is the person sending the pictures, Mrs. Jensen had a lovesick, sex-obsessed, attractive, batshit-crazy lesbian stalker."

"Well, I don't think I can top that. And, of course, as chief detective, I will necessarily have to examine this evidence myself, cough cough, at another time. What I can do is give you boys three key facts: First, Mr. Jensen was apparently hit by a car — a gray car that was a Honda, Kia, Jeep or Chrysler. In addition, we can confirm the blood in the street was that of Jack Jensen — and just to keep up with you boys, I am about to meet a private detective who has pictures of Mrs. Jensen having sex in a car shortly before she was murdered that night."

The entire group blurted out, "Mc-G-Spot?"

"Exactly."

"DeMatha, let's go call our new federal friend and update him again before meeting Mc-G-Spot. Parker, can you arrange all the email and texts in one pile and the associated pics in another pile for me? I want to see the stalker first, and then Mrs. Handly. By the way, I thought you were talking to Handly. Is she a no-show?"

"No. In fact, she called just seconds after I got the report on her affair, so I put her off until the a.m. in order to review all the email communications."

Turning to his daughter, Fitz said, "I'd like to get a warrant for her computer and cellphone. I'd like to see her texts."

"Do you have something more than a love affair to show probable cause, detective?"

"Well, that's your job, counselor. But I will see if I can make it easier by interviewing Mc-G-Spot. Let's discuss that warrant in my office, Ms. Fitzgerald."

Fitz led his daughter down the hall to his office. He held the door like a good father and followed in after her.

"Dad, I don't really think we have enough yet for a warrant on Mrs. Handly."

"I agree, unfortunately. I just wanted to ask you one other important question before Mc-G-Spot gets here."

"Shoot."

"When is your baby due?"

Kelley Fitzgerald turned pink, then pale, and in less than two seconds burst into tears. Fitz leaped to his feet and came around the desk. "Hey ... hey ... why are you crying, sweetheart?"

"I am so embarrassed. I should have told you," she sobbed. "I tried to tell you. I wanted to — it was an accident."

"Kelley, we Fitzgeralds don't happen by accident."

She half chuckled through a sob at her father's observation, sounding more like a snort.

"Honey, you have four kids. I think you know by now, babies are not made by accident. Oops, I fell in your vagina!"

"Dad, this is not funny."

"No. No dear, it's a miracle. It's a gift. You are blessed. I — I am blessed again. Your mother will be so happy for you."

"Dad, the father —"

"The father is the elected commonwealth's attorney, a good man, a great lawyer, a fine public servant. What's the problem?"

"You know about us?" she said moving back from him and looking completely shocked.

"I am the chief detective, dear, and your father. Haven't you read any of my clippings? If I can solve homicides, I can figure out who my daughter's seeing."

"Oh my god, does he know that you know?"

"Who cares?"

"He doesn't know about the baby yet. I couldn't tell him until I told you and Mom, which I wanted to do two weeks ago, and last week, and this Sunday — but I probably would have chickened out again."

"Well, thank God Loudoun's CA isn't a detective. Tell the

221

man. He has a right to know, and I suspect he will be happy."

"As for me, I am delighted. The Fitzgerald brigade keeps growing. Keep up the good work."

Kelley picked her head up and looked at her father. "I love you, Dad. You are still my hero."

"You are still my number one, and I will always love you. That's no accident." Fitz then added, "Putting your little sister up to that bullshit ruse about the Marines was dirty pool — young lady." He winked at her.

****

Buford read the law enforcement bulletin a second time. His daughter's gray Honda Pilot matched the description of the gray vehicle that was the subject of the alert. It was the right make, and the damage was 100 percent consistent with the bulletin's description. More than that, it fit the time period perfectly. And as Buford Mackey looked at it again, he thought, "The subject vehicle is wanted in a connection with a murder in *Brambleton*."

Buford Mackey was no dummy. He wasn't much on coincidences, either. First, Janie called him on almost no notice. Next, she never mentioned a murder, not once, in her own neighborhood. Then she appeared with a damaged car on his doorstep, where her out-of-state mechanic in a retired "body shop" would fix it without question. If this weren't his own flesh and blood, he would be certain he was in possession of the suspect vehicle.

"Janie, baby, what the hell happened?" he thought. Buford Mackey went into the family office, shut the door and turned on the computer. He went straight to Google. In seconds, he had multiple

222

stories on the murder — the murder of Jenny Jensen — his daughter's closest friend.

"*Hole-lee shit,*" Mackey said out loud.

****

"Detective, I appreciate you meeting with me on this delicate subject," Chester McGovern began.

"This is a murder case, McGovern — and right now, I don't have time for pleasantries. Do you have something for me?"

"I want assurances that —"

"No one gives a flying fuck what you want, Chester. Let's see what you have, and then we can talk about what you get," Fitz announced as if was handing down the word of God.

McGovern was the fastest-talking, most unrepentant, smarmy sleaze Fitz had ever come to know. He despised him. Indeed, decent people found him transparently loathsome. More than that, he was pushy and prone to missing the social cues that feed a civilized society. Mostly, he was famous for missing those giant red flares that stop people from saying the wrong thing to the wrong person at the exactly wrong time. But today, looking at Detective Fitzgerald, his best and most useful skill of self-preservation kicked in.

"Here is my complete folder," he said, looking quickly away from Fitzgerald like a frightened child.

Fitzgerald looked through the pictures. He read the correspondence and the client agreement. He quickly rifled through the pictures a second time, stopping at one to turn the 12-by-9 glossy in several different directions, holding it as he did as if wondering, "What the hell is that?"

"The deputy CA told me you had pictures of Ms. Jensen having sex in a car the night of the murder — like right before the murder. None of these look like they fit that description."

"Well, that might be my fault."

"Are you saying you're bullshitting us?" Kelley Fitzgerald interrupted.

"No — no — I took pictures of the sex. It was steamy, and it is clear who the parties were. I mean, wow, these pictures were some of the best I have ever captured."

"And, you sold them to TMZ or what? Where the hell are they, Mc-G-Spot?" Kelley pressed, clearly annoyed by this wrinkle.

"I don't know."

"What the fuck do you mean you don't know," Fitz's voice boomed as he leaned forward, staring right through McGovern, who very well might have pissed himself.

"Someone knocked me out. I was taking these pics, angling in closer — moving up on them, right? I found a perfect spot from different three angles. I mean, I can show you the moles on both of those lady's bodies from these pics. That's how close I was. Next thing you know, it's black. I wake up the next morning in the mud of the construction site about 50 yards from where I was shooting. I mean, shit, I had like seven illegals shaking me and pouring water on me at 6:30 in the morning. I had to go to urgent care. I got 12 stitches and a concussion."

McGovern leaned over, peeled off his classic Irish flap-cap and showed the back of his head. It was a lumpy mess.

"Someone assaulted you while you were taking pictures of the two women having sex?" Kelley asked incredulously.

"Sure did, and they took my camera and everything. But I can tell you for sure, the two I was photographing are the same two

224

people pictured in these photos. I mean, one is Jenny Jensen, and the other is her best buddy, Jane Handly."

"You can positively identify that Mrs. Jane Handly was in that car on that night?" Fitz asked.

"Yes, I can do more than that. I can identify that it was Jane Handly's car, a gray Honda Pilot. And without giving more detail than necessary, you will find Mrs. Handly's handprint on the lower part of the back, passenger-side window. Heck, you might find her footprint on the ceiling in that car. Those two broads were letting it all hang out."

"Seriously, Mc-G-Spot, the term 'broads' went out with high-button shoes, you reprobate," Fitz said, in his best chastising voice. "OK … let's make this easy. We aren't going to jam you up on this, McGovern. Frankly, I don't think we can if we want to. But we want and expect your complete cooperation. I want to walk through every detail of this relationship with your client and then cover every minute you were on the case. You do that, and we might even say a few good words about you. Deal?"

"I am happy to help."

"OK, when did Jack Jensen first come to you?"

****

Janie's phone went off as she was sitting down to dinner. She looked at the Galaxy Note 8 screen and up popped a smiling picture of her and her dad from his 70th birthday, just four years earlier. "Wow," she thought in an instant, "life used to be so uncomplicated." As it rang a second time, Jeff shouted out, "just ignore it."

225

Janie snapped out of her time warp. "I can't, it's my dad. I'll make sure everything is OK and be right back," she said as she dashed from the table down the hall.

"Hi, Dad, what's up?" she said without meaningful affect.

"What's up? *You* are asking *me* what's up, young lady?"

Janie knew, as does nearly every child of any age, 5 to 50, that when your parent calls you *young lady*, it's not good.

"What do you mean?"

"I mean, I have a police bulletin that matches the make and model of your car for the murder of your best friend in your neighborhood. That's what's up! Are you safe? What the hell did your husband do now?

"*What?*"

"Janie — I am not going to ignore this. I can't. If you're in trouble, the time to come clean is right now. If you're being threatened, the time to tell me is now. I'll come down tonight and get you out of there. I'll get you a lawyer. I mean — Christ, honey, what is going on there?"

Janie was in shock. She had her story for the police set. She had this all figured out, she thought. This — this police bulletin, she had no idea about that. And her father, what the hell? She was in stunned silence.

"*Janie!*" Buford Mackey yelled into the phone.

"I am leaving *right* now!" he bellowed as the silence hung in the air for seconds — seconds that seemed like hours.

"Dad. *Do not* come here. It will all be OK. I can't explain now. If you love me, you won't tell another soul what you know until you hear from me again."

The pause was palatable.

"Daddy, promise me you won't tell anyone. Please, Daddy."

"That's a promise I won't make. What I *will do* is give you 24 hours to explain this to me. That's the promise you get."

"That's all I need, Dad, I swear," she whispered, as she fought back tears.

"I love you," she said.

"I'll always love you, Janie — no matter what," his voice said with little comfort to her.

****

"Jack Jensen appeared in my office almost two months ago," McGovern began. "He said he was certain his wife had been cheating on him, and he had to know for sure. He was wound about as tightly as most guys who find out their old lady's riding another guy's rod."

"Hey, Mc-G-Spot, let me tell you this one time and one time only," Fitz interrupted him. "This lady next to me may be the deputy CA, but when you speak in my presence with her here, you will treat her like my 18-year-old. That means you will pretend you're in church, speaking to a priest, making your last confession, hoping for forgiveness so your sorry carcass doesn't burn for eternity in hell. Now, I don't know if you didn't have a father to smack the living shit out of you and teach you some manners, but if you can't give this description like an adult, I am happy to step in and give you the lifetime worth of ass-whoopings you sorely missed." Fitz said as he stared down McGovern.

Fitz then leaned over the table to get closer to McGovern. "Are you fucking reading me, pal?"

McGovern was trembling. This street urchin might not have had a troy ounce of class, but he had smarts. He would choose his words like a choirboy.

"Yes, sir. My apologies, Kelley, I mean, ma'am."

Kelley nearly broke into a smile as she said, "Please continue."

"I am just saying, most of my male clients who suspect infidelity come to me seething in anger. Jack Jensen was red-hot, and he was jumpier and more rattled than most. I swear, I think he couldn't believe it. So he seemed to be caught between the agony of it and the anger of it."

"So why didn't he sign on then?" Fitz asked, noting that the client agreement was 4 weeks old and not 8.

"The guy wanted the all-in surveillance but didn't want to pay. Happens all the time."

"But he came back, right?" asked Kelley.

"Oh yeah, he came back. He showed up the day he signed that agreement and had a cashier's check in hand. He wanted me to get up from the desk and leave that minute."

"Was there some precipitating event he told you about?" Fitz asked.

"All he said was, 'That bitch came home smelling like sex — nail her. The dude looked right through me like — well — like the chief detective here."

"So, when was the first time you got a real lead, and what was it?"

****

Jack Jensen looked up in disbelief. His head was throbbing. His vision was blurred, and he knew he was in trouble. He was bound by his hands and his feet. He was covered in blood, and it was

228

damn sure his. He was pretty sure the moisture running down his head came from a wound. It was pitch dark, and he was gagging and gasping from the rag stuck in his mouth and taped around his head. He was certain he would die in this spot — maybe in that moment.

He tried to evaluate the surroundings for clues. His training made him certain that his current predicament was bad, but it did not appear to be the work of a pro. That he could tell from the bindings. He couldn't remember a damn thing, but that face ... that creepy face staring down at him ... that looked familiar. If he could just focus.

"You never deserved her," he heard the voice say.

****

"I started tracking her that evening. That Jenny Jensen was a lady about town," McGovern announced. "It took me a while to catch on to what was happening. I think that slowed my progress."

"What do you mean, to catch on?" Fitz asked.

"Well, I was looking for her to meet up with a man, engage in classic mistress behavior. You know, sneaking around to out-of-the-way places, going one place while saying she is going another. Checking in with cash at some off-the-beaten-path fleabag motel or just meeting up and sitting too close with another guy. I got none of that."

"Did you bug her phone?" Kelley asked.

"Not until later. I got Jack Jensen's help on that. I did use some of my sophisticated listening devices on her to pick up any conversation with someone I could not readily identify. You know, there's a fair amount of prep and investigative work to identify and make a chart of her contacts and then methodically eliminate people as possible paramours."

"I'm sure you are a regular Dick-fucking-Tracy. How about we skip to the part where a bulb went on and some light filled that space under your mop of hair with a meaningful idea."

"OK — I will tell you — there *was* an aha moment. I had been following this woman so closely, I was surprised she hadn't noticed, to be honest. I mean, I am good, but Jensen was bird-dogging me to find something, anything. So, I might have drawn in a few different times a bit longer and closer on surveillance.

"One evening I see her drop off some kids at the Brambleton fields. I'm basically exposed in those lots, but I am driving a grass-cutting rig and sitting in the corner like I am on a siesta between cuts. The fucking truck is awesome in Loudoun because nobody cuts their own grass, and I blend in like nothin'. It's one of four vehicles I use for what I call intense surveillance.

"And the details that matter are coming when?"

"So, she's about to leave in her car after chasing down her youngest and giving him a water bottle or something. Up pulls her little buddy, Jane Handly. One thing I had was lots of time and eyes on these two. I mean shit, they must change tampons together."

Fitz's fist hit the table like the hammer of Thor, and both Kelley and McGovern nearly jumped out of their seats.

"Oh, I'm sorry, just a vulgar expression. My apologies. I am just saying, it's one thing for girlies to put lipstick on and freshen up together, but these two were closer than close, and I had certainly noted it. It's right in my report, before the big incident."

"How about we skip the sociological study you have made of shameless tarts and go right to the quote, 'big incident,' so I can solve this crime before my youngest is a CA?"

"Yes, well, Ms. Handly lets her kid out, and as he runs over the path, Ms. Jensen leans on the window of her SUV and they are all smiles. Then they start looking around and over their shoulder. Handly is parked behind a big F-250, which shields her car from the fields. So, it's like they are in an open lot but behind a wall. Mind you, they don't pay any attention to me in the grass-cutting truck on the far side of the lot alone. They probably think we are a car full of wetbacks."

"Wetbacks? Really? Mc-G-Spot, what — did — you — see," Kelley asked in slow motion, as if replaying the iconic scene from the TV series *Taxi*. "What — does — a — … yellow — light — mean?"

"Jensen looks all around then sticks her head in the car and kisses the Handly lady, and I mean kisses the shit out of her. Next thing you know, they are swapping spit like 15-year-olds outside the gym at a fall dance. The bell didn't just go off, it hit me right in the head. They broke for a second and started laughing. Then Jensen went in for some more, and I caught that on my camera. You got that picture right in the group there."

"What happened next?" Fitz asked.

"They didn't go any further than that — well, that's not entirely true. Right before she left, Jensen yanked her top and bra down and basically shoved her rack in Handly's face. She covered quickly and laughed, and then took off to her car. I didn't get that on film, but that one is burned into my brain, right here," he said pointing at the front of his forehead.

"The two ladies sped off but in different directions. I was torn, but I decided to follow Jensen, wondering if the two were going to pull the classic, 'leave in two directions and meet up later at the same spot' trick. Jensen went to Wegmans."

"Did you keep the tail on her after that?" Kelley inquired, as both she and Fitz listened like they were watching a soap opera in sweeps week.

"I did more than that. I called my assistant and switched out cars once she went inside the store. I took the sedan, and she kept eyes on Jensen in the building."

"Did they ever meet up that night?" Fitz wanted to know.

"No, but I was hot on her tail. I was sure she made me, but once the sun went down, I decided to trail her no matter what. Sure enough, she took me all over. I was wondering at first if it was a ruse to meet her little friend, but it became clear she knew I was on her. At that point, I wanted to mess with her a bit."

"Is that when Jack Jensen called you and said to get off her ass, you've been made?" Fritz said, laughing.

"How the heck did you know that?"

"It takes real investigation," Fitz smiled.

"I guess I spooked her."

"Why did you write that message in lipstick on her windshield?"

"What? What message?"

"That night, you never wrote something on her windshield in lipstick — and don't you dare hold back on me?" Fitz demanded.

"No, sir, I beat feet, and once she was home and Mr. Jensen dialed me up, I passed her off for the night."

"Listen to me carefully, McGovern. In the course of this sordid surveillance, did you ever notice any other vehicles or people who might have been following Jensen or Handly? Like, before someone whacked your ass over the head?"

"You think someone else was stalking her or following me?" McGovern asked.

"I just want to know what you observed and captured. You say you charted most of the interactions and that you were working the multicar, no BS, tax, tags and processing version of intensive surveillance. So I thought maybe you noticed if someone else was around these two or, in particular Ms. Jensen."

"Well, those baseball moms are always around each other, that's for sure. I can tell you that one day I was tracking Jensen to see if she would meet up with Handly. I had Handly's 20, which was alone at home. So, I thought I might catch these two full-throttle."

"By the way, the PI lingo is really turning me on; please continue," Fritz said, dripping with sarcasm.

"So, bingo, Handly takes off through the neighborhood on foot and even crosses a backyard to get to Jensen's. I have no idea why she doesn't drive, but I had her the whole way. Anyway, I am about to get out of my car and peek in a window or two, in my gas-reader gear, of course."

"Oh, of course — your meter-reader outfit is probably a legend," Kelley said, visibly irritated.

"It gets the job done. Most people don't know the gas company doesn't even read meters anymore. It's hysterical. Anyway, I see one of the baseball moms pull up, go to the front door and knock. I'm thinking, wow, if she only knew who was getting on third-fucking-base in that house, right?"

"Oh, a sex and baseball analogy. Great, now you're fucking Meatloaf," Fitz said, glaring at the cretin.

"Seriously, this lady is at the door, rings the bell, rings again. She peeks in a few windows, and then she is just looking a long, long time, through the side window next to the door, like she's spotted something. Anyway, I retreated back to my vehicle, and the lady went inside. It was that McDougal woman; she's identified in the writeup as one of the moms with regular contact."

"Does your little catalog set out the vehicles each contact drives?" Fitz asks.

"For some of the more regular contacts, it does. I think she is in there."

"Sitting here, right now, without the aid of the chart, do you recall what car Mrs. McDougal drove that day to the Handly house?"

"You bet. It was a white Jeep. It sticks out like a sore thumb."

"You say, Jeep? Is it a Wrangler style or like one of the newer, luxury Jeeps?"

Kelley Fitzgerald didn't have any idea where this was going, or why and how her dad cared about Jeeps, but it was clear he had information on the surveillance of Jensen from somewhere, and Mc-G-Spot was actually filling in blanks.

"She had two, ironically. One is the ragtop, Wrangler-style with personalized plates. That vehicle is classic gray, big black bummer. The other Jeep is brand spanking new, the luxury kind with the cool headlights. It's white, end to end. That's the one she was driving that day."

"You say she has two Jeeps, one gray and one white?"

"Yes — yes, sir, I have seen her in both."

"You have been a very good boy, Mc-G-Spot. Now tell me, do I have every picture you took from that camera before you were knocked out and robbed?" Fitz asked, choosing his words with precision.

"Yes, every relevant picture."

"No. That's not what I asked. I asked if I had all pictures. Are you saying these pictures are selected as 'relevant' by you?"

"That's correct."

"What's fucking correct?"

"I sort through the stick, which might have hundreds of pics, and I print out and catalog those I think are relevant," McGovern explained.

"Do you still have the others?"

"I download every picture I take into a file folder I call raw. Basically, if the name of the client is Jensen, I have a folder titled "Jensenraw." I might make subfolders for the report, but I don't delete any pictures. Those folders are on my system, and I back up automatically to the cloud in case of catastrophic failure."

"McGovern, there are people in this town who think you are one stupid assclown. I am here to testify, you are not stupid. You're an assclown for sure but not stupid," Fitz said as he laughs at his own humor.

"Come on, that's not nice, detective," he said sheepishly.

"No, it's not. The truth hurts. Now, where the hell is that Jensenraw file?"

"I made a copy and put it on this USB for you, sir."

"Kelley, let the record reflect that McGovern here is my favorite assclown. McGovern, Kelley will ask you a few more questions, including how and when you gave some findings to Jack Jensen. The interview will be recorded, which I am sure you will agree to.

"Ms. Fitzgerald, the sheriff's office would like to formally thank Mr. McGovern for his assistance, and we note his cooperation in this matter. We want the CA's office to know that Mr. McGovern's help has been invaluable, and we consider his conduct aboveboard in this matter."

"That's noted, detective, thank you," Kelley said with her father's wry smile tattooed on her face.

"Mc-G-Spot, don't fuck it up — and be on your best behavior in the presence of Ms. Fitzgerald."

McGovern damn near saluted as Fitz tore out of the room with that USB in hand.

Chapter 17: Into the Mystic

"You thought you could tame her, you fucking fool. You *actually thought* she was yours? You pathetic little man. She was never yours. Everyone had her, and she loved it. She loved it in every room, on every floor, on every table — and in every hole. A straight-laced little candy-ass like you couldn't have her — you were fucking furniture to her. Now look at you, lying there dying like a little bitch. You should thank me."

Jack Jensen was too weak to rage, too frail to rise and too injured to live much longer. If this was how he was to go, beaten and psychologically tortured, he never imagined it would be by a "friend" rather than foreign foe. He drifted into darkness as he wondered, "Where is Jenny? Is she OK?"

"That's right, you just die right now for me. I almost have your hole all dug. Meanwhile, your copper friends are searching the world for you, you brutal murdering psycho."

Jack faintly heard the laugh … the weird, sick, stupid laugh … it could only be ….

****

The door burst open, and Fitz came flying in. "Get me every officer we have. Tell them to bring their laptops. Meet in the war room in 30 minutes. Men, we have a treasure trove of pictures to look at, and we need to find each and every instance in these surveillance files of a gray Jeep. Make a log. I am talking about anything that shows a piece of a matching car. Parker, you get a team out to new section of Brambleton — I have the streets right here. You go door to door tonight, on that street, and you find anyone with porch-mounted camera that has a street view. We need to review that film and see if we can catch a gray Wrangler-style Jeep in that vicinity on the night of the murder about 9:15 to 9:45."

"Whoa, chief, slow down," Parker blurted out. "Fill us in, what's going on?"

"Hogan, you get a license plate on any cars registered to Jimmy or Mary McDougal, likely in a Willowsford address.

"Parker, get Richland on the phone in the war room. We will send him what I have, and I want our team to redirect him on his search." Fitz was barking out orders like a Marine under fire.

"Get me a CA — any CA except Kelley; she is finishing up with Mc-G-Spot.

"We need historical cell-tower data on the McDougal phones. We need the last 48 hours right now and the last two months immediately."

"*Chief!*" Parker yelled, finally stopping the Chief's manic yet thorough run. "I thought we were looking at Handly? Who the hell is McDougal?"

Fitz threw three pictures from his stack down on the table. They were different blown-up, high-definition pictures from three different days, all in different locations. They had one immediate similarity. Each was a shot of Jenny Jensen. In one, she was laughing with Janie Handly at a coffeehouse. In another, Handly and Jensen were standing very close to each other, almost intimately, along the fence line of a baseball game. In the third, Jensen was headed into the Wegmans.

Parker peered at them, as six deputies leaned over the table with him, looking, touching and moving the photos. It was like a frantic family fighting to complete a jigsaw puzzle late on Thanksgiving night. The harder they looked, the fewer answers they found. They were waiting for the right answer to leap from one of the photos when Parker got a strange look on his face. "Wait a minute," he began.

Then the rookie, Johnson, screamed, "They all have either a white or grey Jeep and the *same* tan, black-haired woman in the background!"

"Not all of them," Parker protested. "Where is she in the third one?"

"Look, the photographer is shooting Jensen from a distance, inside his own car, and as he does, he catches the passenger-side mirror of his own car. *Now* look more closely. The woman is in the car in the row behind the guy taking the pictures. It's in the damn mirror reflection."

"Holy shit."

"Holy shit is right, people. Three pictures, three different days and three different locations. Mr. Mc-G-Spot is following Handly and Jensen, and so is this woman, *right — fucking — here*. And I'll bet you all I have that her name as Mary McDougal," Fitz announced.

"McDougal?" one deputy asked.

"It gets better. McDougal and her vehicle are positively identified at Jensen's house, and while there, she was spotted peeping through the front window. My guess is we will find a few pictures of that too. What I need to know — tonight — is what she was looking at that day."

"How will we know that?" Johnson asked innocently.

"I will tell you how. Mc-G-Spot was surveilling that day. He says she was peeking in a long time on Jensen, and then eventually Jensen answered the door and let McDougal in. We need to know exactly what happened that day, which was just five days before this murder."

"Wait, you think she might have seen Handly and Jensen together?"

"It's possible."

"Right now, we need that cellphone data and location information. Get working on it."

"I can help with that, detective — maybe," a familiar voice boomed from the doorway. Fitz spun as if on a swivel.

"Harper-O — you're my CA on duty tonight?" the chief detective asked, quite surprised.

Johnson leaned over to Hogan and whispered, "Who is Harpo-O?"

"Harper Alison *Fitzgerald* O'Flaherty — she's one of the boss's daughters."

"No shit?"

"Yes, no shit. And remember two things right now. One, she's married. Two, she'll beat your ass just for sneaking a look at her legs like you just did."

"I bet."

"Detective," Harper-O began saying, "these location data are not easy to get. You have a U.S. Supreme Court case pending on this, *Carpenter.* Lower courts have been holding that to get these data, a warrant is required."

"Great — I want a warrant. We're not getting a damn thing fast enough without one. Hogan, give Harper the relevant facts; we are way past meeting the threshold. Get an affidavit together, and Harpo, get this in front of a competent judge immediately."

She shot him a look.

240

"Please — and Ms. O'Flaherty, I assume we'll see you Sunday for dinner?"

"Of course, detective."

"DeMatha, do you want to run out to the site with the team and see what you might find in the dark on the ground in the area where Mc-G-Spot was assaulted? One never knows what one might find, just looking down, right?"

"Happy to do it. Should I take your Chevelle?"

"That's a good one. Parker, get him some Springsteen-free transportation to the location, please. Let's bring Ms. McDougal in for questioning."

"Whoa," said the ACA, "I don't think we have enough for a warrant to bring her in. It's one thing to get her location data. I agree we should get that on the facts I just overheard, but you *are not* getting an arrest warrant on that."

"You try. Meanwhile, I'll ride over and ask her if she wants to come in voluntarily. I want to know where she is right now. When we find her, I want eyes on her nonstop. Parker, give me Mrs. Handly's number, I'll try her first. If anyone knows what Mrs. McDougal saw that day, it's the frisky Mrs. Janie Handly."

****

As Jack came across the bedroom toward Jenny, he grabbed her very firmly and looked her in the eye: "What the hell happened to you — to us?" He released her, not wanting a physical confrontation with the woman he had come to despise but who was the mother of his children.

Jenny smacked him with everything she had, right across his face. The force broke her nail and etched a scratch on his cheek. He reflexively raised his hand to strike her, but it was not in his nature to cross that forbidden line. He stared at her, and she simply said, "It's over. I am in love with Janie Handly." She bolted from the room, down the steps and out the front door. Jack followed in hot pursuit.

****

Janie Handly looked down at her ringing phone, and again it showed "Loudoun County Sheriff." Her heart jumped a bit, but at the same time she was mildly annoyed. "I thought we had this all figured out for tomorrow," she said to herself. She considered not answering but then hit the green dot on the left of her phone.

"Detective Parker?"

"No ma'am, this is Detective Fitzgerald."

"Detective, maybe our wires got crossed, but I spoke with a Detective Parker earlier, and we agreed I'd come in to try to help tomorrow."

"Yes, yes, you did. No wires have crossed at all. We have had developments and those require your assistance, if you are willing to give it."

"Developments? Have you found or identified the killer?"

"I think I have. And, I think I understand the motive, too, though we still can't piece it all together."

"And you think I have information that will help with that somehow?"

"Ms. Handly, I am going to cut right to the chase because time is of the essence."

Handly's heart began to palpitate. She could feel it racing internally and beating against the inside of her chest. She moved from the kitchen area as Jeff watched TV. She proceeded into the office at the front of the house and shut the door for privacy as the conversation continued.

"I hardly know how I might help with this."

"Ms. Handly, I've been married 51 years, and I don't dance worth a shit. So don't make me dance now."

"Excuse me?" she asked, somewhat surprised.

"Choose your answers to these questions very carefully, Ms. Handly, as you are speaking to the chief homicide detective of this county."

"Should I get a lawyer? Maybe this conversation isn't a good idea," she said trying to push back on his tone.

"You have that right, but right now, I can tell you that I know *you are not a suspect* in this case. Does that help?"

"Why would I ever be a suspect?" she asked.

"Because you and Mrs. Jensen have been engaged in a long, steamy affair, and you were the last person seen with her — and you were last seen in the back of your car, hand on the passenger window, legs in the air, making love to her."

The phone went completely silent, as if the line had been cut. Janie Handly was in shock.

****

Parker and his team were pounding on the doors of homes along Stratford Landing Drive and the corner of Prosperity Ridge Place. Most of the houses were now finished in this latest section of Brambleton, but infill building on the last few lots continued. The streets were classic Ashburn, new construction. They were a broad swath of rough pavement accented with raised manhole covers. The streets were often littered with construction debris, the worst being a minefield of hidden nails.

On one lot sat a brand-new, brick-front home with lush, green grass and cheesy, just planted, builder-grade landscaping. The lot next door, 10 feet from the exterior wall of the finished home, was a marsh of clay and garbage surrounding the concrete mold of a new basement. This was life in one of the fastest-growing counties in America.

"It was on Prosperity Ridge where Mc-G-Spot tracked our amorous ladies," Parker told his team. "They were parked down there on the dark end, near the unfinished homes, just overlooking the retention pond."

"Perfect lover's lane here. Dark, secluded, difficult to get to," Hogan observed.

"Yes, true indeed."

"Let's get samples of tire tracks on the far end. Take as many pics as you can. Also, let's bag and tag this mud from the street."

"Don't we already know this happened in Handly's car?" Johnson asked.

"Yes, of course we do. But we're going to sample this mud up both ends of the street and hope we find a match on the suspect's vehicle to help place her here. Remember, we need tangible evidence to physically place her here — and we don't have that yet. Once we can do that, we're in business. Unless that lady is looking at buying a house on this street, she would have absolutely no reason to be driving to a dead-end corner in a construction zone."

"I assume we're looking further up both roads, as she likely parked some distance from them," Hogan noted to Parker and for the edification of the team.

"Yes, and we want to cover every point of egress into this area and hit every door about those cameras. Many of these residents are new, and they may have installed cameras as part of the construction or simply to protect their biggest investment," Parker noted.

"Don't forget, builders never give this advice, but the reality is hot new construction zones are targets for criminals and even petty theft among a transient population of workers. The builders don't raise that issue to the first residents in the space, but sometimes a good agent will do so. It's a damn good idea to keep an eye out with so many work crews and strangers in the area."

"Christ, I never thought of that," chimed in Johnson.

"Rookie," Parker bellowed out.

"OK, boys, let's fan out and see what we find. I already called Sully and his team about the mud samples. He is assembling the right expertise for that analysis."

"I am going to fish around and see what I can find," DeMatha announces.

"Please do, and try to give us a chance to find some evidence, too," Parker said, half joking.

****

"Be sure to be dead when I get back, limp dick."

Jensen heard the taunt, and he feared he would be dead. He fought the urge to panic. If he could just stay conscious and alive while his tormentor was gone. He lay motionless, trying not to show any movement even while breathing. He wanted his captor to think he was out and could not hear anything. He listened to what sounded like rustling leaves and the fading sound of footsteps traversing and crunching weeds, twigs and thicket. He knew from the first time he became conscious that he was outside somewhere. He also knew, professional or not, his bindings were too good for him to break free and too tight for him to scream. He wondered, though, "Can I crawl, and if so, where would I crawl?"

While being psychologically browbeaten, Jensen had faded in and out. He first had a sense of panic that blood loss would lead to shock and death. It didn't. It was clearly a day later, and he was not dead. Well, not dead yet. He listened for both the direction of the departing suspect, and more importantly he tried to hear the sound of a vehicle, giving him some idea of his proximity to a road or at least a drivable path.

One thing was clear: He heard no moving traffic. Wherever he was, a main road was not close. The cold night, crisp air, seclusion and wooded surroundings convinced him he could be out in the Blue Ridge Mountains. If true, who knows how far he was from civilization or help.

Jensen heard the distant sound of an engine turning over. He surmised it could not have been more than the equivalent of three residential blocks away, though he wondered if his estimate was off due to the otherwise dead silence that hung in the air, broken only occasional by the chirp of birds or the singing of a locust. The car seemed to spit rock or debris based on the sound of the departure, cluing him in that it was not parked on pavement. It could be parked on a gravel pulloff adjacent to a road, but without the sound of traffic, that seemed unlikely.

His captor was now gone, and he could stop singing his favorite songs in his head. Since he woke up, he had drowned out the torments by playing his favorite music over and over in his mind.

The last song had always been his favorite, but it now had a macabre feel to it. Still, it gave him comfort.

He thought of Jenny and how horrible he was to her — and her to him. But Jack Jensen wasn't angry from hate; he was angry at her from the love that stuck to his soul, a love she had betrayed. It was a love he could never extinguish. He sang the lines of the classic Van Morrison song in his head again, just thinking of her:

> *I wanna rock your gypsy soul*
> *Just like way back in the days of old*
> *Then magnificently we will float*
> *Into the mystic*

****

She hadn't smoked a cigarette since high school, when she did it to be cool. Later, that habit was about calming her nerves when she had those fits of rage. After college, she fought the rage through athletics. She ran and ran and ran. She hiked, and she loved the physicality of it all. It chipped away at the tension — not as successfully as great sex, but it was what she needed to quiet the demons.

Tonight the demons were back. "How did that fucking Jensen slut betray me with the little whore, Ms.-fucking-Polly Purebred?" she thought. "That slimy little PI fuck thinks he is going to give up the goods and drive Jenny closer to that Handly whore. Not anymore." The disconnected and crazy thoughts just poured through her head.

She was covered in sweat and mud, still breathing hard from dragging that "fat little doughboy" into the construction site. She paged through the preview viewer of his Canon XLR, and she was torn between rage and titillation as she saw the pictures of the sex acts Handly made "her" Jenny perform.

She took another long draw on that Marlboro. She was there, outside the house where Handly dropped off Jensen. She had to confront Jenny and tell her of her love to save her from "plain Jane." But how? she wondered. She saw the Jensens' bedroom light on, and she wondered, "Is that fucking pathetic Jensen going to try to go down on Jenny after what Jenny just had in her face?" She drew down on that filtered cancer stick again and thought, "What a fucking weak little poseur."

Something had to be done, she was sure of that. She just had no idea what. Still, she was trembling from the rage. Then Jenny Jensen bolted from the front door of the house through the front lawn and across the street.

"Where the hell is she going?" McDougal's mind raced.

Out next came Jack Jensen. He was trailing 30 yards behind her and making ground. He was going to run nearly right in front of her!

The engine revved, and the tires may have even screeched, but the lights were off, and Jack Jensen never knew what hit him.

Hark, now hear the sailors cry
Smell the sea and feel the sky
Let your soul and spirit fly
Into the mystic

Chapter 18: Take Me Home, Country Roads

"Oh my god," she let out in exasperation and panic. "How could you possibly know about Jenny and me?"

"You were followed for over a month by a private detective, Ms. Handly."

"Oh, God, oh, no — my husband —"

"No," Detective Fitzgerald cut her off. "Jack Jensen hired this guy to follow Jenny, and he picked up your scent, pardon the bad metaphor. I just interviewed him and examined more photos than I would like to detail or discuss."

"Does my husband know?"

"Mrs. Handly, I am not a marriage counselor, nor am I your priest. Adultery isn't a crime in the commonwealth anymore, and I only investigate crimes. Your husband doesn't know. What you elect to tell him is up to you. I can't promise this won't ever come out; that's not up to me. I can promise you that I won't work to make it public."

"I need to save my family with Jenny gone. Oh my God, I'm so ashamed," she said beginning to cry.

"Your shame is for another time and another man. I need your cooperation and details, *right now*. And I need the unvarnished truth, because I think I can catch this killer, and I think it is someone you know."

"What?"

"A woman driving a white Jeep, matching the description of Mary McDougal, stopped at Jenny Jensen's house recently while you were there with her. Do you remember that?"

"Yes, she was dropping off a uniform. It was just days before this mess," she said through soft sobs.

"Ms. Handly, what were you doing in that house with Jenny Jensen right before she arrived?"

The phone went silent again, and Fitz heard the not-so-soft heaving of a crying and broken woman. It was followed by a long, deep breath.

"We made love — right in the living room."

"Did you know that Mrs. McDougal was outside, peeking in for some time?"

"What? I mean, no. But, but honestly, we did hear something before we jumped up and well — finished. I basically ran up the back staircase."

"Did you hear their conversation?"

"I did, most of it. Mary really wanted to tell Jenny something, and Jenny was trying to get rid of her — for obvious reasons. Then Jenny promised her they would get together later that week, alone. Wait. Wait one minute — do you think —?"

"Yes," Fitz said, cutting her off. "I think she saw you. I think she also came there to pledge her love to Jenny Jensen, and I think she left pretty upset about what she likely saw."

"Oh my God. Why would she then want to hurt Jenny? Why not me?"

"You are talking about a stalker, and a sick stalker, Mrs. Handly. In her mind, she might already have been 'involved' with Jenny, and she saw your affair as a betrayal of that."

"She has one fiery temper. She can be like a lunatic sometimes, even at baseball games."

"It turns out she was following Jenny and you, and ultimately she was following the stupid schmuck hired to follow Jenny by her husband."

"Jenny was terrified for her life. She said she had a stalker, and she showed me some of the sick, crazy emails the stalker sent. She thought it was all part of a psychological operation by Jack, and she even feared Jack would kill her or me."

"We think she knocked out the PI on the night she was murdered, after catching him photographing you two in that car. My guess is she followed Jensen home, and somehow she murdered Jenny. What we don't know is what happened to Jack Jensen, other than we think she ran him over with her car."

"Oh my God, I thought Jack was the suspect. I saw it on the news."

"You and everyone else were meant to see that. We wanted to flush out the killer and make the killer feel safe."

"This is too much. You think Jack is dead?"

"I don't know, but I am putting a car outside your door for protection. Don't leave your house tonight. I have to run; we need to find Mary McDougal. And Ms. Handly — not one word about Jack Jensen. Do we understand each other?"

"Yes — not one word," she repeated.

Handly put down the phone and broke into a rhythmic sobbing. Jenny was dead. Jack might be dead too, and she was responsible for it all. Her anguish turned to wailing, and Jeff Handly appeared at the door, looking down on her and signaling for her to keep it down. Janie knew that meant the kids might hear her. Still, she couldn't stop.

He walked in, reached down and held her. She sobbed on his shoulder and said, "I never deserved your love."

Handly held her tighter, hoping the embrace would lock in and force down the shame he carried for his affair with Jenny Jensen.

****

"I have a 20 on a gray, ragtop Jeep Wrangler parked in front of the McDougals' house. There is also a Camry here parked in the driveway but no sign of a white Jeep," reported deputy Simpson. "It could be in the garage, I suppose."

"You say there is a gray Jeep parked in front of the house on the street?"

"Copy that, it's affirmative."

"Can you see any damage to the vehicle grille or hood?" Fitz asked, more than a bit excited.

"Not from this angle. It's parked the wrong way, and the front is out of view. You want me to get out and look?"

The sheriff's cruiser had pulled up in front of the McDougal house unnoticed. In the Willowsford neighborhood on the south side of Route 50, like most of the southeastern rim of Loudoun County, the sight of police does not alarm people. And in this case, it wasn't even clear anyone had seen it arrive. Simpson glided up quietly in the dark with the cherry tops off. He parked facing the direction he was driving, but the Wrangler was parked the same way, on the opposite side of the street, a common parking violation often overlooked in most communities.

"Simpson, no, stand pat. I am en route. Sit on the house and car until I get there in about 5 minutes," Fitz commanded.

Moments later a car banged an aggressive turn on the suburban street and raced toward the McDougal home. Simpson first heard the screech and then saw the vehicle moving up the road out of the corner of his eye as it came into view in his rear-view mirror.

Simpson cracked open his door, intending to meet the driver in the street and find out where the fire was that necessitated the speeding and reckless driving.

Rather than slow down, the car exploded toward him. He froze — and that cost him his life. He may never have realized it was the white Jeep of Mary McDougal.

It's hard to know what traveled farther, the open door of the car ripped from its hinges or the lifeless and broken body of the unsuspecting sheriff's deputy.

Mary McDougal never broke stride. She kept going. She rolled past her house with that wretched family she had come to hate. The pathetic husband and needy kids who were obstacles to her love, she reasoned. She never should have left the mountains to fake this charade, she thought: "I'll bury Jack Jensen for good and disappear into the wilderness."

Indeed, a lifetime of training and hiking made her ready for this. After all, her plan all along was to disappear off the grid with Jenny, making love each day with mountain views. They would hike their way deep into the country, and no one would find them. She already had her hiking gear and work tools packed, not to mention her go bag of clothes. She would have preferred the Wrangler for this task, but no time to stop now.

She would disappear, she thought, into the mountains. Maybe she would be "another victim" of that psycho Jack Jensen. This wasn't how she had drawn up the plan, but the plan could still work, she convinced herself.

****

Jimmy McDougal was no rocket scientist. He was the essence of a dumb jock and high school hero who never grew up. Narcissistic, selfish and often a schemer, his best-known skill in the baseball community was making enemies of people he used to further his own interests. Two things you could be sure of, if Jimmy was giving his time to other kids, there was a profit motive.

The McDougals had gone from regulars to outcasts in the famous Loudoun South baseball mafia. So Jimmy started trying to build his own. He wasn't much of a don. While he tried to rebuild profit opportunities upselling his players on paid lessons, his wife handled everything else.

Indeed, Jimmy left all the intellectual obligations to Mary, a computer whiz and the IT director for a large association of private schools. As two dysfunctional people, he and Mary had a relationship that "worked." That is, even if no one else liked them, they worked well together. They seemed to have a symbiosis that fed off their joint narcissism and obsession with climbing the very short social ladder of exurbia.

A day before the crash outside his door, Jimmy was shocked when his wife sent him a long email showing that the crazy Jack Jensen had been stalking her. She included in that message some cut-and-pasted paragraphs she claimed were from emails that Jensen sent her. Jimmy read it once and fumed about that "sick fuck" Jensen. In the email to her husband, Mary told him she was a little afraid, and she wanted to stay away from the house as much as she could until they found Jack Jensen. She wrote, "I'm worried he might have killed her over his obsession with me."

The tawdry and lewd comments she copied from a purported Jensen email made it clear to Jimmy that Jack Jensen wanted to fuck his wife and have her to himself. At the bottom of the email, she told her husband, "Keep a close eye on the kids. I am headed to my aunt's in PA for a visit. He won't track me there."

They spoke by phone that day, and Jimmy was fuming. He wanted to go to the police. She convinced him not to do it, promising to return that night to see him.

The last thing she texted him was, "I'll be home tonight, safe and sound, I am sure. I'll show you what love looks like when I get there."

Jimmy needed that little emotional pat on the head, like a good loyal little dog. He never gave the email another thought until he and his neighbors were outside on their cellphones snapping pictures as one decent man tried to revive the clearly dead Deputy Simpson.

When Fitzgerald arrived on the scene, he hunted down Jimmy McDougal. A neighbor pointed him out.

"Jimmy McDougal," Fitz said moving with dispatch toward him holding out his badge.

"Yes, sir."

"Do you know the location of your wife right now?"

"My wife? Oh my god, is she OK? Did that lunatic Jensen kidnap her?"

"What?" Fitzgerald looked at him, puzzled, as if he'd landed in an alternate universe. "Your wife is a suspect in the murder of Jenny Jensen," Fitz said matter-of-factly.

"Hey, you dumb mope. Jensen killed his own wife, and now he is after my wife, who he's been fucking stalking. Do you even have any detectives working on this case?"

"No, sir, we just thought we would leave the whole incident unsolved until some slap-dick like you in sweatpants and slides tells us how it went down."

McDougal could feel the authority in Fitzgerald's voice, and he retreated to the very defense Mary was counting on.

"Hey, big guy, I have proof right in my house. Come on in and I will show you the email. Jack Jensen is your man."

"You have emails of Jensen stalking and harassing your wife?"

"You bet, and she was terrified he was out to get her. I think he followed her all day and took her right now."

"That's quite an accusation. Can I see the email? And, when is the last time you heard from your wife?"

"Follow me, I'll get the email for you. And she texted me earlier today. I have that right here.

"Jimmy-J, get out of the way, son. I am helping the police," McDougal told his inquisitive young son Jimmy Jr., who was still fuming that he couldn't go outside and see the accident.

McDougal fumbled to pull up the email but found it and dutifully printed out a copy. Fitz looked at it and read it twice.

"This is very helpful. I will take a picture of it and send it to my team. Do you mind if I keep the hard copy?"

"No, go right ahead. See, I told you she might be a victim. She's no damn suspect."

"Yes, you told me indeed. Have you tried to call her or text her since this accident?"

"Both. I get nothing."

"I wouldn't panic, sir, I'm sure we will find her safe and sound," he said paternalistically.

"You better," McDougal announced halfheartedly, more like a wish than a command.

"Oh, one more thing if you can, Mr. McDougal, please. You have been so helpful so far."

"Yes, thanks — anything."

"Maybe your wife checked in at her job for something, is that possible?"

"Oh, heck, no, she's an IT pro for a school association. Most of her work is from home."

"You don't say. Good for her."

"Yes, well, she has all those fancy technical computer skills. They come in real handy in this part of the world."

"No doubt, they can sure help with almost anything," Fitz said as he looked at the seemingly completely clueless Jimmy.

"Jimmy-J," Detective Fitz said in a booming voice to the cute 7-year-old. "Thanks for letting your dad help me. You know how you can be smart like him?"

"No, sir," said the precocious little fellow.

"Keep reading and learning, son, read and learn. For helping me, buddy, I want to give you a very special card. See, this card has my name and number on it. If your friends at school ask who you helped, you tell them, this guy. And, if you ever need my help, call me — just tell them it's Jimmy-J. Deal?"

"Yes, sir," Jimmy-J snapped with a huge smile.

Fitz stood outside as they loaded his officer in the coroner's wagon. He turned to the gaggle of sheriff's deputies who watched him as he saluted the fallen officer. They snapped to attention behind him.

"Simpson doesn't ride alone, you hear me? Someone ride with him, and I want every one of you to guide him home on this journey. Men, some son-of-a-bitch just made this personal to our department. We'll find that bastard, and we'll give Simpson the honor any fallen officer deserves — the respect of his colleagues."

"Yes sir," the deputies shouted in unison.

"Take him home, boys."

****

Jensen had managed to crawl no more than 20 or 30 feet through the heavy brush. The way he was bound, his weakness and the rag in his throat made the heroic effort nearly impossible. He wouldn't reach that road in under an hour, even if he could somehow continue. He had a new plan — and it wasn't great, but he was hoping to buy time. Time gave his FBI colleagues and any locals a chance, albeit small, to find him. He only prayed that when they did, it would be a rescue mission and not a recovery.

Jack thought of his boys and his wife. Even if it was over with Jenny, those boys needed their father. He decided that he was going home to them no matter what it took. He was not meant to die here like this. He wouldn't let it happen.

Now that he had wiggled the blindfold off rubbing his head on the ground, he began to search for two things. He needed anything that could cut his bindings. At the same time, he needed a spot where he might obscure his position. If he could stay hidden in the dark, he could buy more time. The thought of this small chance caused him to smile ever so slightly into the darkness.

He was bloodied, wounded, weak, sick and likely dying. But he felt the crusted blood crack on his face for the first time as his cheeks found a new direction to move. Jack Jensen's smile also broke through the pain and torture to find humanity's greatest weapon — hope. He then began singing a new song in his head. While he made no outward noise at all, the notes were dancing, and the stadium that filled his head was singing in unison.

Almost heaven, West Virginia
Blue Ridge Mountains, Shenandoah River
Life is old there, older than the trees
Younger than the mountains, blowing like a breeze

Country roads, take me home
To the place I belong
West Virginia, mountain mama
Take me home, country roads

Chapter 19: Running With the Devil

"Christ, what the hell happened to Simpson, chief?" Parker blurted out as he answered the call from Fitz.

"He's gone, and that crazy lady killed him."

"McDougal?"

"Yes — 'McCrazy' — she set this whole thing up, and her husband is as dumb as a post. She sent him a bullshit email with some cut-and-paste, made-up lurid lines purportedly from — wait for it — Jensen."

"What? I don't follow at all."

"She bought the news reports that we think Jack Jensen is the killer. So she used her mad computer skills to fool her gullible husband that Jack Jensen was stalking her."

"Why would she do that?"

"Easy. She takes off into hiding, leaves that schmuck and sets the stage to blame it all on Jensen. She must have Jensen's body, which I fear she got rid of today. The whole plan is great, except for the part where we know Jensen isn't a killer on the run but a victim in a ditch or pond or wood chipper. The dumbass husband couldn't wait to run out and show me the email that 'proved' Jensen was stalking her."

"So, she faked an email from Jack Jensen?"

"Well, it was a good fake for Jimmy numb-nuts McDougal, because he's a moron's moron. The email doesn't have any headers or identifying information. Her cut-and-paste quotes in the email are just made-up lines she put in quotes. The lady wrote the whole thing, and dumb Jimmy there thinks it's gospel. He literally thinks Jack Jensen kidnapped his wife and ran over Simpson."

"That guy must be, as Bugs Bunny once said, a maroon."

"How is the search going over there on Little Mumbai's version of Lovers' Lane?" Fitz asked referring to a new section of Brambleton with a very heavy Indian population.

"It's a dry hole here. We can't find a thing. No one has a camera. We have nothing tangible — but I did order the collection of mud samples all up and down the street. I am hoping to tie the mud and clay to her car. I figure we can put her in this neighborhood, on a street to nowhere, by the site of an assault."

"Wait, I'll be right back," he yelled through the phone to Parker.

Fitz leaped out of the car. He walked over and deftly took a picture of the front of the gray Jeep. He then grabbed an evidence bag from the CI team and strolled with purpose back to the street side of the Jeep Wrangler sitting in plain sight on a public street. He used a key off his ring to peel some caked mud off the back splash guard.

"Hey, are you puncturing my wife's tire?" Jimmy McDougal yelled from the lawn.

"No, Mr. McDougal, just her alibi," Fitz said as he walked to the car.

"Parker — *Parker* — you still there?"

"Yes, boss."

"I have a sample from the Wrangler, whose hood is all banged up. Let's see if it matches your mud collection. I am headed back to the war room. What has DeMatha found?"

"He's got a big, fat zero so far, too. He said he will stay the night and walk home. He wants to hit it at first light."

"No, this will all be over before first light. If he wants in, bring him back to the war room. Meanwhile, send a team back to Jensen's and have them canvass the neighborhood for any security camera video too. Let's see if we can put that Jeep in the neighborhood. I have to run; I have Harper-O incoming. I'll take this first, but get back to the war room ASAP."

"Dad, we got the data warrant," Harper told him on the other line, "and we should have the prior location of her phone in 10 minutes. I have worked with someone in that company before, and with the warrant, he pulled this all on an expedited basis."

"Loudoun County only hires the damn finest CAs. Put that on record. I will be in the war room in 10 minutes. Tell the investigative team that McDougal has represented in an email, by text and verbally to her husband that she was in central PA visiting family today. Let's light her up right now and let's see if she is lying. Get my affidavit for her arrest warrant typed up — we will be ready to go shortly. Right now, I need a BOLO from my team out to all local law enforcement. She can't be 20 minutes from this scene."

"Dad, that BOLO is already out."

"What? Yes, right before Simpson was struck, he asked for the BOLO in case anyone saw the car coming inbound to the house."

"No kidding? Good cop — he did us a solid. I should have made that happen the first two minutes I was there, I got caught up in the suspect's husband's nonsense. Simpson was dead on the damned pavement and still he backed me up." Fitzgerald's voice cracked.

"Dad, are you all right?"

"Yes, honey. I am tired of losing good guys. Young, strong, heroic men and women who get up and stand a damned post every day and who die because people are scum. Simpson — he was a cop to the end, and I hate that I lost him on my watch."

"You can't protect them all, Dad."

262

"Maybe, but I don't have to accept the losses lightly. Thanks Harper. I will see you shortly."

"OK. See you."

"Wait," Fitz yelled. "Get my team — direct orders, right now. Tell them to get feedback immediately on the plate readers on the interstates. Let's see if we can find her electronically even if we don't have eyes on her yet. I want to know where she is going."

"Done, and a great call. Some of those readers, like the ones on I-66, for example, are real-time," Harper noted.

****

Mary McDougal was flying out Route 50 to Route 15 and on her way south to Interstate 66. That bustling artery would take her from the exurbs to the mountains in less than 45 minutes.

It was dark, and the damage to her vehicle, including the splash of blood on the hood, was not readily obvious to other vehicles driving at night. Her grille and hood had taken a beating, but remarkably, she hadn't lost the passenger's side headlight, so from nearly any distance her Jeep of death looked normal, minus the little fender bender.

She drew down on another Marlboro. Grabbed the Apothic Red Blend in her passenger's seat and washed her harsh ashtray breath clean with some cheap red grapes. She would make the site in an hour or less and be back to Jensen in 15 minutes after that. She'd park in the camper's lot, which would make the hike a bit longer. But once he was on the ground, she'd be as free as a bird — and living among them, she thought.

She took a long drag again, followed with a gulp of the red stuff, and cranked up the radio. She laughed her distinctive witches' cackle as the radio played the ironic pop hit "The Club Can't Even Handle Me Right Now."

****

Fitz was hauling balls, as he liked to say. He cut over the new finished section of Fleetwood to Evergreen. Once on that windy country road, he opened up the Chevelle to see what she had and to shorten the commute to the war room. He slipped in the mix tape, pounded the pedal and let the amps muffle the roar of his V-8. Van Halen set the exact right pace:

> *Yeah, yeah, ah, yeah*
> *I live my life like there's no tomorrow*
> *And all I've got, I had to steal*
> *Least I don't need to beg or borrow*
> *Yes I'm livin' at a pace that kills*
> *Ooh, yeah*
> *(Ahh)*
> *Runnin' with the devil*
> *(Ahh-hah, yeah)*
> *(Woo-hoo-oo)*
> *Runnin' with the devil*

Fitz couldn't sing a lick, not one note. But no red-blooded American can burn rubber in a '71 Chevelle V-8 playing Van Halen without screaming out the lyrics, so appropriate for his night and the suspect — "Running with the Devil."

When Fitz hit the war room, Parker was coming around the bend with DeMatha. Harper-O and Kelley were working on an affidavit for an arrest warrant. Tankersley was in there trying to look important and in charge while doing nothing. Deputy Houser stopped everyone in the room when he yelled, "I got her."

"What?" Fitz barked.

"Her cell hasn't been in PA today, yesterday or any other time in the last five days. She pinged off towers in Haymarket and then out in Rappahannock. She also lit up a tower in Shenandoah. Now the plate reader just found her on 66 west."

"Jesus Christ," Fitz yelled.

"What if Jensen is alive?"

"What?"

"Why did she go to the mountains and back and then back out there again?"

DeMatha leaped out of the seat he had just found in the room. "If Jensen was dead and disposed of, she'd likely be going any direction but that one."

Fitz jumped back in: "You bet. My guess is she ran out of time earlier today and couldn't finish the job, or she had a timeline to meet and missed it."

"Yes," said Parker. "She rode back in to keep the promise to her old man or to set up the kidnapping story. When she saw the sheriff's car, she panicked and ran him over."

"Or she saw an opportunity to better flesh out the kidnapping idea," DeMatha added.

Fitz jumped in again to the frenetic discussion, "Talk about reckless. Anyone could have seen her on her own street. We are not dealing with a rational person. This isn't just a cold, calculating stalker. She's a psychopath, likely in a psychotic episode."

"I'll tell you something else, Fitz," DeMatha offered. "She bought that news story on Jensen hook, line and sinker. She thinks we're chasing him. She has no idea we know about his injuries and likely death. So she is thinking that if she wasn't seen at the hit and run, no one is looking for her, let alone looking at her as a suspect."

"Why run down Simpson then?" Parker asked.

"That's easy; she's trying to pin that on the dead Jensen with her bullshit stalker tale. It all works in her head. She's not a suspect now — Jensen is. So when she goes missing, she becomes his victim. She's off to disappear."

"Well, we have some friends who can help us track her now."

Sheriff Tankersley jumped in to take over the situation. "You boys get every local sheriff past the last exit she was spotted, and you tell them to follow her ass. Have them set up and stop her if they can on 66. Call those sheriffs, Parker, and you tell them I said old Tank needs every man they have to catch a cop killer."

The room just went silent as Tank tried to take control of an investigation about which he knew nothing and then compounded his felony by directing men who did not respect him.
Fitz jumped on top of the first pause and directed his team.

"We need some air support — and we have a new friend in DC who has air support *and* who is missing a man. I will call the director and see if we can get people in the air on pursuit. Meanwhile, let's direct all attention to video from the park and Skyline Drive for that car. I figure she can't have moved a man that big, by herself, into the mountains very easily. Let's work up some analysis on that reality. If we find the last major location she is spotted, we can build a grid. If there's any chance Jensen is alive, Wray will send an army for him."

After Fitz finished, he put his hand on Tankersley's shoulder and whispered something in his ear. It was a good 25 seconds, and Tankersley looked pained to hear it. When Fitzgerald was done, he left the room.

"Parker," yelled Tankersley, "new plan. Get those sheriffs on the line and tell them to put their best plainclothes on this pursuit. Stay back. We don't want to capture this woman before she leads us as close as possible to Jensen."

"Yes, sir, sheriff, that's some sound strategy, sir."

DeMatha almost busted a gut as he quickly bolted out the door.

Fitz was on the direct dial to the FBI director. He broke down the case and the amazing developments in just the past few minutes. "The bottom line, Director, is that we need your resources to find Jensen and capture the woman who murdered his wife and one of my men," Fitz said through his cellphone.

"I can't say for sure he is alive. I wish I could. We theorize she would not have come all the way back from that location and then return there if he weren't. But we can't be sure. We still have to prepare the reality that this is a recovery mission and not a rescue mission," Fitz added, making sure he had not falsely raised hope too high.

He then simply said, "Thank you, sir, I'll wait to hear from you."

"What did he say, he'd do his best?" asked a skeptical DeMatha.

"He said he has three choppers immediately ready to deploy, including a tactical team to hit the mountains. He reminded me that they have friends in other agencies in them there mountains and he would ask for a courtesy for resources in the air. Basically, he is deploying an army."

"Really? Why do you have to 'wait to hear from him'?" DeMatha pushed back.

"Oh — he's coming to get me with one of those helos, and he said he'll ping me when he's five minutes out. He has two seats; do you like to fly?"

"No shit?"

"No shit."

****

The force of the blow sent Jack Jensen flying. McDougal nailed him as he ran across Conquest from his own home. She never hit the brakes until he landed, and even then, she came to a routine, unpanicked stop. Jenny Jensen heard the crash behind her as she was running. She looked back to see the carnage. "Oh my God!"

Instinctively, she ran to the man from whom she had just been running. "Oh my God … oh my God … Jack, are you all right? How the hell did this happen?" she said aloud. He was out cold and hurt badly, bleeding from a head wound. She looked up and saw a familiar silhouette above her, it was bathed by the backlight of a late-model white Jeep. Before she could ask for help, the all-too-familiar voice spoke.

"He's dead — and lucky for you."

"What, are you crazy? He's not dead. I have to call 911."

"Jenny, it's a blessing. We can finally be together. I took care of him for you."

As Mary McDougal stepped out of the glare, Jenny sprang to her feet. "Mary? Mary, have you lost your fucking mind? Together? What are you talking about? You took care of him? He's the father of my kids, or are you fucking insane?"

"I have never been saner. You know that you love me, and now we can be together forever without this stiff. Help me load the

268

deadbeat in my car," she said with the same tone one might use asking a friend the grab the heavy end of sofa to move.

"You crazy psycho-bitch. Love you? I don't even fucking like you or your limp-dick husband."

Jenny looked at her in shock. She seemingly couldn't move. Mary methodically loaded Jack Jensen's unconscious body into the car and pulled her vehicle over as if to park for the evening right out front — just like she were coming home from the movies. Nothing about her movements indicated panic or rage. But she raged for sure.

Jenny snapped out of it and furiously grabbed at her pockets looking for her phone. She didn't find it, and then, as McDougal got back out of her car, Jenny ran for the house. Mary McDougal followed her, jogging up the pathway of the Jensen house and through the wide-open door. Jensen had a phone in her hand.

"Put down the phone, honey, we have to go if we're going to make it to our cabin for sunrise."

"What. Get the hell out of here," Jenny barked as she turned away and began to punch in the numbers on the handset. She made the 9 and the 1, but she got no further. McDougal smashed Jenny over the head with her son's bright-orange, 30-inch, drop-11, Mako Little League bat. It was now a $400 murder weapon.

Jenny crumpled to the floor, and McDougal slugged her again, muttering to herself, "You *did* love me, you dumb bitch — you *loved* me! Why did *you* make me do this?"

Her rage had betrayed her again. Her Jenny was dead. In a blink, Mary looked almost catatonic. But her mind went to work on a plan. She knew what she had to do. Yes, she would stage the body to look like a sex crime. She would dispose of Jack, and the murder might be thought of as a "husband gone mad after finding out what a whore his wife was," she reasoned. She could see to that, too.

269

McDougal knew exactly what the panties had in them, she thought; "they are damp with the combined love juices of that whore Handly and her sex slave Jenny." She would take them with her and mail them and Mc-G-Spot's photos to the sheriff as a present from Jack Jensen. The note would read, "The whore got the beating she deserved."

McDougal's last deed, the horrific act of sodomy-by-Swiffer, might have been over the top, but it satisfied her burning rage. "Time to clean up your own mess — bitch!" she whispered in Jenny's cold, dead ear.

She strolled right out the front door like she just had a nice glass of wine and was carrying some warmer clothes for the night on the deck. Tucked under her arm was that bright-orange bat her son had obviously lent his teammate.

Mary McDougal lost her mind sometime long before that night. It was just that in this moment, she lost all control of the demons that tormented her. Now it was all about breaking free from her crappy life and living free — free from those who kept her from Jenny. As she jumped back in her car, she realized, "I'm also free now from those who made me do that to Jenny."

First, however, she needed to find a nice place to store Jack Jensen. "He sure didn't deserve a decent view in the mountains," she thought. "But hey, the guy would make some great fertilizer."

****

"Here's a shocker: The mud and the clay are a match from McDougal's old Jeep to the road where Mc-G-Spot was assaulted," Parker announced to the team.

"We have enough for a warrant to search her home. We can get the Jeep on the street, too. I want every detail in that warrant. Our boys will catch her, and if she lives, we need to start building this case. I will check in with the boss and see what the update is on the man — ah — woman-hunt."

****

It was cold, too cold for Jack. He was so weak. He had made it this far, whatever that meant. He did find a small ditch under a large rotted fallen tree. He burrowed his way into it, pulling as much foliage as he could on top of himself. He needed it for cover, and he really needed it for warmth.

He estimated he had traveled over 150 feet from his original location, maybe more. He made his way through some much rougher thicket, and he hoped that to the untrained eye, his path would not be so obvious. He was sure, in the dark, that no one would easily track the otherwise very trackable path of a man who had to slither and hop, lying flat and essentially flattening his own trail.

Jack had no idea what time it was, but the sun had long ago set. His immediate plan was simple. He would stay concealed safely in the dark. If he could just not die of his wounds, his hunger, dehydration, blood loss, hypothermia or shock, he might see the sun rise one more time. By tomorrow night, he thought, "I will be either killed or dead."

Jack never thought of his life as on the clock, but in that moment, he was smart enough to know that McDougal would kill him when she found him, or nature would finish him off by the next night even if he wasn't found.

To keep warm, he resolved to use his energy to work the bindings on his hands across a dull knob in the stump above him.

Lying face down in the muck, sharing a wet, muddy ditch with unknown wildlife was hard enough, but the gag and rag made the position worse for his limited breathing. He feared he might pass out or suffocate. But the reward, the possibility that the effort would both keep him warm and break his bindings, that was a risk worth taking, particularly for a life on the clock.

"Live, Jack — live, damn it. You can do this," he said to himself.

****

"I loved her, Jeff," Janie Handly said to her husband.

"I know, sweetheart. I know how much you loved her."

"No. No, you don't. I mean, I *loved* her — I was *in love* with her. And she loved me the same way, deeply." Janie said, her voice potent mix of shame and sorrow. As the words left her lips, she feared the coming wrath, the loss of her family and the shock and anger from her husband.

Jeff Handly loosened his grip and moved away slowly, releasing the warm embrace that previously held his broken wife. He now looked her in the eye.

"You're a beautiful woman, Janie Handly. That's both inside *and* outside. I don't know if Jenny Jensen was capable of love, but with you how could she not be mad, sick, in love?"

The tears continued streaming down Janie's face. They ran hot down her cheeks and rolled off her chin. In that instant, though, as his words permeated her heart and the river of tears flowing down both cheeks were diverted, Janie Handly broke into a smile. It was a discernable and honest smile inspired by the compassion of her husband.

"I appreciate your love, Jeff, but I don't deserve it, and I am not sure anymore how to reciprocate it. You deserve more."

"Love isn't about deserving," Jeff said softly. "Janie, sometimes love is simply about enduring. The passion sometimes cools to a few graying embers, and the heat is seemingly insufficient for the needs. But it is when our hearts grow colder that we must huddle closest. *That's love's challenge.*"

She stared up at her husband now, captivated by his words, which stroked her broken soul as gently as his large, strong hands again held her. "How had she lost her connection to this man?" she wondered.

"I remember your sweetness when we first met, back in college. That seems like another lifetime. I fell in love with that passion — not just the words but the kindness you always showed. How did we lose all that love?" she asked, genuinely seeking truth.

"Did we lose it? Or did we just neglect it? Lose our love? No, Janie, we lost *our way,*" he explained.

"Look at what love built, right here. Don't look at the material parts of this life of comfort into which the habits of the uninspired fell. Look in the room at the top of the hall and then the one across from it. *Our* love built a family. We persevered at the toughest times, and then forgot to embrace the success of that love. What's love, Janie? Love is my being so happy for you that you found it again. Love is that I can't be angry that you were happy. That's love, and that's how much love I have for you."

Janie pressed her hand against Jeff's cheek.

"Jenny told me about you and her," she said. "She needed me to know. Did you love her, too?"

"Love her? No. I was a fool, just a weak stupid fool who found a thrill in the attention of a woman who lived for that game. I was infatuated by her attention. Later, I simply grew to dislike how wretched I felt for my own weakness. She made me miss the love I had with you."

"I want to love again," she told him, feeling the sincerity in his shame and the love in his words, eyes, touch and heart.

"Then let's love again — forever," he said softly.

She lay her head in his chest, and he ran his arms down her back with that familiarity that is a couple's unique imprint of love.

"Forever," she said softly back to him.

****

As the director's helicopter left the Loudoun Inova Hospital helipad, Fitz was taking real-time updates on the undercover surveillance of the fugitive McDougal.

"She's in the park now on Skyline Drive. We have her tagged by air using your unit, sir," he told the director.

"It's just a matter of time before she stops. Once she does, we will put a tactical team right on top of her," Wray assured Fitz.

"Our people estimate that wherever she parks, she likely can't be more than a mile inside the trail system. There is no way she can carry a man his size farther than that and do so without notice. If I had to bet, she is using one of the handful of off-road car trails that give some deep-site campers access to hiking farther in the mountain."

"Are you coordinating with the park for updated topography and trail info?" Wray asked Fitz.

"Yes, in fact, one of the advantages of being around so long is I have interacted with these rangers for years, and they love their job as much as I do. I've known the head park ranger for two decades. He has been working these mountains for 35 years. He says where she's gone, only three such off-road car trails exist. Whichever one she chooses, we can put your team down in the surrounding radius and work our way in around the grid."

"You think there is any chance Jensen's alive?"

"Her movements are hard to explain if he were not alive. But then, she's a crazy psycho. Still, I think he is either dead, and she couldn't finish the disposal, or he is alive, and she needs to finish him off and dispose of him."

****

When the tape that bound his raw, cramped, bleeding hands finally broke, Jack collapsed from exhaustion. He couldn't even muster the strength to completely break free without resting. There was no adrenaline. He was spent, and he feared his time might be closer than expected. He dozed on and off, battling a dream world where he imagined himself awake and fighting. He wasn't. He was drowsy, passed out and nearing the finish of a fight most men would long ago have lost.

Then he heard the sound. It was faint, no doubt. But he'd heard it hundreds of times before. In his life with the HIG unit, he visited many sites: foreign, domestic, on water, in the mountains and those super-remote, so-called black sites. The primary mode of transportation, nearly always, to those destinations was helicopter. Jack knew the type of helicopter by the sound he was hearing. Jack knew this particular sound really well, because he had been on many tactical FBI flights.

"My boys are in the neighborhood," he thought. *Country roads, take me home.*

Chapter 20: The Sounds of Silence

Mary McDougal was drunk *and* crazy. That unique combination wasn't as combustible as one might think. Her rage had lost a bit of its edge. She was almost a happy drunk — if she had been sane enough to think about it. She knew this: She was going to be even happier when she cracked Jensen over his head, shoved him in that nice hole and headed off to her base camp set up about 6 miles southeast of the trail. "I'll be burrowed into these mountains like a tick on deer. Even if someone thought to look, they'll never find me," she cackled to herself. The plan was easier than she imagined. She cut the engine, grabbed her gear and headed out for the trail.

The myth of the stealth black helicopter was just that, a myth. However, helicopter noise reduction strategies were real, and the FBI's tac team employed that exact technology. It was a distinctive sound, a bit more like a muffled helicopter that one might think is 8 to 10 miles out rather than nearly overhead. The sound Jack Jensen knew so well was completely foreign to Mary McDougal. She never even heard it.

****

"Eyes are on her. She's out of the vehicle and carrying gear. She's on her way up the trail," Fitz reported to the director. Their bird was seconds out from a makeshift command post now taking shape no more than a half mile from where McDougal exited her vehicle. When it put down, Fitz leaped out of it like a paratrooper and met one of his deputies waiting for him.

"Put me within 100 yards of that trail."

"Sir?" he asked

The director got off and yelled after Fitzgerald, "Hey, let's leave this to the tac team, Fitz."

"Give them my position. I am going in. You have nobody with more jungle fighting experience than me, I promise you that."

The director knew he wasn't stopping Fitzgerald, and he barked orders to his team to be ready to take word on the detective's location and entry point to avoid a confrontation. The ranger took Fitz in the upside of the trail about 175 yards to the west of the entrance where McDougal headed. Fitz studied the park map as the vehicle hurried him to the drop point. They radioed back the information to the director and his team, and Fitz grabbed an extra clip and a set of cuffs.

"Tell the director to get his boys on that grid and find his guy," he said. "I'll find McCrazy."

****

Jack Jensen tore the remnants of the duct tape off his face, peeling skin and scabs. Nothing ever felt better. He pulled the rag from his mouth and instantly dry-heaved. He then caught a long, deep, cleansing breath. Ironically, when he did, he immediately realized how bad that rib injury was on his left side. He was drawing in air as if each breath was his first or could be his last. "That cold air never tasted so sweet," he thought. Now, he needed to get the bindings off around his knees and ankles, and he would be a free man — if he could stand.

****

McDougal knew the way back to Jensen from her original point of entry. But this path had been well worn by her, too. In the dark, however, she needed a small camping utility light to illuminate the way. The trail was mostly quiet, but there was the decided sound of rustling that often comes with wildlife on the move. Up here, it was mostly deer, birds and smaller varmints, from the distinctively brown squirrels to beaver. Occasionally, there was a black bear, too.

McDougal was used to the rustling sounds in the distance of moving brush and snapping twigs, so she never thought much about those distinctive noises as she worked her way up the steeper and tough trail. This was no grandpa path here, and tough as it was getting Jensen up from the other side, she wouldn't have been able to do that coming up this side.

Alone, however, she made quick time, even with the haze of a half a bottle of vino.

****

Fitz was moving in bursts. He too had a small light to help him find his way, but he used it only in intervals. He was working on a trajectory with the idea that he could cut off McDougal above her position. Likewise, he designed his sporadic movements to emulate the sound of wildlife, which often shot through the thicket, stopped, waited, listened and moved again.

He not only didn't want to alert her to his position; he wanted to listen for *her* position, if possible. Compass in hand and enough moonlight to stake out his desired direction, Fitz was moving apace and making great time. If she stayed on the trail as he hoped, he would intercept her from above very shortly.

Fitz sure wasn't having any flashbacks. But, he certainly considered the reality that tracking a crazy woman in the woods at night was nowhere near as dangerous as taking point in the jungles of Southeast Asia, memories he'd just as soon forget.

****

Jack Jensen was free — and on his feet, barely. He could not stand well, and his legs were almost useless, as if they had atrophied. He worked to squeeze blood into them, but he feared his grave injuries were more the source of his weakness and problems. Jack no longer heard those choppers, and that worried him.

Had he been wrong? he wondered. Maybe no one was looking for him. Jack knew, however, one person would be back, and that meant he had to beat feet away from this location as quickly as possible. He struggled to get his bearings. He had created markers to remind him of the direction back toward the trail where he heard the car. But in this darkness, even with a bit of moonlight, could he find them? Jack also worried, "Should I risk going that direction? What if I run straight into her? I may not be strong enough to fight her off."

Jack became very still. He was motionless. He needed the break, and he wanted to hear anything around him. It was quiet. It was as silent as he remembered at any time, with just the whisper or chant of insects. Then he heard a rustling sound off to his left — it was not in arm's reach, but it was no more than a short screen pass away. He grabbed the partially rotted and fallen branch he was using to brace himself and prepared to make it a weapon.

The noise ceased. Maybe it was his laser focus on that noise that drowned out the entirety of all sound, but the sound of silence was nearly complete, and it was eerie. Then Jensen heard a whisper, and soft as it was, it clamored through his mind like the clash of a cymbal.

"Jensen, 867. Jensen, 867."

****

Fitz was there, at the trail on his tiny map where everyone agreed McDougal was headed. The question was, had he beaten her there? Was she above him, he wondered, or maybe she already got off the trail? Based on his read of the topography, when she brought Jensen up here, she must have come up the mountain using the trail from the other side. This side was too steep to carry a man of Jensen's size.

Fitz instantly thought of Jensen. He thought it likely that Jensen, if still alive, was above him on either side of the trail or on the other side of the mountain off the trail that headed back down toward the off-road car path. Fitz wasn't sure now if McDougal was close, but he was certain that Jensen had to be.

He sat still, getting a quick breath, relaying his position. He was preparing for McDougal, too. While he processed all these thoughts, his real-life experiences and training, honed in battle decades earlier, had him working to stay aware of his surrounding and the possibility that "McCrazy" could get the jump on him.

Fitz then heard rustling on the path below him and the distinct sound of slightly labored breathing. He spotted a small light and decided that someone was coming up the trail — and that someone was less than 30 yards away.

****

"Jensen, 867, Jensen, 867" — there it was again, Jensen thought, plain and distinct. Into the darkness he repeated back: "Jensen, 867-HIG, Jensen, 867-HIG."

"Jensen, 867-HIG … copy! This is Armstrong, 941-TAC — we are here to bring you home, sir."

Jensen smiled broadly in the darkness. It couldn't be seen, but he felt like it lit up the world: "These are my people using my FBI ID to confirm my identity and find me."

"This is Jensen 867," he repeated, "I am hurt, but I am alone." Jensen realized that it was likely the search team had no idea what danger it might face.

"Copy that, Jensen 867, you're hurt." Then a figure emerged from the darkness nearly right in front of Jack Jensen. It was Special Agent Danton Armstrong.

"You are not alone anymore, Jack Jensen."

Jensen grabbed his arm and fell into Armstrong's grasp. "Thank you — thank God."

"I have Jensen. He's alive. I repeat, *Jensen is alive* — we need medical assistance on my location."

Almost immediately, the director relayed to Fitzgerald that Jensen was found and alive.

"Great news!" he whispered back. "And I have the suspect coming up the path right now."

****

Mary McDougal was slowing as she hit the trail just below the detective. The mix of cigarettes and wine certainly weighed on her, as did her two bags of gear and supplies. In her hand she held her utility knife, which she would use on Jensen to finish him if he were not yet dead.

As she drew within 10 feet of Fitzgerald, he stood out from his position, as if he materialized from an episode of *Star Trek*. He startled Mary McDougal. Before she could even react to the towering figure looking down on her from just yards away, she heard what sounded like the voice of God.

"Mary McDougal, don't move. You're under arrest."

McDougal froze — for a second. Then she cackled that insane laugh that was her trademark even before the insanity kicked in.

"The psycho you're looking for is Jack Jensen," she declared.

"You murdered Jenny Jensen, and you were about to murder Jack Jensen until we just rescued him," Fitz announced with pleasure.

"That little bitch lived," she bellowed, followed by a good laugh. "That's more than I can say for his whore wife."

"McDougal, drop whatever you're holding, get on your knees, lie face down and put your hands behind your back," Fitz commanded.

"I bet you like your women that way, huh — face down and taking orders while you pump them in the can," she sneered.

"McDougal, you have until the count of five, and then I'll assist you."

"Really, just you?" she asked, as she dropped her camping bag to lighten her load.

"Three, two —"

"*One,*" Mary McDougal screamed, as she charged him with the knife extended.

It was a grievous mistake on her part and might have cost her the rest of her tortured life if Fitz had wanted to kill her. He didn't.

282

He disarmed her in one move and faceplanted her on the ground. She banged her head hard on a tree root and was barely conscious after the swift and devastating maneuver.

Fitz radioed in: "I have the suspect. She resisted. Someone tell Peggy Felts I didn't shoot her."

****

Mary McDougal was being transported for treatment for her injuries under heavy guard. At the makeshift headquarters, Director Wray and his team were preparing for a public statement about the rescue of Jack Jensen.

Fitz had just briefed Brad and Tankersley, who were preparing for an 11 a.m. Saturday presser where Detective Fitzgerald agreed to appear.

Fitz and Wray were going to meet in five minutes to see Jensen off to the hospital and to tell him the news of his wife's passing. It would not be a time for all the details, but Fitz insisted, "Jack has the right to know."

Behind the frenetic activity sat one news van. Peggy Felts had just arrived. Fitz had tipped her as he boarded the chopper from Leesburg headed west. She would get her exclusive, as he promised. She was shooting her famous B-roll — which is nothing more than surrounding scenes, people and settings to cut into the production. She'd already prepped her questions and made a few last-minute tweaks to hair and makeup.

Her report would break most of the story of the capture of the murderer. A second news flash by her would then alert the world to the rescue of Jack Jensen, clearing him in this case. Of course, that would not run until Fitz found his kids. For that, he had a quick call to make.

"Bo-dine, it's Detective Fitzgerald," he said after Alan picked up the late-night call on the first ring.

"Detective, it has been a very long day."

"Yes, it has, counselor. And it has ended remarkably. That is why I have called to give you the good news and ask for your help."

"Good news? Please, I could use something."

"We have captured your client's killer."

"You found Jack Jensen?" he asked in complete shock.

"He was not the killer, nor was he involved."

"What — I thought — …"

"Alan, I have almost no time. I need your confidence and cooperation. If you agree to the confidence, I will tell you who we caught and the other remarkable news. Then, I'll ask for your immediate help. Is that a deal?"

"I'll treat it as attorney-client privilege … not a word."

"And, sorry, but that includes Mrs. Bodine, at least until both stories break."

"Yes. Yes, detective, that includes her, too."

"Jack Jensen was taken hostage and left for dead by the killer, who was Mary McDougal."

"That crazy woman killed Jenny and tried to kill Jack, is that what you're saying?"

"An FBI tactical team just rescued Jack Jensen, who is badly injured but expected to make it. I apprehended Mrs. McDougal, who I have nicknamed McCrazy."

"No shit, you got that right. She always had the crazy eyes and the weird cackle."

"Jensen is about to depart for medical treatment. I need you to contact the grandparents and bring the kids to see their father. Give me your number and I'll text you the hospital info once I confirm it."

"I can do that. I am sure I can reach them."

"Jensen has no idea his wife has been murdered, and I'm about to inform him. He can use the support of those boys. There are tough times ahead but times they can conquer as a family."

"Well, Columbo, it turns out you're not a half-bad cop after all," Bodine said with a chuckle.

"Thanks, Bo-*dean* — let the record reflect you're one of my favorite A-hole lawyers."

"Touché," Bodine laughed. "Send the info and I'll connect the grandparents right now."

"Thanks, we need to see that the family hears this news from us first."

"Got it," he said and hung up without a goodbye, another Bodine trademark.

****

"This is Peggy Felts with breaking news and an extraordinary development in the murder case of Jenny Jensen, wife of an FBI special agent attached to the president's interagency High-Value Interrogation Group. Earlier tonight, we reported exclusively from Shenandoah National Park about the capture of a suspect in the murder case. At that time, we told you we could not yet release all the details, pending proper notification of the family.

"A law enforcement source has now confirmed two facts. First, Jack Jensen, the fugitive husband of Jenny Jensen, was rescued in a high-stakes mission by an elite FBI unit, working in conjunction with local law enforcement. That local effort was headed up by the Loudoun County Chief homicide Detective Ronald Fitzgerald. In fact, I will air an exclusive interview at 11:30 tonight with Detective Fitzgerald.

"Jack Jensen, it turns out, was not a suspect in his wife's murder, nor was he in anyway involved. Jensen was seriously injured, kidnapped and facing death at the hands of Jensen's killer. The accused killer can be identified as 43-year-old Mary McDougal. McDougal, it is alleged, had stalked Mrs. Jensen, and while the motive for the killing is not yet clear, it appears she intended to frame Jack Jensen and then murder him as well. Detective Fitzgerald also confirms that McDougal is being charged with the murder of a Loudoun County sheriff's officer, Silas Simpson. Simpson was 34 year old and leaves a wife and two young daughters.

"Jack Jensen is in serious but stable condition. His prognosis, we are told, is good. He has been reunited with his two sons and, sadly, has just learned of the death of his wife.

At 11:30, we will update this report, and you'll hear exclusively from the man who cracked the case and who personally captured Mary McDougal, now a suspect in two murders."

As the local news channel returned to network programming, the producer yelled, "You just went national on that report, Peggy. The cable networks are diving in too, but they're way behind. Great work."

****

"Jack Jensen is an American hero. Let's lead this press conference with that fact," Sheriff Tankersley began. "We grieve for

286

the loss of his wife. Our entire office gives great thanks that Mr. Jensen has been united with his boys.

"The price of justice was heavy in this case. One of our own was killed in the line of duty as he attempted to solve Ms. Jensen's murder. Right before his death, Silas Simpson issued a law enforcement alert that was responsible for helping our team pick up and track Ms. Jensen's killer. He had no way of knowing that his actions would help us find the person who would kill him minutes later. We are brokenhearted for Deputy Simpson's wife, Janice, and their beautiful girls, Tiffany and Daisy. Their dad was a hero to them, and he will forever be remembered as a hero in Loudoun County.

"The rescue of Jack Jensen and the capture of the accused murderer was made possible by the remarkable coordination and cooperation between the FBI and our office. Leading the field investigation and working directly with the FBI at my insistence was our chief homicide detective, Ronald Fitzgerald, who is with me here today. The man we all simply call Fitz or sir cracked this case and personally apprehended the accused. Loudoun County, Virginia, is remarkably lucky to have him. He has served this county for 44 years with distinction, and we hope that continues.

"I am proud to lead such an outstanding group of heroes …," Tankersley continued as his expertly crafted speech slowly turned toward his leadership. Detective Fitzgerald was already exiting the scene.

****

Jeff and Janie pulled into the long driveway leading up to the Mackey house. Only when they were a few miles out had she called her mother to say that she, Jeff, Jackson and Jeremy were there for a surprise visit. As they rode up the winding, narrow lane leading to the Mackey garage on the left and their home 200 yards away on the right, Mr. Mackey emerged from the backyard.

They pulled over, and Jeff jumped out from the driver's side. He met Janie, and they clasped hands as they headed directly for her father.

The boys tracked behind, clueless and still miffed about having to make the trip.

Janie broke her tender grip from Jeff and threw her arms around her dad, whispering in his ear, "I told you, everything is all right. I love you."

"I love you, sweetheart," Mackey said with a tear in his eye, ashamed that he had accused his own daughter of being connected to the murder.

Mackey stepped back and announced, "Your mother is furiously putting together a meal."

"Well, Dad, that gives us time to catch up. Boys, come tell your grandpa what you've got planned this summer."

Chapter 21: Look Who Is Coming to Dinner

Sunday dinner at the Fitzgerald home was like hosting a carnival on Thanksgiving at a Victorian mansion — every single week. The Fitzgerald house was huge, and for decades Fitz had been restoring it inside and out. From the street, it was an impressive home of the period, standing out among all other magnificent homes that decorated the historic landscape of Purcellville, Va. If you rode by the Fitzgerald house, it was the house among many beauties that compelled you to slow down and ask aloud, "Who lives there, and what does it look like inside?"

The house was classic Victorian on the outside. That magnificent façade gave no clue to the unique and remarkable inside transformation. The Fitzgeralds certainly hadn't butchered the customization. Indeed, it was grand in every way. But the restoration required innovation to meet the needs of such a large family. On the ground floor, the Fitzgeralds conceived a dynamic floor plan to make the home all about three rooms.

The kitchen opened on the outside to a huge deck with a sunken fire pit. On the inside, it had three points of access to represent what Fitz called an "egress" and "ingress" from the dining room, while the third opened to the back of the center hall. That door gave easy access to the two bathrooms, one off the back of the hallway, and the added powder room under the hallway steps.

The kitchen was spacious and designed more like a restaurant. Sure, you could entertain and feed an army at the long, custom table overlooking the deck. But the center island was huge too. It sat between the two doors to the dining room to create a circular flow of food going out and dishes coming in. The kitchen was what Fitz called his "cheat" room. It was essentially an entire addition. The Fitzgeralds built this on the back of the house so that they could cannibalize the original kitchen, dining room and front parlor to create Abby's dream dining room.

Abby's dining room was a bit more like the paneled dining hall of a Northeastern prep school. It seated about 5,000, seemingly. The custom table may have held a few less than that, but Fitzgeralds were known to seat nearly 30 for a Sunday dinner. That's a table.

The third room that dominated the downstairs renovation was Fitz's library. It took up the entire left side of the house, and it filled every nook and cranny with custom floor-to-ceiling bookshelves.

Once you entered the front door, assuming you left the spacious, wraparound front porch with its wainscoting and ceiling fans, you hit the grand hallway. From there, it was either reading to your left or dining to your right. Cooking was straight beyond the stairway. A small family room sat off behind the hallway, too, in a round sunroom. Abby hated that it could be entered only from the back hallway, but Fitz refused to cede a door opening from his library. In fact, he closed a door off in the renovation.

He often asked, "Why would I create a doorway from a room where one can sit and get smart just to enter a room where one can sit and get stupid?" The Fitzgerald children had to visit friends to watch TV.

The Fitzgeralds had a simple philosophy built around family. The entirety of their being was about the family unit. They were not the first big family to host a regular Sunday dinner. Many have, and some still do. Growing up, however, Fitz preached the need to put "family first." Like everything he did, he didn't merely preach — his words were met with action.

Fitz said, "You can make the greatest of friends, but that takes a lot of work. That work might pay off or it might not." Fitz proselytized, however, that "family was the unbreakable bond of society and the bedrock of civilization. Lose the family unit, and the civil society will shrivel. On family you can always count, and in family you should always invest."

"It is easier to mend a fence by and between those with whom you regularly break bread" was another Fitzism. Indeed, as Abby liked to remind her kids, "Why mend the fence when regular maintenance keeps it in great shape?"

Sunday dinner was family maintenance. It wasn't a requirement. It wasn't even an expectation. It was a way of life. To skip it would be like canceling breathing that week. It wasn't something one struggled to make work; it was an event that made all the family's struggles much less like work.

If you were a Fitzgerald, you and your friends were welcome to dinner. There were just three requirements. First, bring something, and make at least twice as much as your little group eats. Second, dinner guests at some point had to share two distinct pieces of information: what was the worst thing that happened to you that week and what was the best thing to happen to you that week. This process could take hours, which was good because dinner prep started around noon, and dinner ended around 9 p.m. The third requirement of dinner was that everyone ate, and everyone cleaned.

Most weeks, nearly every week, all the Fitzgerald girls showed up, with spouses, families, friends and sometimes just complete strangers.

Who was coming to dinner most weeks? Well, everyone. Fitz loved it that way.

By 6 p.m., nearly every Fitzgerald that lived was there for dinner, and the house was teeming with activity. Reagan brought three high school soccer teammates. Kelley was there. Harper was there, too. Claire showed up first, as she often did. Kate was late, which technically couldn't happen at this dinner. However, being late was Kate's trademark. Even Carson made it up from Charlottesville with her husband, Tommy, and their three young children.

Of course, Quinn wasn't there — again. She had not been there in nearly 18 months.

Quinn Fitzgerald would have been the baby of this brood if Reagan had not been the geriatric surprise. Quinn was 31 going on 60. She had a Harvard law degree, and she'd made partner at one of the largest litigation firms in the world at just 29, seven years out of law school.

She'd been missing too long from these dinners, and her father told her so. That was over a year ago, and she had not been to one since. "It's not like she lives on the West Coast," Fitz once complained to Abby. "She only lives in goddamn Arlington."

The Quinn "issue" became so sensitive that Fitz did something recently that he nearly never did — he complained about his daughter to his partner, Parker. "You know, she is part of the 'in' set in Arlington — with the flat-earthers." Fitz went on to explain that "the haughty liberal crowd in Arlington thinks the world is flat after the Beltway, so they never drive past it."

This Sunday, however, one other person was missing from dinner so far. It was Fitz.

"Mom, Mom, where is Dad?" Kelley asked. "He told me he would be here, and I'm not sharing until he gets here, period," she protested with the decided tone of her youngest sister.

"He is visiting the Simpson family," Harper-O declared, sending a quick hush over a packed and bustling room. The declaration came with all the seriousness that the Fitzgeralds understood. Honor and duty were not words in their house; they were action.

"Of course," said Kelley. "Goodness, I forgot. That poor woman."

As dinner rolled into the early evening, the sun setting painted a wonderful, warm glow. Ironically, it gave the dining room the most light it saw all day. The room was vibrant, and much of the discussion was over the latest high-profile case. With so many lawyers packed in the room, how could it not?

Just before 7:30, Fitz hit the front door after being forced to park on the street at his own house. He was greeted as a hero, first by a gaggle of the younger grandchildren.

He took his place at the head of the table and spoke of his visit with the Simpson family — who, he reminded the Fitzgeralds, were all now "our family" and "our obligation."

Not long into the confessional part of dinner, the doorbell rang.

"Who the hell is ringing the doorbell," Fitz asked more out of surprise than annoyance.

The kids raced to answer it as if a prize awaited. Around the hallway and into the sight of the archway came the strangest sight.

"Fitz, I'm told this is where the family dinner takes place," said the familiar man with the familiar voice and the all-too-familiar appearance.

Fitz studied him.

"*Parker*, what the hell are you doing here for dinner?" Fitz asked his longtime partner.

Surrounded by nieces and nephews, in strolled next, with dramatic style, Quinn Avery Fitzgerald.

"*I* invited him, Dad. After all, he is my fiancé," she said matter-of-factly.

That did the trick — the entire room went dead silent.

Like a room full of jurors at a death-penalty qualification proceeding, having just heard a judge read the charges of capital murder, every head in the Fitzgerald dining room turned to Fitz for a response.

Before he could speak, Kelley Fitzgerald blurted out, "I am going next. I'm having a baby!"

The room gasped.

"What?" her mother nearly yelled.

As pandemonium erupted, one of Reagan's guests leaned over and simply asked, "Can I come next week, too?"

Still, Kelley's amazing news could not bury the lead or reduce the tension, and quickly the room grew hushed again as Detective Fitzgerald rose from his seat.

"Quinn, dear," Fitz said, "it's always a great day to break bread —"

Quinn then interrupted her father. "And mend fences," she finished for him.

"*Parker!*" Fitz bellowed, "Welcome to the Fitzgerald *family* — *dinner* that is. Come, sit *right next to me.*"

Join the Fitzgeralds for dinner again … in their next adventure …

The ABC's of Murder: Betrayal

Made in the USA
Middletown, DE
28 December 2018